## It was a beautiful moonlit night

Under different circumstances, a stroll like this might have been an exciting and pleasant interlude. A man and a woman together, enjoying the evening and each other's company.

Yet, instead of the soft, whispered words of love, their conversation focused on the ugliest subject of all—murder. Diana suppressed a shiver and wondered when things would return to normal in her life.

Abruptly, Greg stopped and turned. Before she could say anything, he held one finger to his lips. The nighttime shadows had lengthened. Tree limbs dappled the ground with dark images that moved slightly as the breeze shook the leaves. "There," he whispered urgently. "Did you see it?"

## ABOUT THE AUTHOR

Aimée Thurlo says that *Strangers Who Linger* was inspired by one of her nightmares. She woke up in the middle of the night thinking there was a dark figure standing next to her bed. Busy chasing thoughts like "What if someone had really been there?" she was unable to get back to sleep. Fortunately for Intrigue readers, she decided to use the sleepless night productively...thinking about the fact that night is the time of shadows—and of the people and things that linger, hidden, in them. Aimée Thurlo lives and works in New Mexico.

## Author's Note

Although the fine churches and schools in the city of Santa Fe inspired the setting for *Strangers Who Linger,* no actual church or school is depicted.

## Books by Aimée Thurlo

### HARLEQUIN INTRIGUE

# Strangers
# Who Linger
## Aimée Thurlo

# Harlequin Books

TORONTO • NEW YORK • LONDON
AMSTERDAM • PARIS • SYDNEY • HAMBURG
STOCKHOLM • ATHENS • TOKYO • MILAN

To Mary Ann Woodland,
for memories of high school,
dog days and New Year's Eve
freezing in the den

*Acknowledgments*

With special thanks to Dr. Anatole Belilovsky,
for technical advice;
Michael Croom, for legal advice;
and to J.B. and K.B., for helping out
even though they can't take the credit for it.

Harlequin Intrigue edition published May 1991

ISBN 0-373-22162-2

STRANGERS WHO LINGER

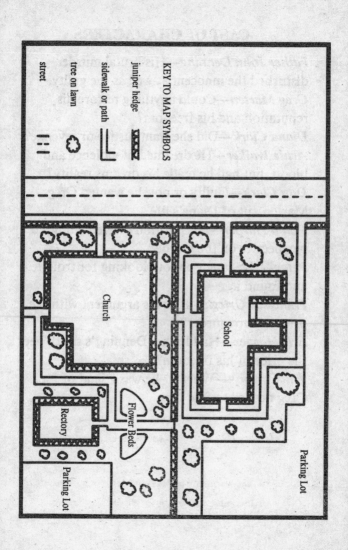

KEY TO MAP SYMBOLS

juniper hedge

sidewalk or path

tree on lawn

street

Church

School

Rectory

Flower Beds

Parking Lot

Parking Lot

# CAST OF CHARACTERS

*Father John Denning*—His brutal murder disturbed the innocent as well as the guilty.

*Greg Marten*—Could anything restore his reputation and his freedom?

*Diana Clark*—Did she want justice or revenge?

*Arnie Walker*—He dreamed of violence and blood, but had he made his dreams reality?

*Don Clark*—Guilty or not, he wanted Greg Marten out of Diana's life.

*Ralph Harper*—His position offered a unique perspective on the murder.

*Petey*—His gang went out looking for trouble, and found it.

*Francisco Ortega*—Had his argument with the priest led to murder?

*Eric Harper*—Had Father Denning's death been the price of his freedom?

*The Cowboy*—Whether he was friend of foe, Greg needed to find him.

# Chapter One

Greg Marten strolled across the grassy Santa Fe Plaza, a large paper-wrapped bundle comfortably slung beneath his arm. As the sun set and a cool desert breeze rolled in from the south, the city of Holy Faith seemed to echo with ghosts of the past. Walking through the shaded portals and cobblestone alleys that lined the plaza, Greg found it easy to call up vivid images of covered wagons, Franciscan friars and Indian traders.

When the sudden blast of a car horn somewhere down the street jarred him from his musings, he checked his watch in the fading light and confirmed that it was time to head toward the church.

He strode purposefully past tourists eager for one last photograph of the Sangre de Cristo Mountains. In the final glow of the fading day, the mountains burned bright red, earning the name the Spanish had given them centuries ago, the Blood of Christ Mountains.

By the time Greg approached the church's carved wooden side doors, twilight had disappeared. The grounds were enfolded in velvety shadows. Through age-rippled glass, the chapel glowed with a beckoning light.

It was a bit past eight and he knew the massive front doors of the church were already locked for the night. But as arranged, the side doors opened easily to his touch.

The few small lights that remained on revealed long rows of empty pews. Votive candles flickered, dappling the walls in unearthly patterns that shifted silently across the adobe walls. He was glad that the carpeted aisle muffled the noise of his comfortable but heavy cowboy boots. There was something about the old church that commanded reverence even though there were no worshipers present to disturb.

As he'd been asked, Greg waited near the communion rail for Father Denning to appear. The priest had been eager to restore the hide painting to its traditional location, now that the restoration process had been completed.

After waiting a few minutes, Greg glanced around. In their previous meetings the priest had been punctual. Noting the light that streaked outward through the slit in the sacristy door, Greg walked up to the priest's small office near the chapel and knocked lightly. "Father Denning?"

There was no answer.

Greg pushed the door open, then froze in his tracks. The priest lay facedown on the floor, his body sprawled like a child's discarded rag doll. A sacrilegious halo of blood encircled his head and flowed outward between the bricks of the floor in gridlike tendrils.

Heart racing, Greg placed his parcel on a chair and knelt beside the injured man. He thought the elderly priest must have fallen and struck his head. But when he reached down to touch the pulse point at the priest's neck, his fingers slid beneath a jagged flap of skin.

Greg jerked his hand back, a cold, sick dread coiling in his stomach. Placing one arm over the man's back for support, he started to turn him gently. As he did, the priest's head lolled back revealing a huge gash in his throat. The slit, just above his clerical collar, extended sideways like a hideous, mocking grin.

His thoughts racing, Greg eased the body back down on the floor and stood up slowly. Except for the priest and himself, the tiny room was empty. He fastened his gaze on the entrance to the sacristy. The dark wooden door frame and white adobe walls on either side were flecked with red splotches, tiny trails running down from their points of impact. Even a portion of the ceiling above the door had been touched by the life-ending spray.

Mentally recording the deathly silence that enshrouded the church, he searched for signs of an intruder. It was possible that the deep shadows were hiding a killer. He remained still for a moment, listening and watching, his senses alive.

He noted the sickly sweet smell of blood that filled the small room, and then became aware of something else. It wasn't incense, though he had detected that earlier in the chapel. There was an unmistakable trace of pipe tobacco in the air. Seeing a vent in the ceiling above the chair where he'd laid the painting, he speculated that the odor had drifted in from another part of the church. He doubted Father Denning would have smoked inside the sacristy.

Greg backed out of the room, his blood-soaked chambray work shirt clinging uncomfortably to his skin. The first thing he had to do now was report the crime, and the closest place with a telephone was the rectory.

He started down the aisle he'd come in, then abruptly stopped. He wanted to ignore the sensation, but some survival instinct tugged at his brain. Someone was there, watching him.

Greg spun around in a crouch and caught a glimpse of movement out of the corner of his eye. One of the shadows was moving. Greg stared into the darkness, hoping for a better look at his opponent as he shifted to face the threat. Then the movement began again, and he realized it was a flickering candle creating the illusion of movement, casting a distorted shadow of a life-size statue of St. Joseph upon the wall.

The sensation of being watched persisted, and Greg noticed again the faint trace of pipe tobacco in the air. He took in every detail, but only the sightless statues stared back. Finally, arguing that his instincts must be deceiving him,

Greg headed for the side exit. He was a few feet from the door when an attractive young woman entered.

They both stopped at the same instant. The woman's gaze dropped to Greg's hands and shirt, and her face drained of color. "Are you hurt?" her voice came out as a near whisper.

He shook his head. "No, but the priest is dead and there's so much blood..." Before he could say anything more, she spun and rushed out the door.

"Wait!" Greg shouted, but she was already gone. He shook his head in exasperation. He'd hoped to ask her to help.

The blood on his fingers felt sticky against the door handle as he pulled the door open and walked outside. Greg wiped his hands on his blue jeans and started across the grounds. He hadn't gone far when he saw a blue and white squad car speeding up the street, lights flashing. He dashed to the sidewalk and began waving his hands in the air to flag it down. A powerful spotlight captured him in its beam, and the car screeched to a halt, its headlights nearly blinding him.

"On the ground, buddy, facedown, arms over your head," he heard one disembodied voice shout.

With the light in his eyes, he could barely make out the shapes in front of him. "Officer, a priest has been murdered..." Recognizing the ratcheting sound of a shell being fed into the chamber of a shotgun, he dropped to his knees. "Will you listen to me? The killer could still be inside!" He squinted, trying to see the officers despite the glare.

"Just do as you're told!" the voice barked. "Facedown on the ground, hands away from your body."

As he lay on the sidewalk, Greg heard a woman's voice from somewhere near the police car. "He's covered with blood, but he said he wasn't hurt. If Father's in trouble, we've got to go inside and try to help!" she exclaimed.

Greg heard a car door slam, and rapid footsteps approaching. As the woman's shape became visible, a policeman grabbed her arm.

"No, ma'am, don't do that," one of the officers ordered. "We'll check out the church. In the meantime, please tell me what you were doing here tonight."

"I was on my way to show Father John a letter I received from my brother, when I saw this man. He told me that the priest was dead," her voice rose slightly. "We can't just stand around here! Someone's got to go inside right now!"

"Ma'am, we'll take care of that. Please stay calm," the officer admonished quietly.

The younger officer searched Greg for weapons. Feeling the handcuffs being placed on his wrist, Greg fought a surge of anger. "Look officer, the priest was already dead when I found him in the sacristy." He forced his voice to remain calm. "I was on my way to get help when I saw your patrol car. That's why I flagged you down." The officer tugged at the handcuffs, indicating Greg was to stand.

Greg looked around and saw the senior officer going toward the church, shotgun ready. A priest and someone else, perhaps a housekeeper, had come out of the rectory. At a signal from the officer, they stopped and waited.

"Maybe you knew the jig was up." Seeing Greg was about to reply, the officer shook his head and advised him of his rights. "Do you understand these rights as I've explained them to you?" he added.

"Yes, now will you listen for a minute?" Greg's voice held a hard edge. Normally he took pride in his patience, but the situation was getting out of control. "I'm sure there was someone else inside that church. I didn't see anyone come out, so it's possible the killer's still in there."

"We've already called for a backup," the officer said. "Exactly what were you doing here at this time of night?" the patrolman demanded as his partner emerged safely from the church.

"I was hired by the church to restore a painting. I came to return it to Father John Denning tonight."

The senior police officer stopped to speak to those who'd come from the rectory. Moments later, he came toward them, his face pale even in the headlights. "The father is dead all right, but there's no one else there."

"Sarge," the young officer spoke, "the suspect claims he was here to return a painting. Did you see anything that might confirm his story?"

"It was wrapped in brown paper, and I set it down on a chair near the body," Greg explained.

"There was nothing near the body," the sergeant said flatly, "except a lot of blood."

"I'll show you where I put it. That painting will establish my innocence."

"No one's going back in there until the crime scene unit gets a chance to go over everything."

"I didn't kill him," Greg insisted angrily.

"How do you explain being covered with blood?"

"The priest was facedown when I found him. It was impossible not to get blood on me when I turned him over to check for signs of life!" Even as he answered, Greg knew he was in trouble. He was a stranger in town, and the murder of a priest was not going to be taken lightly by the community.

He took a deep breath and forced himself to speak calmly. He had to convince these cops to look for the real murderer. "Sergeant, even with that massive loss of blood, the body was still warm when I found it. That means Father Denning hadn't been dead long. You've got to do a careful, thorough search of the place right now. I thought I saw movement in the shadows as I was leaving to get help. I also smelled pipe tobacco. If you act fast, you might be able to catch the killer tonight."

The senior officer rested his hand on the butt of his pistol. "Or we might have done that already," he answered in a level tone.

Hearing footsteps behind him, Greg turned his head. The woman from the church was staring at him. Her face was an ashen color against her ebony hair, but her eyes were alight with cold fire. "You won't get away with it," she said flatly. "For once I'm glad this state has the death penalty."

Her words made a cold chill seep through him. Surely there wouldn't be enough evidence to put him in jail. "Ma'am, you're upset, and you're not thinking clearly. Just because I was there doesn't mean I'm guilty."

He saw a flicker of doubt cross her face, but in an instant it was gone.

"There was nobody else there," she said with conviction. "The church was empty, and no one was outside, either. I would have seen them."

"Nonetheless, someone else was in that church tonight," Greg insisted.

His wrists were still handcuffed tightly behind his back, reminding him of his predicament. He glanced around, trying to gauge the situation. Several patrol cars had pulled up and were now parked in front of the church, along with a security guard's car. A yellow tape line was being erected around the side of the building. Two plainclothes police officers, badges on their belts, met with one of the arresting officers, then walked into the church. In the meantime, other officers questioned the people from the rectory.

After several minutes, one of the detectives emerged from the church. His gaze was cold as he fixed Greg with a glacial stare. "You mentioned a painting. Do you want to tell me about it?"

"I placed it on the cushion of a small chair near the body, away from the blood. Then I knelt beside Father Denning and checked to see if there was anything I could do to help him. Look," he glanced down at his pant legs. "I've still got bloodstains on my knees."

"Take him in," the detective replied with a disgusted look. "There was nothing there."

Greg swallowed hard. The tobacco scent could have dissipated, but who had removed the painting to discredit his story? He'd have to contact his attorney in Houston as soon as possible and get some help. Max took all Greg's business calls, negotiated contracts and handled his legal matters. This was outside of Max's usual field, but he would know what Greg should do.

The officer led Greg to the squad car. They were only feet from it when the policeman stopped in mid-step and cursed loudly. Bright red graffiti had been spray painted all over the police insignia.

"What the hell happened to our vehicle?" the sergeant demanded as he joined them.

"It's the plaque of the Diablo Locos. The paint's still wet! My guess is that it's initiation time, and while we were busy with the suspect, one of them left this here."

"Great," the sergeant muttered sarcastically. The officer opened the rear door of the squad car and pushed him inside roughly. "We'll never hear the end of it at the station."

Two hours later Greg sat in a stark office facing two plainclothes detectives. His clothes and boots had been taken away and he'd been given some jailhouse garb that was too small for his six-foot-five frame. Even the sneakers were tight. At least he'd been allowed to wash off the blood, after samples had been taken from his hands and fingernails for evidence.

He'd also made a telephone call and asked Max to find him a good local attorney as soon as possible. In the meantime Max had advised him to withhold all comments. Yet he had nothing to hide. He figured answering a few questions with the truth couldn't hurt as long as he didn't allow the police to play word games.

"Okay, Mr. Marten. What happened to that painting you were talking about?" The blond-haired detective had the kind of cherubic face that would have better suited a bible salesman, but his tone was hard.

"I don't know. It's my guess the person I sensed inside the church took it with him. Have you contacted the bishop yet? He'll verify who I am and what I was hired to do."

"His Eminence is out of town and it's taking some time to track him down." The middle-aged detective with the protruding belly sat on the edge of the table and gave Greg a skeptical gaze. "But the fact that you were employed by the church won't clear you, Marten. This could all be part of a plan you concocted."

"My reputation is solid, Lieutenant. Check it out. I make a good living restoring Western art. I have no reason to jeopardize my career by stealing, and I certainly wouldn't have had any reason to kill Father Denning. If you're considering profit as a motive for me, then there's something you should know. The church's hide painting is not nearly as valuable as some of the museum pieces I'll be working on later this year."

"I've already checked you out, Marten." He looked down at some notes he had taken. "Let's see, after college you worked for some hotshot art institute in San Antonio, Texas, right?"

"No. I attended the institute to study the techniques used to restore Western art. I didn't get paid, I paid tuition," Greg answered wearily.

A short, slightly balding man in his early fifties walked into the room. "I hope you're not questioning my client, Don. I'd hate like hell to think you're trying to take advantage of his good will in this matter." He straightened the clasp of his bolo tie.

The detective's mouth tightened into a thin line. "A. J. Crowley, you're all I needed to top off a rotten day," he muttered.

"Glad to know I'm appreciated. Now I'd like some time alone with my client, please."

Twenty minutes later Greg stood in the lobby of the police station. "Mr. Crowley, I appreciate your coming down. I was beginning to think I'd have to spend the night in jail."

The man shook his head. "They had nothing to hold you on, son. I knew that right after I spoke to Max in Houston. He told me everything I needed to get you out." He grinned slowly. "I'm just sorry I couldn't get you any better clothes than those."

Greg shrugged. "It'll do till I get home."

"By the way, it was pretty sharp of you to ask for a home-town boy to represent you. One of the fastest ways to get these fellows against you is to bring in a hired gun, especially one from Texas."

"I don't think they're going to be 'for' me no matter what I do. They didn't find anyone else in the church, and I'm the closest thing they've got to a suspect." Greg rubbed his chin with one hand. "Then there's that woman."

"The one who saw you leaving the church? Hell, boy, that's not enough evidence to support an arrest. You had an appointment, the police found it recorded on Father Denning's desk calendar. It stands to reason you'd be there. Besides, the preliminary investigation indicates that several items are missing from the church. Someone forced the locks in the sacristy and behind the altar. So far a gold chalice has been reported missing, a jeweled cross, several smaller gold crosses, some *santos* made out of gold and some silver candlesticks. Yet you didn't have any of the stolen items or any burglary tools when they searched you. Also, they found nothing they could link to the crime in your apartment or van."

"Maybe that'll convince them that the real killer is still out there." Greg shook his head slowly. "It's too late for me to help Father Denning now. What I can do is try to see that the painting he entrusted me with gets back to the church where it belongs. That theft took place *after* the murder, and I feel responsible."

"Son, take my advice. Let the police handle it."

Greg said nothing for several moments. "Thanks for coming down, sir," he said finally.

"Which means that you're not taking my advice." A. J. Crowley reached into his pocket and pulled out a business card. "Keep this with you at all times. You're going to need it. Now, I better get back," he said, shaking Greg's hand. "I have some other business here that's going to take a while." He strode down the hall.

Greg started toward the exit, eager to leave the station and go home. What he needed now was a cab. He reached into his pocket and pulled out his wallet. All he had was a five-dollar bill, and unless he missed his guess, that wouldn't be enough to get him home. He considered trying to ask Crowley for a lift, but that would require hanging around the station until the man finished his business. He'd just have to walk.

Greg hadn't gone more than a mile when it began to rain. It fell lightly at first, then in a downpour that sent him under a tree for shelter. A short time later the summer cloudburst had passed.

Invigorated by the clean, cool air that followed the rain, Greg made his way through the nearly deserted neighborhoods. Fate had certainly placed him in an awkward position. Despite what the cops thought, he wouldn't have been in Santa Fe at all if his only concern had been money. He'd turned down a far more lucrative job in Phoenix in favor of working here. But one conversation with Father Denning had convinced him that this was where his skills were needed most. The meager funds the parish had available would have made it difficult, if not impossible, for them to get another qualified conservator. Thanks to that generous decision, he was now in some very serious trouble.

Almost an hour later he reached the street corner across from his studio apartment. As he glanced at the tenants' parking lot, a light inside his van caught his attention. Someone was standing on the far side of the van, aiming a flashlight in the window. The man, who stood as tall as the van itself, seemed intent on the contents of the vehicle. His hand, resting on the roof, held a weapon. From where Greg stood, it looked more like a long-bladed knife than a gun.

Greg's muscles tensed. An ordinary car thief wouldn't carry a weapon. It was possible that the story of the priest's death and his own release from jail had stirred up someone intent on revenge. Or perhaps the real murderer had come to eliminate a potential witness. Either way, his opponent was bound to be formidable. Anyone that tall would have a dangerous reach with a blade.

Greg looked around, searching for a way to create a diversion. He needed to take the offensive before his presence was discovered. Crossing the street silently, he grabbed the lid off a trash can and hurled it over the roof of his van. The metal projectile clanged loudly as it hit the adobe wall on the other side, then clattered on the pavement. His silent, shadowy opponent started, then dashed in the opposite direction.

Greg waited by the curb, stepping out at the last possible second. Grabbing his opponent's arm as he dashed by, he twisted it in a painful hammerlock. To his amazement, his adversary cried out in a decidedly feminine voice. He realized suddenly that the person he'd captured was neither tall, nor particularly strong.

Only one explanation made sense. There were two of them, and he was being set up. He had to act fast. "Drop your weapon," he ordered.

# Chapter Two

"What weapon, you big jerk? My umbrella? Let me go this instant!" she demanded. She had to think fast, the man was a giant.

She felt him lean to one side and glance at the object that lay at her feet. Lighted by the glow of the streetlight, it was obviously exactly what she'd claimed—a small rolled-up umbrella.

"You're the woman from the church!" he whispered harshly. "Where's your partner?"

"What partner?" she replied loudly. "If you don't release me immediately, I'm going to start screaming my head off."

"Fine, then when the police come, you can explain what you were doing and where the tall person who was shining a light into my van is," he rasped.

She didn't want the police here now if it could be avoided, but she was getting more frightened by the minute. She had expected to have plenty of time to examine his vehicle while the police held him in custody. With his unexpected arrival, she was in real danger. She hadn't dropped her flashlight, but it was a plastic one and wouldn't do much good as a weapon against this man, even if she could have reached his head.

"I was the person shining the flashlight inside your van," Diana replied haughtily. "I stood on the running board so

I could see inside." She took a deep breath and hardened her voice. "Now release me this instant."

He held her arm firmly behind her as he glanced around. He was probably still searching for her nonexistent partner. Diana fought the wave of panic that now threatened to engulf her. Her ace in the hole had failed. She'd learned long ago how to take command of situations by using a certain tone of voice. It made most people do what she wanted before they even had a chance to think about it. Growing up poor and being only five feet tall had meant learning and perfecting this kind of survival skill. Yet this man hadn't even flinched! She tried again.

"I warn you. There are others who know where I am and what I'm doing. If I go missing, the police will come for you."

"You know, if you really think I'm guilty, you should be terrified. Yet you sound more angry than afraid." He loosened his hold slightly. "Maybe your instincts are trying to tell you something."

"You're right. I'm not afraid of you," she shot back, relieved that her bluff had fooled him. "You wouldn't risk another murder now, particularly one that could be connected to you so easily. What I can't understand is why you're out on bail. You shouldn't have been released!" she added angrily.

"I wasn't charged with anything because I'm innocent." He looked around one more time, then finally released her. "I guess I was mistaken about you having a partner." As she spun to face him, he caught her gaze. "How did you get my address?"

"The detective I spoke to had the preliminary report on his desk. I didn't have to look hard." As she straightened her coat, he picked up her umbrella and handed it to her. The courteous action surprised her. "Thanks," she muttered grudgingly.

"So, you protected yourself by telling others where you were going tonight. That was good thinking," he commented with laughing eyes.

The signs were unmistakable. He wasn't taking her seriously. All her life she'd had to work hard against her looks. She was small, well proportioned, and attractive in a perky way. Woman generally wanted to mother her, and men wanted to put her in their pockets and take her home with them. Either way, few ever bothered to notice that she had a good brain and plenty of common sense.

She took a deep breath. "I knew precisely what I was doing." Tossing her shoulder-length black hair away from her face, she readjusted her silver barrette expertly.

His jade eyes were unreadable. "We're off to a very bad start. Let's give it another try, okay? As you probably know, my name's Greg Marten. Now, why don't you tell me yours."

For a man his size, she would have expected a booming voice, but heck, hers was louder than his. You had to *listen* to catch everything he said.

"My name is Diana Clark," she replied almost formally, as if they were meeting to conduct business. He was being so polite and reasonable about the whole thing, she found it annoying... and contagious. "Father John Denning was my friend, and right now you're the only suspect the police have in his murder. There was nobody else in that church, and Father's blood was all over you. The cops might have been forced to let you go because the evidence is still circumstantial, but *I'm* not giving up." She was going to do whatever she could to help the police bring the criminal to justice quickly. She knew that, left to their own devices, the departmental investigators could draw everything out, making the process ineffectual and painful for all concerned. She'd had firsthand experience with their work in the past and the bitter memories lingered.

"Do you want to catch the killer, or just have somebody arrested and charged with the crime?"

"I'm not trying to railroad anyone, but I intend to make sure Father Denning's killer doesn't get away with what he's done," she countered angrily.

Greg stared at her for the space of several heartbeats. "It was chance that placed me at the church ahead of you, Diana. If you'd arrived a few minutes earlier, it could have been *you* rushing out to look for help, all covered with blood, not me."

Her body tensed as the picture he'd laid out took shape in her mind. The agonizing horror of it left her feeling weak. Compassion mingled with dark shadows of doubt as she regarded him thoughtfully. Then again, this was exactly the response he'd wanted from her. If he was the killer, he could have planned to use her own sense of fair play against her. "If you're as innocent as you claim, then what I'm trying to do shouldn't worry you at all."

Greg shook his head in quiet resignation. "Look, you can't hang around parking lots at this time of night," he said, gesturing toward the ornate turquoise and silver ring she wore on her right hand. "What if you get mugged for your jewelry? There's an easier way to find out what you want to know about me. We could get together and just talk."

"Oh sure, and I'm to trust your word automatically, right?" She gave him an incredulous look.

"Come to my place right now and I'll show you what I do for a living. That should answer some questions for you, like what I was doing at the church tonight."

"I don't know..." She wanted to believe him, but couldn't quite bring herself to trust him. Not yet.

"Are you afraid of finding out you're wrong about me and losing the only suspect you have?"

There was a great deal of truth in what he was saying, and that's what bothered her. Without him, she and the police would have little to go on. The possibility that Father John's killer might never be found made her feel cold. After all

Father had done for her, she couldn't fail him now. "If our positions were reversed would you find it easy to trust me?"

"Well, actually, it might be wiser for us to talk out here. If you take another look at our situations you'll see that we both have a reason to be concerned," he answered. "I know someone else was at that church, but the only person I actually saw there was you. Granted, you seemed to be coming in, but you could have set that up. For all I know, you're the murderer."

Anger welled inside her and spilled over like a tidal wave. "How dare you accuse me of hurting Father John!"

He faced her calmly, his eyes holding hers. "You're angry because you feel I've insulted you. How do you think your accusations have made me feel?"

Her heart constricted as she put herself in his place and saw all too clearly what it must have been like. "But it's not the same thing at all," she argued halfheartedly. "Father was my friend." Diana stared at him, completely confused. Greg Marten seemed so well mannered and even tempered! Then again, if someone as big as he was ever lost control, there'd be no telling what could happen. With his curly, copper hair and enormous shoulders, he could have passed for a Viking.

"There's another element we both should keep in mind," Greg continued. "If *we're* both innocent, then whoever else was at that church is the killer. Since he can't be sure we won't remember a vital clue, we're a dangerous liability to him. It's very possible he might try to silence us permanently."

"That's another reason why I want the murderer, whoever he is," she qualified sharply, "behind bars." She looked down the street casually, wondering if they were being watched right now.

Greg walked to the front step of the old, thick-walled, earth and wood duplex. Individual adobe bricks were visible where the mud plaster had fallen away. "My studio is right here. Now that we've cleared the air, I think we should go in. Either one of us could have been followed."

She hesitated, looking into the shadows once more. Greg Marten was an unknown quantity. Yet some of the answers could be waiting on the other side of the door. "I *would* like to find out more about your work."

"Good," Greg answered, opening the door and walking inside. Automatically he flipped on the light switch. As his gaze traveled around the room, he swore softly. "I knew that the police had searched my place, but I didn't expect them to leave this big a mess."

The sketches and detail photographs on his scarred drafting table had been scattered, and some now lay on the floor. His paint box had been dumped on the counter. His palette knives had all been set in a line, each one apparently inspected. Fortunately, the small wooden sculptures he'd carved remained safely on their shelf. If something were to happen to them, he'd be in even more trouble. They represented the money he needed to travel from job to job nowadays, as well as his emergency funds. "In a way, I'm grateful they were this thorough. This may help clear me."

"It won't hurt, but my guess is they're not through with you yet."

"Do you think the police consider you a suspect, too?" he asked, picking up his sketches from the floor.

"No, of course not! There's no evidence against me. I arranged to see Father because he'd wanted to read the letter I'd received from my brother. I went to the rectory and got his message asking me to meet him near the sacristy."

"I also had an appointment with him there," Greg replied. "The police saw it written down in his date book. If nothing else, that should tell you I'm not the murderer. I'd have to be a fool to kill Father Denning at a time when I was scheduled to meet with him."

"Maybe," she conceded reluctantly, "but that would depend on the circumstances and how strong your motive was." She stared at the dilapidated condition of his studio.

The plaster was chipping off the walls, and the wavy hardwood floor showed signs of damage from cigarette burns and water leaks. Old memories of hard times with her migrant farmer family came back to her in a painful rush of emotions. She'd lived this way half of her life, going from one town to the next, never having anyplace to call home. She knew intimately how a life-style like this could breed desperation and make people capable of things they'd never do under other circumstances.

"You aren't going to trust me until this hide painting I restored is found and verifies my story, are you?" he observed pensively.

She said nothing for a moment. The past few years had been filled with harsh lessons, and she'd learned a great deal about being on her own. She'd become a skeptic out of necessity. "If you went to the church to return it, then where did it go? You claimed you set it near the body, yet there was no painting there by the time the police went inside. I don't know about them, Greg, but I find it difficult to believe that the killer rushed back to the sacristy just to steal it. On the other hand, he couldn't have been hiding in that small room when you found the body. You'd have seen him. Also, what happened to his tracks? Whoever killed Father must have had blood all over him."

Greg dropped down onto the worn cushion of a misplaced chair. "I can't explain any of it. All I can tell you is what I saw. I have a theory about what happened to his tracks, though. The murderer could have taken off his shoes, or wiped them on something the police haven't found yet." He stared at his drawing table. "Tell me, are you an artist too?"

"Me?" she smiled ruefully, wondering if he was teasing her. "I can't even draw those little puppy faces on the back of matchbooks. What made you think I was?"

"There are traces of paint, or maybe ink, on the bottom edge of your cuff."

"It must be ink from an advertising flyer I ran off the presses this morning. I own and manage a print shop." She studied the faint smears. "You have terrific eyesight," she replied, amazed.

"It's my job to observe. That's what an art conservator does."

"I thought it was protecting what was already there."

"It's more involved than that," he answered. "I have to be part historian, radiologist and detective. Paintings sometimes have to be X-rayed to make sure that there's no work buried beneath. Samples of paint have to be analyzed under a microscope so pigments can be identified and the work dated. Under certain circumstances, I'm also expected to reconstruct or inpaint areas that have been lost." He ran one hand through his thick, curly hair.

He looked so bone tired she almost felt sorry for him. "Tell me, how long did it take you to finish the painting you restored for the church?"

"You're still wondering if I'm connected to the murder, aren't you? Do you think I ruined the *Madonna* I was restoring, somehow, and did all this to cover up?" His eyes flashed.

"I considered that possibility. You could be the worst kind of con man," Diana answered, realizing uncomfortably that she hadn't fooled him.

"Well, that's one motive you can cross off your list," he answered, sounding more disappointed than angry. "The old hide painting was in terrible shape when I picked it up. It was warped from water damage caused by a leaky roof, and smoke and dust had darkened it considerably. I spent four weeks of painstaking work restoring and protecting the *Madonna* against further deterioration. It was the best work I've ever done, and I was very eager to show it to Father John." He walked to the armoire at one end. "These are the before and after photos."

She stared at them for a few minutes. Greg was right, he had done an excellent job of bringing the *Madonna* back to its original condition. "There's a considerable difference between these. The colors are much brighter, and all those horrible water stains are gone."

"Not gone, but decreased substantially. A good cleaning revitalized the work."

She handed the photos back to him. He'd effectively countered all the motives she'd thought of so far. "Does your job keep you moving constantly from place to place?" she asked, distaste inadvertently coloring her words.

"You don't approve," he observed. "Why? Don't you have any interest in art?"

"No, that's not it. I just find your life-style puzzling. It seems to me that a man who enjoys restoring beauty would want to surround himself with the finer things in life."

"I believe I already am. I've seen the sun rise and set in places that would take your breath away. I've learned about cultures and beauty that goes way beyond the things we see. I don't view myself as deprived at all."

There was a basic simplicity and honesty about him that touched her. She'd spent her adult life striving for something better. She'd worked hard to make a home for herself and to be able to fill it with the luxuries she'd never had as a girl. Yet this man seemed to care little for the material things she valued. Was he a saint, or the worst kind of con man and murderer?

"I have a little brandy in the cupboard. Would you like a drink?"

Diana shook her head. "It's time for me to go."

Greg stood up slowly. "Let me change clothes, then I'll take you home or walk you back to your car."

"Thanks, but it's not necessary. I'm parked right across the street."

He walked to the door with her. "Diana, what will it take for me to convince you that I'm innocent?"

His gaze was so unflinchingly direct it was hard to believe he had anything to conceal. "Evidence," she replied after a moment's pause.

"Believe me, for my sake as much as for the father's, that's exactly what I intend to find."

Car keys in hand, she glanced up at him. "What do you mean?"

He shook his head. "Just remember that we both want the same thing—facts that will prove who the murderer is."

As Diana walked outside, Greg remained at her side. Silence stretched out between them. It was obvious he wasn't going to elaborate further. She considered the problem. If Greg was up to something, she had to find out what it was. Despite the possible danger, she owed it to herself and Father John to take the risk.

Within seconds they reached her car. Out of habit, Diana glanced inside and checked to make sure everything was as she'd left it. Satisfied, she said good-night to Greg, unlocked the door and eased herself into the driver's seat.

She'd only traveled half a block when she became aware of a peculiar scent. It was an odd mixture of wet leather and pipe tobacco. But how on earth had it found its way inside her locked car? She hadn't noticed it on the way over. Feeling with her right hand, she checked the ashtray. She didn't smoke, and it was empty. One quick look told her the floorboards were clean of tobacco or ashes.

The odor seemed to grow even more pronounced as she continued to drive toward home, and she had the feeling that she was being watched. A prickly sensation coursed up her spine and the feeling intensified. Fear slipped into her, touching her at a level she'd never experienced before.

Reaching a stop sign, she glanced around. The streets were empty. Yet she could feel eyes, cold and staring, following her every move.

This was no time to be irrational. What on earth was the matter with her? She took a deep breath, trying to calm herself, but was only marginally successful.

Diana pressed on the accelerator, eager to get home as quickly as possible. As the car picked up speed, she felt the stirring of a breeze. She looked around, trying to locate the source of the cool air, but her windows were all rolled up. Slowing down, she searched for an explanation and discovered she'd left one of the vents open.

Relieved, Diana chuckled softly. Everything was going to be fine. She was overtired, that was all. Casually she glanced in her rearview mirror as the car passed beneath a streetlight. Her breath caught in her throat as she saw a dark figure seated behind her. She slammed on the brakes.

# Chapter Three

Her car skidded to a stop, and she turned quickly to face the intruder. "Get out of this—" The words died in her throat. As the headlights of a passing vehicle illuminated the interior of her car, she realized that there was no one in the backseat.

Diana's hands were shaking badly, and perspiration coursed down her body. Her imagination had never played tricks on her before, but maybe the strain of today's events was finally catching up to her.

Getting the flashlight out of her purse, she aimed the beam at the rear seat. A couple of business flyers had come loose from a bundle, and had lodged on the shelf behind the backseat. The handouts promoted the Jobs for Teens program and contained the portrait of a young man.

She breathed again. That must have been what she'd seen. The darkness had fooled her and led her to interpret it as something far more menacing. She started her car moving and concentrated on the road before her. The strange scent she'd detected before was now gone, she noted gratefully, probably dispelled through the open vent. Undoubtedly that also explained how the smell had filtered in earlier. Someone must have stood by her car, smoking.

Fifteen minutes later Diana pulled into her driveway. To her right stood the small "mother-in-law" cottage where her friend Anita Talbot lived. The lights of the cottage were on, telling her Anita was still up, waiting to make sure she had arrived home safely. Diana hadn't been lying to Greg about having let someone know where she'd be. Anita was her "insurance."

As Diana left her car, she thought about the first time she and Anita had met. They had each been waiting for Father John Denning in his outer office. Anita, a spry woman in her early sixties, had been the victim of a retirement home scheme that had bankrupted a number of elderly in the area. At the time Diana too had been in desperate straits. She was over thirty, unskilled, on her own, and facing a stack of bills. The print shop she'd inherited from her late husband had been on the verge of bankruptcy and she knew nothing about bookkeeping or running a business. She'd managed to stall and gain some time, but the future looked grim. Creditors demanding payment had repossessed everything, including her car. Only one small press and the printing supplies remained at the store.

The half hour Anita and she had spent in the priest's outer office that day had turned both their lives around. Anita had suggested that Diana use her last twelve boxes of paper to print advertising flyers. Then, working together, they had hand delivered them to as many merchants as they could. Their joint efforts had saved the print shop and Diana from bankruptcy. Through hard work and mutual support, they'd accomplished the impossible. They'd been partners ever since.

Diana walked to the narrow cottage door, flanked on both sides by bunches of dried red chiles. Her knock was answered almost immediately by a tall, gray-haired woman.

"I've been really worried about you!" Anita said with a martyred sigh. "I had no idea you were planning to be gone this long." She waved Diana inside.

"Things got much more complicated than I'd anticipated," Diana answered truthfully. "I appreciate you waiting up to see I got home okay."

"I sure wish you'd let the police handle this on their own, Diana. Father Denning wouldn't have expected you to take matters into your own hands. He knows, from wherever he's watching," she glanced up at the ceiling tiles, "that you're not a detective. You have trouble finding your coffee cup!"

"You're right," Diana conceded grimly, "but I have to do this."

"You're risking your life."

"After Bob died, I needed help. Father John was there for me. He didn't stop to count the cost then, or wonder if calling in favors for me was going to place him in an awkward situation. He just helped and treated me with respect. I owe him for that. And you know how I feel about repaying my debts."

"Okay, so you're not going to listen to reason." Exhaling loudly, Anita sat back down in her easy chair. "At least tell me what happened tonight and why you were gone so long."

Diana recounted the entire story, omitting the incident in the car on the way home. She was certain now that had just been nerves. "Greg Marten's a hard man to figure out. He doesn't even raise his voice. A murderer has to be more prone to losing control, don't you think?"

"Not necessarily. But then again, I'm not an expert on the subject. Just remember that Father John wasn't stupid. If Greg Marten killed him, he must have taken Father in completely." Anita stood and began to work with her small collection of bonsai. "Diana, I like to think of life as something precious and worth celebrating." She watered the smallest one, then pruned back a branch. "To me, murder is unforgivable. Whoever killed Father should pay. But it's wrong for you to jeopardize your own life to make that happen."

"I'll stay alert, believe me. Try not to worry."

"Why are you insisting on doing this yourself? Does it have something to do with your husband's death?" she asked softly. "I don't know the details, but Father mentioned that you went through a very difficult time then."

"I'll never forget what the police department put me through. First they said my husband committed suicide. Business hadn't been good, and they'd found him in the car with a bullet in his head and a pistol on the floorboard beside him."

Diana's voice quivered, but she swallowed and continued. "Then, my brother-in-law pointed out the week's receipts had been found in Bob's jacket, and so they ruled Bob was the victim of an attempted robbery instead. They ordered a reexamination of the physical evidence, which revealed that the pistol had been fired from waist height. That ruled out suicide. Don convinced everyone that in the struggle for the thief's gun, the weapon had gone off. The thief must then have fled in a panic, not bothering to complete the robbery."

Anger filled her and she gripped the sides of the chair to keep her hands from shaking. "Then, weeks afterward, a new forensics study ordered by the courts discarded that theory based on the trail of powder burns on Bob's shirt and the car seat. If someone had been struggling beside him for the gun, some of the powder marks wouldn't have reached the seat. The experts in homicide looked into the case some more and found that Bob's friend Larry had brought the gun to the shop so Bob could look at it. Bob had wanted something small to keep at home for defense. The experts then concluded that Bob must have slipped the gun into his winter coat pocket and forgotten all about it until he got into the car to drive home. When he tried to take it out his glove caught in the trigger mechanism and he must have yanked at it, because the gun went off."

"Diana, I'm so sorry." Anita crossed the room and gave her a hug.

It was a few minutes before Diana could trust herself to speak again. Then, taking a deep breath, she continued. "What worries me is that this investigation is starting to go back and forth in exactly the same manner. At first the department was convinced they had the murderer. But after a few hours they released him, so they must have changed their minds. Since talking to Greg Marten, I'm not sure he had anything to do with the crime, either. Now the police are starting all over, looking for more evidence or another suspect. If they don't find something soon, they'll have to put the case on hold and work on something else."

"They don't have enough cops for everything, Diana. Still, they do their best. I don't see what you expect to accomplish on your own."

"I'll tell you what I can do. I have a personal stake in this crime, and not just because of what Father John meant to me. The killer could be looking for me and Greg Marten, wanting to get rid of us, too, because of something we might have seen or heard. I have to find him first. And if I have to hand feed clues to the police to keep them on the case, so be it."

"And if Detective Don hears what you're doing?" Anita asked, using their private nickname for Diana's relative.

"Actually I'm hoping to keep it from him," she answered sheepishly. "He'll be furious that a 'civilian' is interfering with police business." She exhaled softly. "Don is a good person. I know he's trying to watch out for me and take care of me, but he can be such a pain in the neck."

"Well, if you're going to act crazy, then, as your friend, I'm going to have to insist you do something for me. And unless you agree, I'm going straight to Don."

"What would you like me to do?" Diana asked.

"I want to know everything you learn, where you'll be, and what your plans are. If you'd like, you can think of me as your life insurance."

"You've got it." Diana stared at the wall of cattle Anita had painted in the adjoining room and whimsically referred to as her low-maintenance house pets. "I'm going to follow Greg Marten tomorrow and see what he's up to. Can you open up the shop alone?"

"Sure, but promise me you'll be careful?" Seeing her nod, Anita reached inside her purse and handed Diana a small container. "This is tear gas, keep it with you. If anyone gives you any trouble, use it!"

Diana tried not to smile. "How long have you been carrying this stuff in your purse?" She held up a hand. "No, never mind. I don't want to know." Diana stretched slowly, then glanced at her watch. "It's been a long day. I better say good-night before I'm too tired to even go home."

Diana left the cottage and walked across the graveled driveway to the small rear patio of her home. Stepping up onto the red brick, she unlocked the door and went inside.

Diana walked to her bedroom then kicked her shoes off with a contented murmur. Her quilted calico bedspread, a Christmas gift from Anita, looked warm and inviting. She sat on the edge of the bed, then plopped backward, enjoying the softness of the mattress. She'd never understand a man like Greg Marten. How could he opt for a nomadic lifestyle out of his own free will?

Diana picked up the brass clock on her nightstand and set the alarm for six. That would give her plenty of time to be at her post by seven. Eager to slip into bed, she undressed quickly, allowing her clothes to fall in a heap on the cool brick floor. A moment later she was tucked beneath the cotton sheets.

Despite her best efforts, sleep eluded her. Images of Father John flashed through her mind. She'd miss him terribly. Silent tears stained her pillow as she rolled on to her side and stared into the darkness.

By the time sunrise rolled around, she was eager to get going. The short letter she'd penned to her brother, Frankie, upon rising had been a struggle. He was out at sea somewhere, and she had no idea when he'd get word of Father John's death. She prayed he'd be able to deal with the news when it came.

It was a bit past seven when she parked down the street from Marten's studio. Within minutes Greg emerged wearing a gray sweatsuit and old worn sneakers. He stopped at his van for a moment and took out a basketball. Then, moving at a slow jog, he dribbled expertly down the sidewalk. Diana started the car and followed at a distance. He stopped a couple of blocks down at a basketball court next to a public school and began to shoot baskets.

He was incredibly light on his feet for someone as large as he was. Whenever he shot a basket, his sweatshirt revealed his flat, muscular stomach and torso. Diana tried to ignore it and failed.

Finally, thirty minutes later, Greg retraced his route, and she followed him back to his apartment. An hour passed, but Greg did not emerge from the studio. The strident trumpets and guitars of mariachi music coming from inside the café across the street kept her awake through the boring vigil. As more time elapsed, however, she began to worry. Diana searched her memory, trying to recall whether there was a back exit to his place. She was fairly certain there wasn't one.

It was around a quarter to nine when she finally saw him come out of the building. As he slid into the driver's seat of his van, Diana started her car's engine and prepared to follow.

GREG MANEUVERED the van slowly down the narrow street, having finally decided upon a course of action for the day. He'd been awake for hours. At first he'd tried to keep his mind occupied by straightening the mess the police had left in his studio. But his thoughts had drifted continuously back to Diana Clark. Despite her porcelain-doll appearance, he'd sensed an undeniable core of strength in her, and that intriguing mixture drew him.

Almost in self-defense he'd gone for his regular morning workout. His short run and shooting a few baskets helped him maintain his hand-to-eye coordination and stamina, skills he needed to use constantly in his work. Yet even physical exertion hadn't done much to put her out of his thoughts. The last thing he needed now was to be distracted by a woman.

After a short drive Greg pulled into a parking space across from the church. Sheltered beneath an enormous old cottonwood, he studied the area. People seemed to be entering or leaving the church at a slow but constant rate. Parishioners, he concluded, probably coming to say prayers for Father Denning.

Reluctant to go inside, he remained seated. He had mixed feelings about returning to the scene of the crime. Nightmarish images of what he'd witnessed in the sacristy yesterday flashed through his mind. Yet he knew he had to go in. It was possible he'd missed some detail that could shed light on the case and help him learn the truth.

Unwilling to put off any longer what had to be done, Greg left the van, walked across the street and entered the chapel. He retraced his steps of the night before, noting the signs of cleaning that had removed all traces of blood from the carpet and floor. The sacristy door was open, a housekeeper was busy inside scrubbing the walls. The smell of cleanser and disinfectant reminded him of a hospital.

Greg moved away quietly and headed toward the statue of St. Joseph. He looked around carefully, as he had when he'd searched for an intruder. The recessed area, without outside windows, wasn't any brighter now than it had been last night. Suddenly, Greg's body went cold and a spidery, tingling sensation coursed down his spine.

He closed his eyes and then opened them again, willing the feeling away. As his gaze came to rest on the wall before him, his blood turned to ice. Last night St. Joseph's statue had cast a shadow—he remembered the black shifting outline against the wall. But now there was nothing there.

As it has been the evening before, all the votive candles on the small stand before the statue were lit. The floodlights overhead that illuminated the figure cast only two overlapping shadows at its base.

Puzzled by his discovery, Greg walked around the chapel slowly. Perhaps a recently burned-out bulb could explain the mystery.

When he found nothing, Greg's confusion grew. Was it possible that he'd seen the killer standing there last night? But how could the man have appeared so dark and shadowlike? As an artist he knew much about light and shadow, yet all of his knowledge failed to provide him with any answers now.

Greg left the chapel abruptly. Troubled, he wasn't sure whether or not to call the police and report his discovery. He sat in his van, watching a work crew graveling and leveling the adjacent school parking lot. Finally he decided against telling anyone. He still had no description to offer, except a vague shape he'd seen against a white wall. He had to find out more.

TWENTY MINUTES LATER Diana followed Greg's car down the street. Her heart raced as she saw him park near one of the art galleries on the plaza and go inside. If he was the killer, it was possible he was trying to fence the missing painting or the other stolen articles. Yet there was no way she could confirm that from where she was.

Diana left her car and approached the gallery. Cautiously, staying to one side of the large glass front, she peered inside. Greg was standing by a glass display case talking to a man who appeared to be either the manager or owner. She edged in furtively until she was only inches from the door and listened to the exchange.

"Mr. Santeiro, I understand that Taylor Goodwin, the curator of the Tucson Western Museum, spoke with you earlier this morning."

"Yes, and you must be Greg Marten. I've been expecting you. But as I told Mr. Goodwin, I'm not sure your coming here is a good idea. The police have issued a bulletin alerting all the dealers about that hide *Madonna,* and I gather you're the person who was detained for the robbery and murder."

"I didn't commit either one of those crimes. That's why I'm trying to get a lead on the painting. It'll corroborate what I was doing at the church last night."

"If I had any information, Mr. Marten, I would have turned it over to the police already. Just what is it you want from me?"

"Art dealers in a town the size of Santa Fe tend to know each other, by reputation if nothing else. The police probably have a list of the ones known to have contacts with criminals, but there might be others who are more discreet."

"I have no idea who they might be," Santeiro said, rubbing the back of his neck with one hand. "I wish I could help. That murder took place only a few blocks from here. If it was the result of an art theft, the man responsible could hit my gallery next. Some of the artists I display here are known the world over."

Greg nodded. "Good point."

Santeiro walked to the counter, picked up a piece of paper and a pen and handed it to Greg. "Leave me your telephone number. If I hear of anything I'll let you know."

"I appreciate it," Greg answered, jotting his number down.

"I don't think any galleries in this area would touch the missing art, but there's always a market out of state. I'm sorry I couldn't be of more help," Santeiro said, walking Greg to the door.

"It's a . . ." Greg paused ". . . start."

"I wish you luck."

As she saw the men approach, Diana ducked out of sight into the doorway of another gallery. If Greg was guilty, surely he would have known precisely where to find the hide painting. Was he doing all this for show? Either way, she had to admit, he had a good idea. Finding the painting, then backtracking to the thief, certainly made sense.

Diana continued to trail Greg around the crowded Plaza. As he stepped inside the large courtyard of a Spanish-style building, she rushed forward. She knew that the building housed dozens of stores. If she lost Greg now, it would be nearly impossible to track him down in there.

She was only a few feet from the entrance when a man came out from a restaurant and blocked her way. "Diana! I'm glad I saw you going by. I needed to ask you about my order."

Diana stopped abruptly, barely managing to avoid a collision. "Mr. Garcia, hello," she said, recapturing her balance. "I can't talk right now, but I'll give you a call this afternoon." She tried to go past him, but he refused to be put off.

"It'll just take a second," he assured her. He was holding a white waxed bakery bag of Indian fry bread, and the aroma made her mouth water. "I need to give you the new kachina design I want on my menus." He handed her a sheet of paper. "Can you add it to the print order I gave you last week?"

"I'm sure I can," she answered glancing at it quickly and placing it inside her purse. "I'll call you." Not giving him a chance to reply, she shot past him, heading toward the courtyard.

Greg was nowhere in sight as Diana rushed beneath the arched gateway. With at least twenty shops to choose from, there was only one hope of finding him now. She'd have to go down the line and check all of them.

Diana sprinted to the entrance of the first store, stopped and glanced inside.

The soft, steel-edged voice from behind took her completely by surprise. "You're playing a very dangerous game, lady."

## Chapter Four

Diana spun around. Greg stood inches away from her, his green eyes probing her own. "How did you know I was following you?" Diana managed.

"When I was getting ready to leave Santeiro's gallery, I saw your reflection in the glass. Would you mind telling me what this is all about?"

She led the way to one of the benches inside the courtyard and sat down. "Last night you said you planned to find some evidence against the killer. It was obvious you had something definite in mind, so I decided to keep an eye on you and find out what it was."

He rubbed the back of his neck with one hand. "Don't you realize you're risking everything? If anyone notices I'm being tailed, it'll destroy my chances of learning anything important."

"Then let me go with you."

Greg allowed the silence to stretch out between them, then nodded. "At least then you'll know when I need you to stay out of sight."

She ignored the sharp remark. "So, what's next on the agenda?"

"I'm going to contact some people I know out of state and find out if there're any collectors who'd be interested in that hide painting."

"What makes you think they would be? Its value is primarily as a religious object, isn't it?"

He gave her a startled look. "That hide painting is an antiquity, and that alone adds to its value. It's also a beautiful example of primitive folk art. And I've heard that there were other artifacts taken as well. That tends to support my idea that the murder was an unexpected consequence of an art theft."

"What else was stolen?"

"My attorney had a list. They were small religious objects, items crafted out of gold and silver."

"Okay, I'll concede your theory has merit, but that's only one place to start. The murder of a priest is sacrilege, as well as a crime and that could appeal to some cults. The same applies to the theft of religious objects. I think we should look into that possibility also, and I know just where to begin asking questions.

"There's a record store about a mile from here, a hole in the wall, really. It specializes in all kinds of hard rock paraphernalia like posters and T-shirts taken from album covers, as well as fan magazines, books and jewelry. Some of the groups and their fans really go in for gory imagery, including the satanic, so the place attracts a lot of kooks. Kids, hard core or not, love the place. From what I hear, business at the store is booming. I'm sure most of the teens who hang around there are harmless, but it may be a good place to search for a lead."

"Some of those kids may not be as harmless as you think," he warned, jamming his hands into the pockets of his denim jacket. "Let me take care of this."

"I appreciate your concern, but I know the place. My brother, Frankie, used to work there, and he got to know the owner real well. The guy dresses as crazy as the kids to hype the business, but it's all show. Before he came out here, the man used to run a shoe store."

"Okay, while you're talking to the owner, I can talk to the kids."

"I'd better handle that too. They aren't going to trust you. They'll just give you the runaround and waste your time. You don't understand what you'll be up against." Frankie had been hard like the kids at the store, she remembered, until Father John had helped him turn his life around.

"It's my time to waste. And if all else fails, maybe they'll get tired of looking at my ugly face and tell me something useful just to get rid of me."

His face wasn't at all ugly, in fact quite the opposite. His deep green eyes contrasted vividly with the light bronze cast of his skin. His square jaw conveyed strength and determination. Yet, he also had a certain weathered, rugged look about him that eradicated any illusions of perfection. Instead, it added a touch of pure maleness Diana found very appealing. "You're going to have to be very thick-skinned and persistent," she warned.

"I can be that way when I'm trying to accomplish something that's important to me," he replied, his voice was deep, and vibrated with unspoken sensual power. "I've always believed anything that's worth having is worth working for."

He held her gaze longer than was necessary, and a shiver of excitement coursed through her. She had no business letting him affect her this way, but Greg awakened yearnings she'd never expected to feel again. Around him she was acutely aware that in the two years since her husband's death there'd been no one special in her life.

She stared at the ground, trying to focus on logic instead of emotion. "Okay, if we're going to work together, we might as well start with this lead." At least this way she'd be able to keep an eye on him and make sure no evidence was tampered with or missed. She glanced at him, wondering if he'd had the same thought. Somehow she managed to get the distinct impression he was way ahead of her.

"My van's right here," he pointed ahead. "Why don't we drive out there now?"

She stared at the weather-beaten vehicle. This was the first time she'd seen it up close in daylight. "Is it safe?"

"It looks like it's ready to fall apart, I grant you, but it's very reliable. I've traveled all over the West with it."

She shook her head. "I don't know how, unless you're a part-time mechanic."

"Actually, I have a knack with mechanical things. Nothing electronic, mind you, but I'm good with brake jobs, old clock mechanisms, fishing reels and that sort of stuff. I enjoy tinkering, it helps me relax."

"Is that what attracted you to your work?"

"In a way. In college, I landed a part-time job at the university's museum where they were doing some conservation and restoration work. I discovered I had a knack for it."

"Was it difficult to become qualified in that specialty?"

He shrugged. "Getting the financing I needed took some doing and there were strings attached." The muscles in his jaw clenched. "I learned the hard way that everything has a price and sometimes money is the least of it."

She wanted to ask him more, but before she got the chance, Greg smoothly switched the topic of conversation.

"What about you?" he asked. "How did you get into printing?"

She didn't want to talk about herself, but after all her questions, she couldn't exactly refuse him. Stalling, she gazed out the window. They were passing through one of her favorite neighborhoods, where the flowing forms of the adobe homes blended perfectly with the piñon-covered hillsides. But she didn't have the luxury to dwell on the beauty today. If she wanted to learn about Greg, even if only from an investigative point of view, she had to be willing to open up, too.

"I didn't exactly choose that business," she admitted, going on to tell him what had happened after her husband's death. "But it's turned out very well for me. I like the work and the shop's successful."

"How much did you know about the printing business before you had to take over?"

"I started working there just before Bob died, but he was always the one who managed the operation. Being his own boss was a matter of pride with him. He wasn't much of a businessman, I'm afraid. He worked long and hard, but any real gains just seemed to slip through his fingers."

"That must have been hard on you, too."

As memories flooded her mind, she stared off into the distance. After a few moments, she glanced at him. "What about you? Have you ever been married?"

"No. My family's back in Texas, but I don't have much to do with them."

Diana shifted, studying the items that filled the rear of the vehicle. There were no backseats, and cardboard boxes lined both sides, two rows deep. Leaning forward, she tried to figure out what was inside the smallest, near the driver. "Are those building blocks?"

He laughed. "In a way, I suppose. I make puzzles out of wood. The pieces, when fitted together properly, make squares or spheres. It's a hobby that helps me relax and maintain my eye for detail."

"Does that lamp mounted on the side over there really work?"

"It sure does. Those two cartons beneath it contain books on Western art and legends of the Old West. I live in the van when I'm traveling and I like to read."

There was a rootlessness to his life that filled her with sadness and evoked memories she would have much preferred to forget. "Turn at the next block and park in the first spot you see."

"Is this the shop where all those teenagers are?"

"No, that's a hangout for one of the street gangs in the area. The Gargoyle is on the second story of the corner building, further down."

He parked, then helped her out of the van and silently fell into step beside her.

"The kids hang around here on weekends and at night," she commented. "They have no other place to go. That's part of the problem. I know. My brother Frankie was mixed up with one of the gangs a few years ago."

As memories came rushing back, guilt assailed her. Frankie might have still been one of those boys if it hadn't been for Father John. And what was she doing in return? Letting herself become attracted to Greg Marten, the police's primary suspect in Father's murder.

Determined not to let Greg distract her, Diana started walking toward the door of the Gargoyle. As she passed the boisterous teenagers on the sidewalk, conversations stopped. Usually the young members whistled, or made rude comments when she walked by, but today there was only silence.

She paused at the base of the wooden stairs that led up to the store and glanced back. Greg was standing right behind her. He towered above her protectively. He hadn't said a word, he hadn't needed to. She suddenly understood why Greg was so easygoing. He must have discovered a long time ago that it was unnecessary for someone as imposing as he was to be unpleasant to anyone.

Envious of his gift, she strode up the steps and entered the shop. Greg remained outside. If he was planning to try to talk to any of the kids, he sure had their attention.

A short but powerful-looking man glanced up from the cash register as Diana walked in. "I'll be with you in a minute," he said in a gravelly voice.

She watched him for a moment, unsure if he'd recognized her. Bubba Mackenzie, the owner, hadn't changed much, except for putting on about twenty additional pounds. He was dressed in black stone-washed jeans and a black T-shirt depicting a bony hand reaching out from a grave. His wrists were decorated with studded leather bracelets. Bubba's hair was unusually long for someone in his late forties, and his beard was trimmed to a dramatic point in an attempt to convey a "satanic" appearance.

Diana tried to look at him through the eyes of his young customers, but it was no use. To her, he looked like a retired professional wrestler promoting a new grudge match.

"Diana Clark?" Bubba said as he came toward her. "I haven't seen you in ages!"

"I was afraid you'd forgotten me," she said with a smile.

"How's Frankie? Heard from him lately?"

"He writes occasionally, but not nearly often enough." She remembered his last letter, the one she'd brought to the church to show Father John. Her chest tightened. "I really miss Frankie, but I'm glad he's happy."

"And you?" He glanced around the room. Suddenly his gaze fixed on one of the teenagers looking at the silver skull jewelry.

Before the young man could take a step, Bubba lunged forward. He grabbed the youth's hands and pinned them firmly against the wooden counter. "Wanna buy some trouble, punk?" Bubba's deep voice reverberated throughout the room, and everyone stopped in their tracks.

"Let's have the stuff back now, kid. Put it on the counter with your left hand." Bubba's voice was low but menacing.

The young man, too terrified to speak, scrambled into his jacket pocket with the hand Bubba had released, and pulled out a silver chain and earring. Both had store tags still on them. "I was going to pay for them, honest. I just put them in my pocket by accident."

Bubba sneered at the young man, then grabbed him by the collar and lifted him inches off the floor. "Accidents like that can get you busted up real bad, punk. If I ever see your mangy body in here again, you're dead meat. Now get out!"

The teenager practically flew from the store, almost knocking over a customer who was just coming in the door.

No one looked up or made a sound for about fifteen seconds, then a girl by the posters giggled nervously. That seemed to break the tension, and conversations began again among the half-dozen kids present.

Bubba fastened his cold gaze on Diana, then winked. He cocked his head toward the office. "Come on. I can't talk to you out here." Stopping briefly, he yelled at the tall college-age kid behind the counter, "Joey, take over out here."

"No problem, Bubba."

As they moved toward the back, Diana saw Greg outside, at the top of the stairs, watching her. She gave him a quick nod, signaling all was well and followed Bubba into the back room. The minute the door was closed, Bubba broke into a wide smile. "I handle my own security, so I have to be firm with the kids. If I ever called in the cops, some of my customers would never come back. I've even been taking acting lessons. What did you think?"

As his expression softened the change in him was startling. He looked like a kid who'd found a brand new toy. "It's very effective," she admitted.

"I've got to stay one step ahead in this business, otherwise the kids will rip me off. Or worse, maybe get bored and stop coming."

"From what I saw out there, business is great," she replied.

"Sure, right now it is, but kids grow up and move on. You gotta keep them interested. And their interests can be pretty strange."

"Which brings me to the reason I'm here," Diana admitted. "I'm sure you've read about Father Denning's murder. Father didn't have any enemies that I know of. That's why I wondered if the murder might be associated with one of the cults in the area. Do you know of any groups that might be prone to violence?"

Bubba leaned back against the wall and regarded her silently for several seconds. "The police have already been here about that, but I didn't have anything I could tell them. I have an opinion, but I'm not going to speculate without facts. It's not fair to the kids. And if these kids start thinking that I'm betraying them in any way, they'll put me right out of business."

"Bubba, I give you my word that whatever you tell me will stay between us."

His eyes narrowed and he stared across the room deep in thought. Finally he nodded. "Okay, but let me warn you first that my impressions are just guesswork. I don't get close to the kids who come in here, even the regulars. I need to come across as just a little dangerous."

He walked to his desk and took a seat on top of it. Then, with a wave of his hand, he gestured to one of the chairs. "Most of the teenagers I see here are okay. They might get a little rough on occasion, but most of their energies are spent trying to impress each other. Peer pressure is very strong. There's one boy, though, who's a real loner. He's very intense, and he gives the rest of the kids the creeps. From what I've heard, the other kids think he's crazy. It's like he *really believes* all the hype."

"Has he ever done anything that would make you suspect he might be violent?"

"No, it's what he's interested in that makes me wonder. He always buys the most violent books and posters I carry. He even tried to trade me his own drawings once for some merchandise. Believe me, if a psychologist ever saw those, he'd have the kid locked up before dark. He's a good artist, but his subject matter is really sick." Hearing loud voices outside the door, he stood. "He usually comes in at about this time, I think he lives nearby. If you stick around, you'll see him. He always dresses in black, and has a bright silver pentacle around his neck. Only, if you want to try and talk to him, wait until he leaves my store. The other kids will get nervous if you approach anyone here."

"No problem." Diana followed Bubba to the door of his office. "I'll make sure he's a block away, at least. When he comes in, would you give me a sign? I'd hate to get the wrong kid."

"Believe me, you'll know this one when you see him."

As soon as Bubba emerged from the room, his jovial expression was gone. Diana saw him fix his stare on Greg, who was outside on the porch surrounded by a small group of kids. The two boys beside him were arguing the relative merits of hard rock bands.

"What's going on?" Bubba asked in a clipped tone.

"We're just talking," Greg assured the shopkeeper.

"See that you keep it that way," Bubba glowered at the boys, then fastened his gaze on Greg again. "Is there something I can help you with?"

Diana came forward. "He's with me, Bubba," she said quietly.

Bubba shrugged, then returned to his place behind the counter.

The next twenty minutes passed slowly. Diana made a show of browsing while she waited. Hearing the laughter coming from outside, she glanced at Greg enviously. Kids were milling around him, talking freely and obviously enjoying themselves. She was still trying to figure out what made people relax around him when she heard one of the two girls near her whisper to the other.

"Check out the guy coming in. He's a *strange* dude."

"Oh, yeah! I heard him talking to Bubba once and you're not going to believe this! The guy had built a small replica of the guillotine the Grave Robbers use in their act. Only his really worked, and he was planning to test it out on rats he'd caught at the dump."

The other girl shivered. "Yuck. Let's get out of here before he comes over."

Diana glanced at Bubba, and he gave her an almost imperceptible nod. A young man with shoulder-length black hair and piercing eyes came into the room. He seemed to take it in at one glance, then relax and step toward the book section. His black sweatshirt and jeans showed signs of age, their color having faded to a dark gray. Yet the silver pentacle he wore around his neck gleamed brightly, attesting to the care it received.

Diana turned to Greg, and saw that he too was watching the boy. It was almost impossible not to, really. The young man exuded the restless energy of an animal in a cage. His wary gaze would dart around the room periodically, then return to the books in front of him.

It took a great deal of willpower, but Diana forced herself to leave the shop and meet Greg outside on the porch. "Are you ready to go?"

Greg glanced at the boy, then back at her. As Diana shook her head in silent warning, he exhaled softly. "Give me a minute."

It took him a few moments to take his leave of the boys, but by that time Diana was halfway down the block. Greg jogged to catch up to her and said, "You won't believe the weird stories circulating about that kid! His first name's Arnie."

She gave him a rundown of what she'd found out. "I want to speak to him, but Bubba asked me not to do it in the store. I figured we'd wait for him out here."

"Getting him to talk to us might be tricky. We'll have to take whatever opportunities come our way."

"Here he comes now," Diana said quietly, moving forward.

Greg placed his arm around her waist and held her back. "Give him plenty of room. See the way he keeps looking behind him? We don't want him to figure out he's being followed." The boy reached the corner and stopped abruptly next to a small grocery store, glancing around.

Reacting quickly, Greg went inside the courtyard of an apartment building, pulling Diana in with him. "That was close."

Diana peered around the corner of the adobe wall. "He's bought a newspaper. Now he's heading down the side street."

"Let's go by and see what he's up to. Maybe he's meeting someone."

Diana stepped to the other side of Greg, angling to be the one facing the side street as they walked past.

"No, let me stay on your left," he countered. "I can look right over you without any problem. You're going to have difficulty seeing around me."

A moment later they strode past the side street. Diana casually turned her head and glanced in, unable to resist the temptation. Arnie stood about twenty feet away, newspaper in hand, leaning against a dumpster.

Greg stopped on the other side of the grocery store. "I don't think he's waiting for anyone. He didn't even glance up when we went by."

"Then this is our chance to approach him, and I know exactly how to do it." She pulled several leaflets from her massive cloth purse. "These are handouts promoting the Jobs For Teens program the Businessmen's Association sponsors. I'll duck in there and pretend I'm sneaking a breakaway from my partner."

"Sounds good, but just in case he decides to bolt, I'm going to jog around the block and come up from the other side. We don't want to alarm him if he tries to avoid us, but we don't want to lose him, either. It would help to find out where he lives."

"Okay, let's get started." Without delay she walked down the block and entered the narrow side street.

Hearing footsteps, Arnie gave her a quick glance, then looked back down at his newspaper.

Diana sat down on the crumbling sidewalk near the wall. "Handing out these leaflets is killing my feet," she commented. "My partner's so darned tall, I have to practically jog to keep up!" She reached for the pile of flyers beside her. "Here, take this," she said. "It'll be one less I have to give out."

Arnie turned his back to her and continued looking through the newspaper. "Throw them out for all I care, lady. Just leave me alone."

"Lighten up, will you? I'm just trying to unwind before my partner finds me and I have to go back to work." She saw him tear out something from the newspaper. Curious, she started to walk toward him. "Something interesting?"

Arnie spun around to face her. His eyes were blazing with a strange inner fire. "Back off, lady." He started walking slowly toward the other end of the alley, keeping his gaze on her. As he was about to reach the halfway point in the alley, Greg appeared at the far end, blocking his path.

Arnie froze, his head turning from Greg back to Diana.

"Relax," Diana said softly, continuing to approach him. "All we want to do is talk to you."

In a flash the boy ducked behind a large garbage bin on wheels, then with one mighty shove, started it rolling.

The giant bin wavered unsteadily as it hurtled forward on a collision course with her. Unable to get out of the way, Diana leaped up onto the edge of the bin, clinging desperately to its side. She tried to pull herself into the container, knowing she was about to hit the wall.

## Chapter Five

That's when she saw Greg out of the corner of her eye. He'd grabbed a wooden pallet from beside the building and jammed it against the wall. An instant later the dumpster hit the low pallet, partially collapsing the wooden framework with a loud crunch. The jarring stop loosened Diana's hold on the metal side. As she fell, Greg caught her and pulled her into his arms.

"Are you all right?" He lowered her gently to the ground, but didn't let go.

"I think so," she answered.

She tried to convince herself that the shiver that coursed up her spine was just a reaction to her close call. His body felt hard and warm and for a moment at least, she knew she was safe in his arms. Then, as he rubbed his hand over her back, she had to admit another more dangerous emotion had begun to flutter to life within her. A thrill ran down her body as he tightened his arms slightly. She could hear the hammering of his heart as she pressed her cheek against his chest. He tangled his fingers in her hair, sending fiery sensations rippling through her.

She moved away from him reluctantly and fastened her gaze on the smashed pallet. She'd been lucky this time, but danger and violence were an ever-present reality she'd have to guard against. She forced her thoughts back to the task she'd vowed to see through. "Any idea where Arnie went?"

Greg glanced around. The side street was deserted, and the only sound came from traffic a block away. "I think he climbed over that coyote fence." He pointed toward a wall made of six-foot-tall branches bound together with rope. "He's long gone by now."

"We almost had him!" Diana said, her face lined with frustration.

"Count your blessings. You could have been really hurt."

"Thanks to you, I wasn't," she admitted unsteadily. "I guess I owe you one."

"A simple thanks is enough. Besides," he added with a grin, "if anything had happened to you, I would have had a devil of a time explaining it to the police. Based on my experiences with them so far, I'd have probably been doing all my talking from jail."

Despite his kidding, the fact remained that he *had* come to her rescue. His actions were more in line with the caring, gentle man he appeared to be than the murderer she had suspected. "You were there when I needed you, and that's what counts."

He gave her an embarrassed half smile. "Does this mean I've graduated from low-life to knight in shining armor?"

"Let's just say you're moving in the right direction," she answered in a soft voice.

Diana picked up the torn newspaper the boy had left behind. "I'm going to take this with me and find out what's missing. Maybe that'll give us a clue."

"Good idea." Greg rubbed his shoulder near a spot where the seam of his shirt had been torn by the refuse container.

"Are you okay?" She came up to him. "Maybe you strained a muscle."

"I'll work the kinks out on the way back," he said, stretching his arm slowly forward.

"Does this help?" Diana reached up and began to rub Greg's shoulder and upper back with her fingertips. She liked the feel of his muscular body and the way it seemed to yield, then tighten into rock hardness in response to her touch. Her mind raced and she began to visualize scenes she had no right to consider. Angry with herself, she stopped abruptly and moved away from Greg. "That's enough," she snapped more for her benefit than his, and started walking toward his van.

"Thanks, I think," Greg said, regarding her sudden change of attitude with confusion. He caught up quickly and fell into step beside her. "By the way, you have my address and the phone company can give you the number, but how can I reach you?"

She pulled a business card out of her purse and wrote a number down on the back. "If I'm not at the print shop, try my home number on the back of the card. I usually get off work between five and six."

Greg nodded, placing her card into his shirt pocket.

An overwhelming sadness seeped through her. "You won't be able to get hold of me at home before eight or nine tonight, though, even if something does come up. I'm going to go by the church this evening and say a prayer for Father John."

"We'll get together tomorrow then and figure out what to do next. Maybe my out-of-town contacts will have a lead for us on the stolen painting. I'll also ask my attorney to give me a list of the other stolen items," Greg said.

"Okay. By then, too, I should know what article Arnie was reading. That boy is involved in something, I can just feel it."

WHEN DIANA ARRIVED at the print shop, things were already hectic. Giving Anita a chance to take a break, Diana dealt with the customers who were waiting and then packaged the orders ready for pickup.

"By the way, how did things turn out today?" Anita asked when she emerged from the small coffee room at the back.

"All I managed to end up with are more questions," Diana grumbled.

"Anything I can do to help?"

"Yes, there is," Diana replied, pulling the folded newspaper from her purse. "Could you find out what article was torn out of this newspaper?"

"Sure," Anita answered, taking it from her. "Mine is still sitting on the kitchen table."

Diana helped Anita lock up the shop. "I'll be late getting home tonight, so don't worry. I'm going to stop by the church."

"Light a candle for Father John for me, okay?"

"I will," Diana replied.

As she drove to the church, memories of Father John Denning filled her with an infinite sense of loss. If only she'd arrived earlier at the church, maybe she could have done something to prevent his murder. Yet, even as the thought formed, she knew that she was not to blame. Fate had conspired against them both.

Diana pulled into the parking lot adjacent to the chapel and walked inside. The church was nearly empty, except for one woman sitting at the front and another just leaving. Diana went to the votive candle stand before the statue of the Virgin and lit a candle. As she started back toward one of the pews, she caught a glimpse of a tall, thin man at the back of the church. He was standing next to a recessed doorway, partially hidden in the shadows.

Diana shivered slightly, unable to ignore a vague, but persistent sense of uneasiness. Taking a deep breath, she struggled to view the situation in a clear and logical manner. There was no reason for her to feel apprehensive. The church was a public place and being tall and thin was scarcely a crime. She tried to push the man from her thoughts as she sat facing the altar. Her efforts failed as some innate sixth sense warned her of his continued presence and interest in her.

Curious, she turned her head slightly and verified her instincts were right. The man was still there, watching her. Diana could feel his eyes on her, boring into the back of her skull as if she were a display in a store window. Perspiration ran down her back.

This just wasn't like her! She'd always confronted problems head-on. Yet there was something about this that felt all wrong. If only the church hadn't been empty! The other two women she'd seen were now gone.

As she detected a faint trace of pipe smoke, she remembered Greg's words the night of his arrest. Her body began to shake as she realized the danger she was in. If Father John's killer had returned, she wouldn't be allowed to leave the church alive.

Trying to map out her best possible defense, she shifted and gave the man a long sideways glance. He was wearing a long top coat that bulged slightly on one side of his waist. Light gleamed off what appeared to be a large shiny button or pocket watch on his vest. Her gaze drifted upward and fastened on the dark bandanna around his neck. Above that, his features were hidden in dark gray shadows made even more pronounced by his wide-brimmed Stetson hat. Only one object stood out clearly, the briar pipe in his mouth. A thin tendril of white smoke curled lazily toward the distant ceiling.

He had to be crazy, or an actor of some kind, no one else would go around in public dressed like a turn-of-the-century cowboy. She waited a bit longer, hoping he'd make the first move and she could duck him by moving in the opposite direction. Yet the man made no attempt to come any closer.

The church, ordinarily a serene and peaceful place, offered her little solace. She swallowed back her fear. She had to try to get away. Her palms moist with perspiration, she jumped to her feet and ran toward the opposite side of the chapel. When she finally risked a glance back, she realized the cowboy had disappeared. She stopped in her tracks and looked around quickly, more afraid now of what she could not see than of what she had. Maybe he'd anticipated her move.

Bile rose in her throat. Bracing herself, she walked to the back of the church. It would be the last thing he'd expect her to do and perhaps that would give her a slight advantage. Diana peered warily into the shadows searching for the cowboy, but he was nowhere in sight.

Puzzled, she remained still and listened. The tomblike silence remained undisturbed. Moving about cautiously, she went to the place where she'd seen him last. The scent of his pipe tobacco was particularly strong there, a tiny wisp of smoke still lingered in the air. Yet the cowboy had vanished like the trace of smoke that dissipated before her eyes.

Weak at the knees, she reached for the nearby stand of holy water and steadied herself. He must have gone outside, that was the only explanation that made sense.

Dreading what she had to do next, she peered out the doors and glanced around furtively. It was still light outside, and people were strolling by on the sidewalk. The normality of the scene, in stark contrast to her experiences moments before, caused her to breathe a sigh of relief.

Diana approached a couple sitting on the grass near the front of the church, and asked if they'd seen anyone come out before her. Their negative answer only added to the mystery. Diana spoke to several more passers-by, but no one had seen the cowboy she described. Of course it was possible he'd tossed off his coat and Stetson. A tall man in blue jeans wouldn't have stood out any more around here than rabbit brush out on the mesa.

As she turned the corner, she saw Greg standing near the side door watching a few tourists. "So it was you," she muttered softly, her fists clenched in anger.

Spotting her, he smiled and came forward. "Hello. I thought I saw your car parked out on the chapel side."

"What are you doing here?" she demanded harshly.

"You're angry," he observed. "Sorry, but I didn't think you'd care if I came here. I thought it might be a good idea to ask people in the area if they'd seen anything the night of the murder."

"What was the big idea of stalking me inside the church wearing that dumb costume?" she demanded, unable to keep her temper in check any longer. "Though I see you've discarded it already," she observed, glancing at his blue chambray work shirt and jeans.

"What are you talking about? What costume? And what do you mean by stalking?" he protested.

As a breeze swept past her, she caught a whiff of pipe tobacco still on his clothes. "And I suppose you're going to tell me that you don't smoke a pipe either."

He gave her a wary look, his muscles tensing slowly. A shadow crossed his eyes, but then was gone. "I do smoke a pipe sometimes when I'm unwinding, but I have to be careful never to get it around anything I'm trying to restore. That's why I don't smoke very often." He clamped his lips in a straight line. "Okay, I've answered you. Now I want to know what happened and why you're asking me these questions."

She took a deep breath, trying to make up her mind. The tobacco scent wasn't quite the same as the one she'd detected inside the church. And the cowboy had seemed taller and thinner than Greg. But, considering her frame of mind at the time, she wasn't quite sure she could trust her perceptions.

She glanced at the low juniper hedge next to the church wall. Could he have stashed the clothes there? She decided to take a look.

"Will you please tell me what's going on?" he insisted, his voice gaining a harder edge. "If there's someone around here I should be on the lookout for, I'd like some advance warning."

"First, I want to check and see if there's a stash of clothing anywhere around here. In the meantime, if you see a man who's tall and on the thin side lurking about, please let me know."

She crouched by the hedge and parted the prickly branches carefully, peering into the areas beyond. She worked her way along the hedge slowly. Besides a plethora of whining gnatlike insects, there was nothing to be found.

Reaching the end, she faced Greg and told him about the man she'd seen inside the church. "He was waiting and watching." A shudder traveled over her. "I was afraid he was the killer."

"If he'd wanted to hurt you, he had the perfect chance. I think you can rule that out as his intent." He considered the matter. "I can understand why he made you uncomfortable, but it's possible he hung back trying *not* to scare you."

"Then why stay in the shadows instead of sitting in one of the pews?" She shook her head. "His actions were peculiar, Greg, and believe me I'm not prone to an overactive imagination. What bothers me most is the way he disappeared when I started to make a run for it."

"When you came out, did you see any sign of him?"

"No, but it's possible he got into a car and left, or perhaps someone picked him up."

"If this guy could have had something to do with Father Denning's murder, then we should continue looking around. It'll be dark soon, so let's not waste any time." He studied the people on the sidewalks. "Forget about the guy's costume for a minute. Think back. Tell me everything you remember about the man."

"I didn't get a real good look at his face," she conceded, walking alongside him toward the Plaza. "What struck me most was his height. I wouldn't swear to it, but I think he might have been an inch or more taller than you. I also got the impression he was very thin."

"You mentioned the smell of pipe tobacco," Greg added, his voice taut. "Can you describe it?"

She thought about it for a moment. "The scent reminded me of cinnamon and burning piñon wood mixed together."

He furrowed his eyebrows and remained silent for several moments. "We may be on to something. When I found Father Denning's body, there was a faint but unmistakable trace of pipe smoke in the sacristy. I told the police, but they didn't believe me. Apparently they didn't notice it themselves. Did Father Denning smoke?''

"No. And even if he had, he never would have lit up in church. Do you think we're dealing with the same man?''

Greg shrugged. "It's possible, but the evidence is too circumstantial at this point. Remember, I smoke a pipe, too, and so do many other people.''

She considered it for a moment. "The pipe tobacco on your clothing smells more like cherry, and it's less pungent. The cowboy's blend was *strong,* of course I detected it while it was being smoked. *He* didn't hesitate to keep his pipe lit in Church, though I thought anyone would know better than that.'' She glanced at the people strolling around the plaza, but the tall cowboy was nowhere to be seen.

"I have a suggestion. There's a pipe shop not too far from here. That's where I found my favorite blend. They're really well stocked. Why don't we stop by there and see if you can identify the brand the cowboy used? It might tell us something about this person, especially if the tobacco is expensive or imported. And if we're lucky, maybe he bought his tobacco there and it might give us a way to locate him.''

"It's worth a try,'' she answered. "I'd sure like to find that cowboy. He's too good at vanishing into thin air. I haven't seen anyone who even remotely resembles him.''

Greg led the way to a small pipe shop next to one of the hotels. "Good thing the shop stays open until eight, or we couldn't have come in tonight.''

The shopkeeper greeted them with a smile. He listened to Diana's description of the blend, then brought out a handful of tobacco tins from beneath the counter. "I'm not familiar with what you've described, but let's see if we can match what you're looking for.''

The minutes passed slowly as she went from tin to tin, and the shopkeeper's smile began growing thin. "Perhaps you could get me the name . . .''

"I don't know it, that's what makes everything so difficult." She continued until she'd checked all the blends he carried. "It's not here. What he smokes is stronger, and more acrid. I'm sorry I've taken up so much of your time."

"No problem at all," the shopkeeper answered, trying, but not quite succeeding, to keep the annoyance out of his tone.

As they walked across the plaza, Greg gestured toward a coffee shop on the next block. "I think we should have a bite to eat and talk this out."

Diana thought back to the scene at the church, trying to recall some other clue that might help them find the cowboy. "Whenever I try to picture the guy we're looking for, what I remember most is the costume he was wearing. It was so peculiar! Why would a criminal go around in something that makes him so conspicuous? He has to be a real psycho."

"Or a very smart man," Greg answered, then glanced at her. "Look at it this way. The costume is what you remember, not the man himself. Almost anyone else would have had the same reaction."

"You're right." She pursed her lips tightly. "Let's go have that coffee," she muttered, slowing down.

He hustled her past the door. "Keep going, then turn at the next corner."

"The coffee shop's right here," she said, confused.

"Just go along with me. I want to see if I'm right about something."

"What?" Greg's arm was draped loosely over her back, and the warmth of his skin seeped through the thin fabric of her blouse. She struggled to suppress a shiver, knowing it would give too much away.

"*Don't* look back, but I think we're being followed."

She tensed instinctively. "The cowboy?"

"No, a couple of kids. I spotted them when we first went into the tobacco shop." He angled sideways slightly as they turned the corner. "They're still back there."

"If it's just kids, let's go back there and confront them. They'll probably run off," she suggested.

"No, let's just ditch them. The diner up ahead has a rear exit. I eat there a lot and use it often since it's a short cut to my studio. The owner knows me by now so he won't mind if we just walk through."

"I'd rather go back and force the issue. I've dealt with kids like that before, and it's all a matter of how you come across. If you show them you're not going to stand for any nonsense they back down."

"Maybe that's the way they react to you, but with me along it could be a completely different story." He let out his breath slowly. "I've seen this type of situation before. Most adults wouldn't try to mess around with someone my size, but with kids it's different. They're constantly testing themselves, and picking on the largest guy around is one way of doing that."

"I hadn't thought of that, but you may be right," she conceded. "Let's do it your way."

He led her inside the Mexican restaurant and gave the manager a wave. "Enrique," he said as he approached the small, overweight man, "there are some kids outside who are looking for trouble. Would you mind if we took the rear exit and avoided them?"

"Amigo, any kids who'd pick on you have to be a little *loco,* don't you think?"

Greg grinned. "I agree, that's why I'd like to keep the lady out of their way."

"Go ahead," Enrique answered loudly. "I'll make sure they don't come through my place."

"Thanks, Enrique. I appreciate it." Taking Diana's hand, Greg led her through the restaurant and out the rear door. "The employee parking lot connects with the same street the church is on."

They were about twenty feet from the restaurant when two angry young men appeared a few feet in front of them. A third came up a moment later.

Greg stopped in mid-stride and stared at the boys. Casually he stepped in front of Diana. "Something on your mind, fellows?"

"You're on our turf man." The tallest one challenged Greg. "We don't need a reason to be here. But you do."

The boy's stained shirt had the sleeves torn out and hung down almost to his knees. Yet what struck Diana most was the lack of emotion in the boy's face. He had the same look she'd seen on the hardened criminals who occasionally made the evening news.

"Look guys, I don't think you really want to pursue this. So let's call it a night, okay?"

"You scared?" The boy's sudden grin was as lethal as it was mirthless.

The fat kid behind him stepped up and stood beside his friend. His eyes jumped from Greg to Diana, then back to the third teenager with them.

"Cops patrol this area about every five minutes, guys," Diana warned. "You know that as well as I do. If you start something, you're going to end up in jail. What's the point?"

"The cops don't know nothin'," the fat kid spat out. "They been trying to push us around like we're trash. Let 'em come."

"So they've seen a few of our plaques around here," the leader said defiantly. "We've got a right to our own art," he added, and started to move to outflank Greg. "They're declaring war on us, so we're returning the favor."

Greg made a move that left the kid with his back to a wall. "Don't do it, kid. You *know* you can't win."

"You've got more to worry about than we do," the leader shot back. "There's three of us against you. And you're going to have to look out for your chick, too. You've got the problem, not us."

"I guarantee you'll have more than you can handle," Greg answered in a quiet voice. "Just walk away."

Diana watched him, fascinated. It was Greg's calm that made him appear even more menacing than his size. He held his body perfectly still, and she had the impression that when he did move it would be with purpose.

The third boy angled sideways slowly. Then, without warning, his arm flashed out, feigning a punch. His fist stopped inches from Greg's side.

Greg never flinched and the leader regarded him warily. "So why don't you show us what you got, man?"

Greg held his ground, but made no move toward the boys.

The boy worked his way over to the other side, trying to edge closer to Diana. "If you're worried about getting hurt, take a walk, and we'll entertain your chick."

Diana's patience snapped. "Okay, that's enough!" she stepped around Greg. "You've had your fun, now *back off*!" As the leader started toward her, she kicked him hard in the shins. "Don't even think of it. My foot could have reached higher, so count yourself lucky."

Before she realized what was happening the overweight teenager moved in behind her. Diana heard him and spun around, but before she could react, Greg grabbed the boy by his collar, lifting him off the ground. He held him aloft with one hand and swung around to face the others.

As the leader stepped toward him, Greg grabbed the dangling boy's belt in the back, ready to throw the kid right into the other two.

The teenager froze, his mouth slightly agape. "Whadda you gonna do to him?" he demanded.

The boy trapped in Greg's grasp made a tiny sound as Greg shook him slightly, effortlessly. The kid, Diana surmised, must have weighed one hundred and sixty pounds. Yet Greg held him in the air, and looked no more burdened than a fisherman proudly holding up a string of trout.

Impressed by Greg's strength, the leader backed off, giving Diana plenty of room. Stopping about ten feet away, the two remaining kids glowered at Greg. "We're not going anywhere without Bullfrog, mister," the leader said, "and neither are you. We have friends who'll be showing up any minute now."

## Chapter Six

Three more boys appeared from around the corner before he even finished the last word. "What's going on, Rob?" a short, Hispanic-looking boy glanced at the leader, then glared at Greg.

"This chump's not going anywhere until he puts Bullfrog down," Rob growled. He threw back his shoulders, trying unsuccessfully to look imposing.

The Hispanic boy leered at Diana. "Don't you worry. We won't hurt you a bit."

"You don't impress me, kid," Diana shot back. "And I don't think Petey's going to be too thrilled that you're giving me a hard time."

The boys looked at her in surprise. "How do you know Petey?" Rob asked, then quickly shifted his attention back to Greg.

"Why don't you ask him?" Diana smiled at the muscular-looking boy approaching. His brown hair fell over a red bandanna. His face was void of expression, but the lines that edged his features attested to the harshness of his life. "Diana?"

"Hiya, Petey."

"Rob, what the hell's going on here?" He glanced at Bullfrog, then at Greg. "Diana, why don't you take off?"

"That chick's not going anywhere, Petey. For crying out loud, look at the size of that dude. She's our bargaining chip."

Petey stared at the boy until he looked away. "Take off, Diana."

"I'm not going anywhere," she shot back. "Petey, we didn't start this. We were checking out some leads on Father John's murder when we spotted your guys tailing us."

"This guy's with you?" Petey asked.

Diana nodded. "Bullfrog tried to grab me from behind, so he picked him up."

"Picked him up?" Petey met Greg's eyes. "What are you going to do with him?"

Greg eased Bullfrog down, then gave him a little push away. "He's all yours. All we wanted to do was go our way."

"Now we got you!" Rob signaled the other boys to move in.

Greg pulled Diana behind him as he took a defensive stance with their backs protected by the wall.

*"No!"* Petey's voice was sharp. "Rob, can't you get anything right?"

"You wanted us to roust people so they'll swamp the cops with complaints. What's the problem, all of a sudden?"

"This is Frankie's sister. We don't hassle our own," Petey spat out.

Rob's eyes narrowed. "The lady who gets us jobs decorating walls with our art?"

"Some of you are really good," Diana said. "You should get paid for your work."

Rob shoved his hands into his pockets. "I remember Frankie. Nobody ever messed with him more than once."

Bullfrog flashed her a smile. "He was the one who gave me my nickname."

"Yeah, who else can catch flies right out of the air?" one of the others said.

"Father John was all right," Petey commented thoughtfully. "He even got the cops to cut us some slack. You're trying to find his killer?" Petey gave her a puzzled look. "I thought the cops already had him."

Diana glanced at Greg, wondering how he'd handle it.

"I'm helping Diana find leads," Greg answered. "The artist who was arrested was quickly released. He was working for the church restoring some paintings." He paused long enough to make sure he had their complete attention, then added, "He didn't do it. I know, I'm him."

"You're the one they arrested?" Rob asked, surprised. "Hey, you might be able to con the lady, but don't try to put one over on us," he warned. "No one would come out and admit to murder, man."

"If my story hadn't checked out, I'd still be in jail. Father Denning hired me. That's why I was at the church." He challenged the boys with a direct look. "You guys have a problem with that?"

The gang members exchanged quick glances, and Diana could see that they weren't eager to force another confrontation. "If Diana says you're okay," Petey answered slowly, "you're safe from us." He paused then added, "For now."

"We could really use some help, Petey," Diana ventured. "We're trying to find a guy I've seen around the church. This character is either very smart, or a real lunatic. We're not sure which."

"We can handle that. Count us in," Petey replied, then glanced at the other boys, who nodded.

Diana gave them a description of the cowboy she'd spotted inside the church. She looked around uneasily as she talked about him. She'd never forget the terror she'd felt inside the church. Her sense of helplessness and vulnerability had filled her with an acute dread. As much as she wanted to find the cowboy, deep down she was terrified of their next encounter. "Have any of you seen this guy hanging around?"

Bullfrog shrugged. "There's some kind of play going on in a place about two blocks from the church."

"The Corral Dinner Theater?" Diana asked.

"That's the one," Bullfrog answered, more animated now. "They're doing some kind of Western. I saw some of the actors in costume hanging around the back smoking cigarettes."

Diana glanced at Greg. "It's worth checking out. Let's go right now."

"We'll keep an eye out around the church, Diana. If we see anyone who could be the guy, we'll let you know," Petey said.

"Thanks, I appreciate that."

Greg remained close by her side as they walked away from the gang.

"It's okay, they won't bother us anymore," Diana assured him. "Petey'll see to that."

"Kids can change their minds."

"They seem tough, Greg, but it's mostly for show. I know, Frankie was just like them. Only he was one of the lucky ones. Thanks to Father John, he got out and made something of his life." Her voice was taut. "When I see those boys I remember Frankie, and parts of my own life, too. Those kids strike out at others in anger because that's the only emotion that survives inside them. They're unwanted and that leaves an empty spot inside them that never stops aching. After a while, most of them see it as a weakness that can be used against them, so they bury it under resentment and hostility. There're very few people like Father John who actually try to change the odds stacked against them."

"I don't doubt they're troubled, but that's why it's foolish to trust them. At first their hardness is mostly an act, but eventually it becomes a part of them. They learn to enjoy the power that comes from victimizing people, and eventually that destroys their humanity. Think about Petey's face. The adult he'll be someday is etched there."

When they reached a building edged in small colored floodlights, Diana walked up to the young woman who stood just inside the doors. "We'd like to talk to the manager, please."

A moment later a middle-aged man wearing the costume of a turn-of-the-century gambler approached. Seeing the distinctive dress, Diana's hopes soared. "We're trying to track down a man we believe might be one of the actors appearing here. It's possible he might have witnessed an accident that happened a few days ago," she said, couching her terms carefully.

The manager shrugged. "Why don't you buy tickets, have dinner, then enjoy the show. The actors circulate after the performance."

"Would it be possible for us to come in and talk to the actors *before* the play gets started? We won't take much of their time."

"I'm running a business, ma'am. The same policies that apply to the other dinner guests also apply to you. Theater patrons only, *no* exceptions." He was about to say more when an irate looking chef strode over. After a hurried exchange, the manager excused himself and walked away.

Diana checked her wallet. "I've only got two dollars."

Greg reached into his and produced a five. "I don't think I'm going to be much help."

Diana exhaled softly. "Well, that's that." As she glanced around the room, her gaze fell upon a display of photographs promoting the current play. She walked to the wall to study them more closely. "None of these actors seem to have the same type of costume or build as the cowboy I saw."

As a waitress came by, Greg flashed her a wide smile. "Ma'am could you tell me which one of these actors is about my height?"

"Honey, we don't have anyone built like you." She gave him a wink. "Too bad for us."

"Any who are even close?" Diana insisted, annoyed by the woman's flirting.

The waitress considered it for a moment or two. "The tallest actor we have here is the man who plays the saloon keeper," she pointed to one of the photographs, "but he's barely six feet tall."

"Thanks," Greg answered with a quirky grin.

The waitress smiled coyly. "You come back soon. We'll take good care of you, I promise."

As they left the dinner theater, Diana gave him a dour glance. "Well, it looks like you made quite an impression."

Greg chuckled softly. "Does it bother you?"

"No, of course not." But the smug grin on his face irritated her beyond belief. She quickened her pace and he fell easily into step beside her.

"Tell me more about Frankie. You've never said how Father Denning helped him. Did he talk him into quitting the gang?"

"It was much more involved than that," she answered. "My parents sent my brother to live with me the year after they started managing a corporate farm outside Los Angeles. The job took practically all their time, and Frankie was left alone too much. There were too many influences there working against a boy with too much free time on his hands."

"What happened?"

"My parents found out that he'd joined a street gang in Los Angeles. They were terrified of the trouble he'd get into and insisted he quit, but Frankie refused. Dad called and asked me to help by talking to him. I did, and suggested they send Frankie to live with my husband Bob and me. I knew that what Frankie needed most was someone who'd be there for him."

She paused for a moment, painful memories making it difficult to keep her voice steady. "Then Bob had his accident. His death took us all by surprise, and the aftermath nearly destroyed me."

"You must have loved him very much," he commented in a soft voice.

"I did, but it was the circumstances that made things even more difficult." She recounted the details of the investigation. "Every time they revised their opinion, I'd have to try and come to terms with it all over again. It practically tore me apart. I wasn't able to deal with Frankie and his needs on top of that."

Diana shoved her hands into her jacket pockets so Greg couldn't see them tremble. "Of course Frankie felt abandoned again and the inevitable happened. He got involved with the street gang you met earlier. You think Rob and Petey are tough? You should have been around Frankie."

"You can't blame yourself for the choices your brother made," Greg said, sensing the guilt that lay beyond her words.

"But I do. You see, instead of drawing him into my life and allowing him to help, I pushed him away," she said, her voice filled with sadness. "If it hadn't been for Father John, I'm not sure what would have happened to Frankie."

"He spoke to your brother and helped straighten him out?"

Diana smiled, remembering. "Father John made Frankie his business. He found a myriad of jobs to keep Frankie busy and away from gangs. He played up to his 'tough guy' image, and got him involved with the youth boxing program. He also managed to talk him into doing 'security' during church-sponsored dances. He slowly built up Frankie's self-esteem by constantly reminding him of how the other kids looked up to him. Six months after he arrived, Frankie took the high school equivalency test and joined the Navy." Diana glanced up and met Greg's eyes. "Father John turned my brother's whole life around and that's a debt I intend to square."

"I guess we both have a lot at stake." Greg stopped near the church parking lot and looked around thoughtfully. "Everyone agrees that whoever murdered Father John must have left a trail of blood. The police believe I obscured it when I went into the sacristy, then left the church." He paused. "But it's also possible they didn't search a large enough area."

"They had the church, the grounds and part of the street cordoned off. If there had been a trail, they'd have found it."

"They searched the logical area, but maybe the killer was prepared for that. If he got complacent at all, it would have been after he was away from the church grounds. If we take our time looking, we might be able to find something the police missed."

"It hasn't rained in this part of the city since the murder," she said glancing around at the sidewalk and curb, "but it could at any time. If we're going to search, we'd better do it tonight."

"It's already dark," he protested. "Even with flashlights we'd be hard-pressed to find anything. Let's wait until morning."

"Blood spots will glow under a fluorescent light. I can borrow a battery powered lamp from a friend of mine who's a geology buff. If there are traces of blood anywhere in the area, then you can bet they'll be minuscule. Our best bet of finding anything is to use this method at night."

"Okay, let's go find your friend."

They returned with the lamp twenty minutes later. "Let's start by searching the school grounds. If the killer rushed away from the church on foot, that would have been the most likely escape route for him," she ventured.

"Good thinking. He would have had plenty of cover while making his getaway. Had he headed in the other direction, he would have been going toward the plaza and bound to encounter quite a few people."

They divided the ground into sections and worked with methodical precision. Fifty minutes later, they still hadn't found anything. "Well, maybe my theory wasn't as good as I thought," Greg said, as they took a break.

"It's bound to be slow going," she argued. "The lamp can only do so much, and there's a vast area to cover."

"We've searched the parking lot and the sidewalk. I'm not very hopeful at this point."

"There's a section of the curb that borders the parking lot. We haven't checked that. Let's go give that a try."

Working together they made their way around the curbing. As they reached a section near the school, Diana rubbed her back. "We struck out again," she muttered. "It was worth…" She stopped speaking, seeing the look on his face, and followed his line of vision. Spots glowed faintly in the beam of the lamp she held wearily in one hand. She stared at the maroon dots that shimmered with a peculiar green cast.

Greg crouched down and studied them. "I think it's blood. If it belongs to Father John, then we've found a trail," he added, standing up. "We've got to contact the police." He jammed a stick upright into the graveled ground next to it.

"I suppose we should go to the rectory and call from there," she said hesitantly. Uneasiness began creeping through her, filling her with apprehension and a twinge of fear.

"I know it's a shock to find Father Denning's blood," Greg said gently. "Do you want to sit down for a minute?"

She shook her head. "It's not the blood. It's…well…I just have the strangest feeling that we're being watched."

Greg searched the shadows, his gaze taking in everything around them. "I don't see anyone, but it's dark. That puts us at a disadvantage. Let's get going."

She switched off the lamp, a shudder running over her. Everything had grown quiet all of a sudden. The absence of sound around her seemed to magnify her tension. Even the night insects had stopped their humming.

They were heading back to Diana's car when, without warning, Greg stopped.

Her heart jumped to her throat as she saw the cowboy. The man stood about thirty feet away from them, outlined in the pale glare of a street lamp.

"I'm going to talk with him," Greg said resolutely.

"I'm going with you," Diana answered.

As they approached, the man slipped around the side of the school building and disappeared from sight. Diana and Greg rushed after him, but when they turned the corner seconds later, the cowboy had vanished.

"Where the hell is he?" Greg grumbled. "He has to be around here somewhere." He glanced in the hedge that bordered the grounds.

Diana gestured toward the street gang gathered at the far end of the block. "Maybe the kids can tell us what direction he went." Diana rushed forward, Greg at her side.

Petey nodded, seeing her come up. "You again. This is getting to be a habit."

"I have a question, guys. Did a man in a cowboy costume just go by here?"

"Nobody's gone past us," Petey answered. "Are you looking for the same guy you told us about before?"

"Yes. He was here a minute ago," Diana answered.

"We'll help you look." With a few hand gestures he split up the group, then hurried them on.

Diana rushed back toward the school grounds with Greg at her side. "Where would you hide if you wanted to escape people following you?" she asked, glancing around.

"Inside the school, if I could find a way in."

"There are no windows on this side, but maybe he cut through the hedge, and went down the street that way," Diana suggested, looking at the residential section behind the school. "That's the only way he could have gone and avoided Petey's gang."

"I don't know," Greg replied thoughtfully. "I think we would have seen him running, at least at first. He wouldn't have been able to hide very well until he reached the houses. Those streets are well lit, and empty."

Fifteen minutes later, after a fruitless search, the boys rejoined them. Petey looked glum. "Are you sure you saw him, Diana? We looked everywhere and there's no sign of him."

"I saw him all right," Diana replied.

"It's dark, fellows," Greg added. "Somehow he managed to give us all the slip. But we had to try. Thanks for the help."

Petey shrugged. "We'll keep our eyes open. Is there anything else?"

"I've got to call the police," Diana said, "so you guys might want to make yourselves scarce."

"Our pleasure."

As the kids walked away, Diana turned toward the rectory. The lights had all been turned off. "If we knock now we're going to wake up Father Sanchez," she said. "He's very old and has to be up early in the morning to say mass. Why don't we use the telephone at the gasoline station down the street instead?"

"That's fine with me." Greg strode down the crumbling sidewalk, his face lined with worry.

"You're so quiet all of a sudden. What are you thinking about?"

"I don't like the idea that someone's dogging our footsteps. This guy's sharp Diana. We shouldn't underestimate him. I was keeping an eye out, yet he sneaked right up on us."

Reaching the telephone, Diana collected some change from her purse and called the police. After a brief exchange, she replaced the receiver. "They'll meet us over by the school. They're dispatching the crime scene unit."

They returned in time to see two sedans approaching. "Maybe that's them in unmarked units."

Greg didn't take his eyes off the vehicles. A moment later four men emerged and came toward them. Greg stepped in front of Diana and moved forward to meet them. "Can we help you?" he asked.

The man at the front flashed an ID. "Detective George Morales, Santa Fe Police Department. We're looking for Diana Clark."

"That's me," Diana said, coming up to them.

"You made the call to the station?"

"Yes I did," Diana said. "We found some traces of blood we believe might be Father Denning's and thought you should know about it."

"Why were you out here looking for blood now?" he countered.

"We got the idea of expanding the area you guys had searched, and figured that the fluorescent lamp would give us the edge."

"Civilians shouldn't get involved with police business," the detective replied. "If you had any reason to believe there was evidence here, you should have told us about it and let us check it out."

"We didn't know anything for sure," she protested. "We just decided to take a chance."

The detective gave her a sour look and focused his attention on the technician working near the curb. The man carefully chipped off the sections of concrete that had been stained with blood.

"Did you find any more using your lamp?" the technician asked, glancing at Diana.

"No, that's it."

The man's attention shifted to the detective. "I'd like to have this area taped off. We didn't search for blood this far from the scene so we're going to have to do it now. We have a special chemical, Luminol, that's for use only in darkness. It'll come in handy now. It doesn't establish the presence of blood, but it does react with certain chemicals, some of which are found in blood. It'll pick up even a trace and make it glow. We'll go over areas that are suspect, and see if we can find any more. Then our boys can take the sample to the lab and run a test to determine what it is."

"I really doubt that's Father Denning's blood," the detective commented. "It's not likely the killer could have avoided leaving a trail until he got this far out."

"He might have carried his shoes for a while," the technician ventured with a shrug. "That's one way to explain it."

"There's something else." Diana told the detective about seeing the cowboy.

"This is the second time I've seen him. I haven't been able to get a clear look at his face, but the costume and body build were the same."

"Nothing you've told me proves he's tied to the murder, so don't go jumping to conclusions. You could have an admirer who's got a few connections loose." He twirled his finger next to his ear. "You know what I mean?"

"I know perfectly well what you mean," she shot back acidly.

"In either case we'll check it out."

Diana watched the crime scene unit as they worked. The area was sealed off, and soon more technicians arrived.

A few minutes later the detective strolled over. "Which one of you spotted the blood first?"

"I did," Greg answered, locking eyes with the detective.

Seeing the mistrust in the cop's eyes, she recounted the details. "I'd have seen it in another minute too."

"So it was just luck and hard work?" The detective grew quietly pensive, then added, "Or you might have had more of an advantage over the department than you realize, Ms. Clark." He challenged Greg with a direct gaze, then walked away.

Diana kicked the pine tree next to her. "That was a cheap shot."

Greg smiled. "I know. Only I've got to admit it was worth it to see you react this way." His voice was deep and as gentle as a caress. "It's good to have an ally and a friend."

His words made a pleasant warmth course through her. Yet, in its wake came an intense longing for the caring and closeness that bound a man and a woman together. She'd had it once and the loss had opened a wound inside her that had never quite healed.

A moment later the detective came up to them. "There's no need for either of you to remain here. We'll handle things from here on."

Diana nodded and they started heading back to her car. "I think it's time to quit for the night."

"I should get back to the studio and check my answering machine. I telephoned some art dealers in Phoenix and Dallas earlier, and they're supposed to call me back if they turn up anything interesting. The thief will have to market the stolen items sooner or later, or may have already tried to do so. Maybe I can track him down that way."

"Will you let me know as soon as you can if you do hear from them?"

"Why don't you come back to the studio with me? We really should map out an overall strategy together, even if we have to modify it as we progress."

"Shall I give you a ride?"

"My van's parked a bit further up. It seems a lifetime ago, but I met you at the church, remember?"

"I'll follow you," Diana said with a nod.

As she drove through the nearly empty city streets, her thoughts remained on Greg. The more she got to know him, the less she believed he could have had anything to do with Father Denning's murder. He was the least violent person she'd ever met. Gentleness and protectiveness were too much a part of his character. She sighed, thinking that Anita would have insisted that it was much too soon to lower her guard.

Diana pulled into the parking area next to Greg's apartment building and found an empty space near the back. Greg met her as she was getting out and led her toward his studio. "What do you make of the cowboy, Greg?" she asked.

"I'm not sure. He's made no attempt to harm either of us, so I don't think he's an immediate threat. We'll have to keep an eye out for him, though, until we figure out what he's up to."

As they approached his studio Greg slowed his pace, his gaze fixed on the area directly ahead of them.

His tension communicated itself to Diana, and she felt her heart start to hammer. "What's wrong?"

"That corner window facing this end of the building belongs to my studio," he said, gesturing before him. "Only it wasn't broken when I left."

"There's light coming from inside," Diana warned.

# Chapter Seven

As he quietly approached his front door, he listened for sounds coming from inside. "I can't hear any movement in there, but just to be safe, wait here," he whispered.

Diana watched him nudge the door open with the tip of his sneaker. He obviously had no intention of calling the police. As the door swung wide, Greg stood with his back to the wall for several seconds, then went inside. He emerged moments later. "You can come in. No one's here, but it's a mess."

Diana followed him into the studio and glanced around, her stomach plummeting. Curtains had been torn from the windows. The contents of cabinets and drawers were scattered about, and the walls were covered with reddish spray paint. She recognized the gang's plaque prominently marked on each wall. "It's the Diablo Locos. I expected better from Petey. I never thought they'd pull a stunt like this!"

She saw Greg walk around, picking up broken pieces of glass and debris from the floor. There was no anger in his face, just a stoic acceptance that made her heart wrench with sympathy. "I'm going to find Petey and the boys and haul them back here. They can either clean this up or explain it to the police."

Greg started picking up his paint brushes. "Don't bother. We wouldn't be able to prove anything without a witness.

And they're minors. I doubt anything would be done about it.''

She crouched down and picked up parts of what appeared to be a shattered camera. ''They've destroyed some of your equipment, too.''

Greg moved to the other side of the room and picked up a black metal tube. ''This used to be my microscope. I'd use it to study brushwork, and to date certain pieces.''

''Here's the phone,'' she said, retrieving it from beneath the overturned sofa. ''You really should call the police and report this. And don't touch anything else.''

Greg pulled a chair upright, and dropped down into it. ''There's no sense in rushing to clean up anyway. The damage has already been done.''

He telephoned the police, then as he placed the receiver back in its cradle, a thought occurred to him. ''What if the kids planted something here that could incriminate me?'' He studied the debris around him. ''Some of those boys have a grudge against me. They might have left a knife or almost anything else among my things. I don't need more trouble with the police if it can be avoided. Let's have a quick look around just in case.''

Diana helped Greg look through the mess, but they didn't find anything he couldn't account for.

''The closest thing to a deadly weapon I have in here are palette knives, so keep searching. If you find anything that looks suspicious, show it to me.''

They had just finished when a squad car pulled up. As the uniformed officers came in and looked around, Diana prayed that calling the police wouldn't end up creating an even bigger disaster for Greg.

Eventually the patrolmen filled out a report and prepared to leave. Diana stared aghast at one of the officers. ''Aren't you going to even try to lift fingerprints?''

''Ma'am, this looks like an ordinary breaking and entering. We don't have the manpower or budget to follow up on something like this. Besides, Mr. Marten said nothing appeared to be missing." He diverted her attention to the wall. "We already have a good idea who did it. That plaque belongs to the Diablo Locos, but those kids will vouch for each other. It's almost impossible to pin anything on them, unless you actually catch one of them in the act."

"What's he supposed to do now?" Diana demanded. "They've destroyed practically everything in here."

The officer shrugged. "I suggest you call your insurance agent, Mr. Marten." Taking another look at the small studio, the patrolman added, "That is, if you have one."

Greg remained in his seat as the officers left. Diana watched him. "How on earth are you going to replace all this?" she asked softly.

"I'll think of something," he muttered, rising and walking to the bed. "At least they didn't find the box with my carvings." He bent and pulled out the cardboard box. It looked to be full of old clothes.

"More wooden blocks?" she asked, wondering why those would mean so much to him. "Why did you pack them in with old clothes? They don't look that fragile to me."

He smiled and shook his head. "These aren't the blocks," he answered, pulling out an intricately carved wooden figure of a cowboy riding a bucking bronco. "These are fragile, as you can see."

"The ones from the shelf. I thought they were bronze castings when I saw them the first time I came here."

"I decided after the police had done their search that I should be more careful where I placed them. So I stored them for safekeeping." Pride was evident on his face as he watched her examine his work.

"This is beautiful," she exclaimed as she took the sculpture from his hands and held it by the base. "Just look at the expression on the rider's face! You've captured his determination and something else..." She paused, searching for the right word. "Satisfaction. The cowboy likes what he's doing."

He brought a second carving out and placed it in front of her. "This one's my favorite." A weather-beaten cowboy stood holding a rifle. His other arm was draped gently over a boy hugging his knee. The man's fingers were laced lovingly in the child's tousled hair as he stared ahead defiantly.

"It's as if the wood was still alive," she said in a whisper. "The man has an incredible toughness etched in his face. Yet he's conveying love and strength at the same time. You can see it in the way he's touching the child. How do you capture those emotions in your work?"

"Whenever I sculpt, the tools become an extension of my mind. I carve what I feel, not just what I see."

"Do you exhibit them in galleries?"

"Not usually. The carvings are too much a part of me. I know there's a market for them. The collectors and galleries who have seen them always make offers, but I rarely sell one. Maybe it's not a smart business move, but not everything an artist creates has to be on the market."

He placed the pieces back inside the box, wrapping them carefully in old clothes first. "I better put these back beneath the bed. They would have been destroyed for sure if I'd have left them out in the open."

She helped him pick up all the clothes that had been strewn out of the closet and drawers. "They've made such a mess, but at least they didn't ruin your clothes, too."

"My jeans and shirts have been through worse," he said, restoring some order to the closet.

"Do you want to pick up everything else?"

"No, I'm ready to call it a night. The bed's been cleared off, the rest can wait until morning. Come on, I'll walk you to your car."

"If you need anything call, okay?" It was obvious Greg didn't have much money. If their situations had been reversed she would have been desperate. Diana wanted to help him but she wasn't sure how to go about it.

Greg accompanied her outside. "If I find the answering machine, I'll see if there were any messages on it. That is, if it still works. If not, I'll call the dealers tomorrow again and check with them."

Diana stood by the car, reluctant to leave. "Are you sure there isn't anything more I can do?"

He smiled gently. "It's enough to know that you care, Diana."

Saying good-night, Diana drove home, but she couldn't quite force Greg from her mind. His home was in shambles, and the things he valued, with the exception of his carvings, had been destroyed. Every time she put herself in his place, her chest tightened. As she pulled into her driveway, she saw that Anita's lights were still on.

"I've been waiting for you," Anita called, rushing out to meet her. "How did things go?"

Diana invited Anita into her kitchen and filled her in on the evening's events. "He can't win with the police or the kids. Now, on top of everything else, he doesn't even have the equipment he needs for his work."

"Don't be too quick to feel sorry for him. If Greg Marten turns out to be a thief and a murderer, he'll probably have plenty of money stashed away."

"The guy doesn't have much. Look at his life-style. His van is a disaster and his studio was certainly nothing to brag about." Diana filled a plate with chocolate chip cookies and placed them on the table between them.

"By the way, I tracked down the article that was missing from that torn newspaper," Anita said. "It was a story about Father John's murder."

Diana sat up, relief and excitement coursing through her. Even though she'd all but ruled out Greg's involvement, anything that pointed away from him was still welcome news. "I have a feeling that Arnie's either mixed up in this, or knows something about it. I need to find him."

"How? You don't even know his last name."

"I'm not sure how I'll manage, but I will. Arnie's got something to hide and I'm going to learn what it is."

DIANA SCARCELY MOVED from her desk the following day at the print shop. Orders needed to be sorted, bills paid and account books balanced. Despite her hectic schedule, she kept glancing at the phone hoping to hear from Greg. Her attempts to telephone him had proved fruitless. It was a bit after five when she decided to drive to his studio.

As she reached the parking lot outside his complex, she saw him walking up the street, a bucket of paint in each hand. "I've been trying to reach you. How are you doing with your studio?"

He walked with her to his door. "The owner provided the paint and fixed the window. I've got to put one more coat on the walls, but it looks decent now." Greg led the way inside.

"You have been busy," she said, surprised at the difference he'd been able to make in less than twenty-four hours.

As her gaze drifted around the room, her astonishment became mingled with a trace of suspicion. She hated to doubt him, yet the evidence before her was hard to dismiss. Next to the telephone was a brand new answering machine, the tag still dangling from the wire. A camera, still in the box, had been placed on top of the worn sofa. New paint brushes and an expensive looking gray microscope stood on the corner of his table. She blinked, taking it all in. "Where on earth did you get the money to replace everything so fast?"

"I sold the carving of the cowboy on the bronco to a collector who's been after it for years," he explained.

"I'm sorry. I know how much that carving meant to you," she sympathized.

"It's okay. As I told you, I part with them occasionally. It's just not something I want to mass produce and sell for a living. And it'll be appreciated by the man who bought it." His voice held a hollow ring.

"I'm sure it will be. It was a beautiful piece of work."

"Let's not talk about it anymore," he commented. "Would you like to stay for dinner? I make a mean Texas chili."

"I can't. The morning paper announced that there's a memorial service for Father John tonight at the church and I want to be there. This is the only chance our community has to say goodbye. The actual funeral is going to be in his Michigan home town."

Greg nodded, his expression remote. "I had nothing to do with the murder, but I feel that I've failed Father Denning. He entrusted me with the hide *Madonna*," his tone grew quietly pensive. "I need to go to the service, say goodbye to him, and . . . assure him that I won't give up." He held her eyes for a moment. "Can you understand that?"

"Yes," she said in a quiet voice. "If our situations were reversed, I'd do the same thing."

"I'll wait until after the service has started and stand at the back of the church. My presence there could be awkward under the circumstances."

"I doubt you'll be noticed. My guess is that the church will be overflowing."

He walked with her to her car. "I'm glad you came to see me." His eyes held hers longer than was necessary. "You're the closest thing I've got to a friend in this town, even if you're still not positive about me."

His words were unemotional. Yet his need to be believed communicated itself to her and struck a chord deep within her. She wanted to offer some comfort, but she wasn't sure what she could say that would make a difference. "I'll call you later tonight. We still need to get together and plan what we're going to do next."

As she drove away she realized she hadn't told him about Arnie. That omission pointed to the biggest problem with their investigative partnership. She was getting too close to him. Her wish to prove him innocent had become almost as strong as her need to find the person responsible for Father John's death.

She had to pull back into herself, to keep her distance. If she failed Father John in this, she'd lose the one thing that had always sustained her, her ability to count on herself.

GREG WATCHED HER GO, then returned to his studio. He'd tried to fight it, but Diana was making a place for herself in his heart. She was attractive and intelligent, but those surface attributes had little to do with the intensity of his feelings for her. Her rare smiles warmed him, bringing a sweet ache he'd never experienced before. It tore him apart inside to see that she was still reluctant to fully trust him. He would have given ten years of his life to gain a share of that unflagging loyalty she showed her friends.

Tossing his jeans and shirt on the top of the bed, he showered and changed. He was about to leave his studio when a plainclothes detective appeared at his door. He recognized the man from his initial interrogation at the station.

"Let's go, Marten." He flashed his ID. "We have a few more questions for you."

"I've told you guys all I know," Greg replied irately. "Is this about the bloodstains Diana Clark and I found yesterday?"

The detective clenched his fists. "Downtown, Marten."

"Am I being arrested?"

"Not yet, but that can be arranged if necessary," the detective growled.

"What did you say your name was?" Greg insisted.

"Clark. Same as Diana's." He brushed past Greg and stepped inside the studio. "What the hell, we can talk here."

Greg watched the man carefully. It didn't take a genius to see that he was looking or hoping for trouble. If he was related to Diana's husband, then undoubtedly this was connected to her, not the case.

Greg shut the door. "What's this all about?"

The detective looked up at Greg, who was a good six inches taller than he. "Listen, dirt bag, I heard the story about you happening to notice the blood on the ground, and I know it's pure crap. You knew where to look. You've got enough problems right now, Marten. Believe me, you don't need the kind I'm going to bring you if you don't stay away from Diana."

Greg met the other man's gaze without flinching. "Are you finished now? I've got an appointment I'd like to keep."

"You're a cool one, I'll give you that." Don Clark strode to the door. "Just don't do anything you'll live to regret."

Greg watched him leave, then picked up his keys from the hook by the door and walked out to the parking lot. As he drove to the church he thought about Detective Clark. The man had the disposition of an angry bobcat, but he couldn't fault his motives. There was something about Diana that made a man want to protect her.

By the time he arrived, the service had started and the church was filled to overflowing. People crowded around the front steps. Greg joined the multitude pressed around the open doors. A loudspeaker carried the service out to them. Deep in his own thoughts, he bid the Father goodbye and vowed to find and return the hide painting.

As a prayer rose from the crowd around him, he glanced up. Detective Clark stood glowering at him about fifteen feet inside the church beside a seated Diana. The venom in the detective's glare made him stiffen his back, but he met the man's eyes with a stare of his own. He would not be cowed by anyone, particularly where Diana was concerned. Even if that fool of a detective didn't know it, they were both on the same side. They shared mutual goals: finding the priest's killer and keeping Diana safe.

AFTER THE SERVICE ENDED, Diana and Don left together.

Fifteen minutes later, Diana sat down across from Don on the sofa at her place. It was clear something was on Don's mind. Her guess was that he'd heard that she was investi-

gating the father's death. "Don, let me save you some time.
I'm going to keep looking into Father's murder. Whether or
not you agree, the department needs help. I can give them
that. Look at what happened last night. Thanks to Greg and
me there's a trail for you guys to follow."

Don's lips were compressed so tightly they became white
at the edges. He stood and paced for a moment before answering. "Diana, I've done my best to help and watch over
you since Bob died. Sometimes I know you've hated that,
but you're family, and I'm doing what I feel's right."

"I know." She smiled. "That's why I've done my best to
put up with it."

Seeing her expression, he chuckled softly. "You sure
don't make it easy, lady." He paused, growing serious once
more. "I've really tried to respect your need to make your
own decisions, but this time I've got to step in. It's bad
enough that you're trying to investigate a murder, but
what's even worse is that you're relying on Marten's help to
do it." He returned to the sofa and sat down. "Do you realize that it's still possible *he's* the murderer?"

"I don't think so. The more I know him, the more I believe his story. He's a gentle person—"

Don let out a cynical laugh. "He's sleazy, Diana. Look at
how he lives. He does that by choice."

"So he doesn't make tons of money, so what? You can't
judge someone on that basis."

"Fine, then let me give you a few other facts. He lives like
he hasn't got two dimes to rub together, yet he's got a top-
notch attorney representing him. I'm not at liberty to dis-
cuss police business with you, but you've got to start using
your head. Marten's showing you the side of himself he
wants you to see. Trusting him could be a deadly mistake."

"I'm not trying to convince you that he's innocent, Don,
not without proof. But don't be so quick to convict him,
either. Even the police department let him go for lack of
evidence. And don't forget. He did find the blood. I might
have missed it." Seeing his expression, she held up one

hand. "He didn't lead me there, or manipulate me into following that course. Don't insult my intelligence, Don."

"All right," he conceded, "so you happened to go in the right direction. Maybe he pointed it out when he thought you were about to see it anyway."

She shook her head. "That wasn't the way it was." She met his eyes. "Now you tell me one thing. Was it Father's blood we found?"

He hesitated. "I don't suppose there's any harm in telling you. The newspapers are going to carry the story tomorrow," he muttered almost to himself. "It was Father's blood, and we think it was carried there by the sole of the killer's shoes. We just aren't sure yet how he managed to avoid leaving a more obvious trail closer to the church."

"This should clear Greg." She answered with a wide smile. "He was arrested as he came out of the building. He wouldn't have had a chance to get that far."

"It doesn't rule out an accomplice," he countered. "That's the problem with amateurs. You make snap judgments without sufficient evidence."

"It seems to me that you're doing the same thing. You're assuming he's guilty and working from that premise."

"I admit I'm a cynic when it comes to human nature."

"Are you on the case officially now?"

"We don't have that many guys on homicide, so we all share the work load. You know that." He started toward the door. "Do one thing for me. Don't trust Marten, not even if he's charming as hell." He walked out onto the porch. "And if he gives you the slightest hint of trouble, call me. Remember that not everyone is as nice as I am."

She laughed. "Right. A charming, sweet cop with a disposition to match."

"I may be a little gruff at times," he admitted with a sheepish smile. "But I only have your best interests at heart."

Diana returned inside and turned off the porch light. She'd just poured herself a glass of iced tea when she heard a knock.

Thinking that Don had returned, she didn't hesitate to open the door. "Did you forget..." Her smile gave way to confusion. "What are you doing here?"

Greg leaned against the door frame and gave her an embarrassed grin. "I've been waiting for Detective Clark to leave. I saw him with you at the church and I didn't want to have another confrontation in front of you."

All of a sudden she understood why Don had seemed so tense through the service. "Come in," she invited. As she led the way to the living room, she filled Greg in on the latest developments. "So the police still haven't ruled you out. Their theory is that you might have had an accomplice."

"What do you believe?" he insisted softly.

She remembered what Don had said about Greg's attorney, but it wasn't something she could simply ask Greg about. She needed facts and knowledge gained from something more than his word. "I wish I could say I'm one hundred percent sure about you Greg, but I'm not. I know that's not what you want to hear, but it's the truth."

Greg stared across the room, disappointment etched on his face. "I came to tell you that the art dealers I contacted for information on the hide *Madonna* have not been able to help us. At least not yet."

"There's something else we can look into in the meantime." She told him about the article Arnie had ripped out of the newspaper. "We have to learn what his interest in Father John was. Tomorrow I'm going to go back to the Gargoyle. If I can't find Arnie at the store, then I'll ask around the neighborhood. Surely someone will know where we can find him."

"That's going to be tough, but it's worth a try. We'll go together. Judging from what we know about this kid already, you shouldn't approach him alone."

"Can you meet me at the print shop at about noon?"

"I'll be there."

Diana walked with him to the door. "What happened between you and Don earlier today?" she asked, wanting to hear his side of it.

"We talked, that's all. He's trying to protect you, and he sees me as a threat to your safety." He met her eyes. "But I'm not, Diana. I would never hurt you." He stepped closer, and held her gaze. "I'd give anything to have you believe me, without reservations."

She wanted to wrap her arms around his neck and press herself against him. The memory of the last time he'd held her flashed through her mind—a memory that was embarrassingly and intensely physical. She glanced away. "I . . . won't lie to you."

"I know," he murmured. He smoothed his hand across her cheek and held his breath while she instinctively leaned into it. "I'd better go," he said, his voice low and hoarse, "right now."

She nodded, struggling against the desire that flowed through her. Diana watched him walk out into the night, then went back inside. The sound of the door shutting accentuated the emptiness she felt. In her heart she knew Greg was as innocent as he claimed to be. Yet there were discrepancies in Greg's life that were impossible to ignore. They indicated that there was more to him than met the eye. But whatever his story turned out to be, she couldn't believe it would prove him to be different from the caring, gentle man he appeared to be.

Diana walked to the bedroom and undressed. Crawling between the sheets, she wiggled and stretched, trying to get comfortable. Only cool emptiness greeted her no matter which way she turned. The bed seemed impossibly large all of a sudden. She thought of Greg, images of him flashing through her mind. The hollow feeling inside her intensified and she sighed long and loud in the silence of her room.

# Chapter Eight

At the print shop the following morning, Diana finished packing two large orders while Anita took care of customers. Everything was running smoothly and on schedule.

Anita placed the telephone back on the receiver and glanced up at Diana. "You're still determined to go with Marten to look for that boy?" Seeing her nod, Anita added, "If Don calls, shall I tell him where you've gone?"

Diana cringed slightly. "You don't have to lie, but I'd appreciate it if you didn't volunteer any information." As Greg stepped through the door, Diana reached for her purse and went to join him. "Thanks for taking over for me here, Anita. And don't worry. I'll be back by two o'clock."

"Let's go in my car," Diana suggested, preferring her own driving to his slower pace.

She zigzagged through the daytime traffic around the plaza, then headed out toward the edge of town. As they approached the Gargoyle, she slowed.

"Bubba said Arnie doesn't usually visit the shop until later in the day, so let's check out the area first and see if we can spot him." She parked in the first available space. "It's lunchtime so we may get lucky. If not, we'll go back where we lost him before and ask people if they've seen him."

"That kid should stick out like a sore thumb. Someone's bound to know where we can find him."

"We're also going to have to figure out a way of getting him to talk to us. Any ideas?"

"Not really." Greg matched her pace as they made their way down the sidewalk. "We're going to have to play it by ear, but at least this time there's no way he's going to take us by surprise."

They tried places a boy like Arnie might frequent, but their search proved fruitless. "If we don't turn up anything today, I'll come back later and keep looking," Greg assured her. "Sooner or later, he's bound to show up."

"Good. This kid is our best lead so far."

Greg stopped abruptly and gestured to the restaurant ahead. "It looks like we just struck pay dirt. Look at the corner booth near the window."

Diana smiled. "We've got you now, Arnie," she muttered.

Greg stopped in the waiting area and glanced toward the tables. "Arnie's sketching," he said quietly. "He doesn't know we're here."

"Smoking or nonsmoking?" the hostess asked, greeting them.

"We'd like to talk to that young man," Greg answered pleasantly. "Do you mind if we go on ahead?"

The hostess shrugged. "Good luck," she muttered.

"I gather he's not one of your favorites," Diana commented.

"He's a real nuisance. Every day it's the same. He orders a cup of coffee, then sits at the window sketching while getting endless refills. In the afternoon, when the light shifts, he leaves. He never talks to anyone or tips the waitress." She shrugged. "If you're going to talk to him, be careful. He's a real jumpy little guy."

Greg glanced at Diana. "I'm going to slide into the booth next to him. You sit on the other side."

"He's facing the room, Greg. He's going to see us coming."

"I don't think so. He hasn't looked up yet. Whatever he's working on has all of his attention. Let's go now before that changes."

They were ten feet away when loud laughter erupted near the doors and Arnie looked up. As he saw Greg and Diana, the surprise mirrored on his face quickly turned to anger. In the blink of an eye, he slid out of the booth and bolted down the aisle that led to the kitchen. A waitress emerging from the double doors saw him a second too late. Food-laden dishes crashed onto the floor as he shot past her into the kitchen.

Mumbling an apology, Greg hurtled over the mess and sprinted after Arnie. He reached the kitchen in time to see him ducking through the rear doors. Determined not to lose him, Greg dodged the cook and his helper who were yelling at him in Spanish, and raced after the boy.

As he stepped outside, Greg glanced around the employees parking area. Arnie was nowhere to be seen. Quickly he dashed to the street. That's when he saw Arnie. The boy was sitting on the back of a flatbed truck that was speeding away.

Muttering an oath, Greg returned inside. He'd never been less welcome at a restaurant. The cook and his helper yelled out an endless string of Spanish words he didn't understand. He could make a good guess as to their meaning. Then, as he entered the dining area, the waitress transfixed him with a lethal glare and lambasted him.

Greg helped her gather up the pieces of broken glass, then, mumbling an apology, moved away. He could see Diana still at the table Arnie had occupied. She held several sheets of paper in her hand. Her face was unnaturally pale, and she looked as if she were about to be ill.

Under normal circumstances she would have followed him in pursuit of Arnie. Whatever she'd found must have had the import of a guided missile.

He placed a hand on her shoulder and turned her to face him. "Are you okay?"

Her hands trembled as she handed him the papers Arnie had left behind. "They're disgusting," she managed in a shaky voice.

Greg studied the drawings. They were simple but realistic pencil sketches showing, from several different perspectives, a man with his throat being cut by a large blade.

"You two have caused enough trouble." The hostess came toward them, her eyes glittering with anger. "Our other patrons are all upset. I'd like you both to leave."

"Come on. I need some fresh air." Diana strode directly to the door. "I should have helped you," she said apologetically, "only I wanted to gather up what Arnie had left behind. Then I saw what it was." Her voice shook and she paused for a moment by the sidewalk. "By the time I got my act together, you were on your way back in." She cleared her throat. "I'm sorry. If you lost him, I'm as much to blame as anything."

"Forget about Arnie for now. Are you feeling any better?" He could still see the signs of strain on her face and fought the urge to pull her against him and hold her.

"I thought I was ready for anything, but I guess I wasn't," she said, starting back toward the car.

"You're human." He kept his pace slow, matching hers. "You don't have anything to apologize for." He could sense her fear and the embarrassment she felt for not having helped him.

"I want to find that kid more than ever now," she said, her voice hard. "I don't know why anyone would hurt a priest, but I do know Arnie shouldn't be running around loose."

"I admit that he seems to be a good suspect, but remember what Bubba told you. Arnie has a real penchant for gruesome art. These drawings don't prove anything."

"Okay, so the evidence is inconclusive, but that doesn't mean it should be discounted. I'm going to tell Don what we've learned. With his contacts maybe he can locate Arnie."

Moments later they reached Diana's car and started back to the shop. Greg watched her as they drove east. A frown creased her face and her fingers were clenched around the wheel. Diana was strong and she'd handle this, but he wished that she would reach out to him and let him help. He hated to be shut out of anything that concerned her.

"Diana..." He struggled to find the right words. "It's impossible for anyone, man or woman, to always be tough. Sometimes we confront our vulnerabilities when we least expect it. You faced yours when you saw the sketches. Mine came when I realized I needed—" He clamped his mouth shut. He'd almost said too much. Damn, he would have ruined everything, telling her something she didn't want to hear from him.

She parked next to the print shop. "Finish it," she insisted quietly. "What were you going to say?" Nervous, she moistened her lips with the tip of her tongue.

Heat flashed through Greg. "I've never cared what people thought of me. I was at peace with myself and that was enough. Then you came into my life and things changed. I needed to have you believe in my innocence," he said slowly, "and believe in me as a man. That's as important to me as what I think of myself. I care for you, lady, and that makes me as vulnerable as a man can be." He tore his gaze away from hers before he lost himself in it. "And it's because I care that I'm not going to rush you or do what I'd really like to do right now. Only I'm going to have to leave, or my good intentions are going to go up in flames."

She reached for his hand and held on to it. "What exactly do you have in mind?" Her trembling voice was scarcely more than a whisper.

He was on fire for her. He touched her cheek, his eyes lingering over her lips. They were soft, full and impossibly inviting. She looked beautiful with the afternoon sun playing on her hair. Angling his head, he pulled her to him, pressing her mouth with his own. He urged her to part her lips and drove his tongue into her warmth.

She moaned and the soft sound was practically his undoing. He held her neck gently in his hands and increased the pressure of his kiss. Hunger tore through him, and he ached to feel her moving against him. His body was so taut, he thought he'd explode. With a ragged breath, he broke off the kiss, but couldn't tear his gaze away. Her lips, still moist, tugged at his restraint.

Shivers of desire made her body pulse. "I'd better go inside," she managed in a shaky voice.

"And away from me," he growled. "Maybe Don was right. You're not safe with me." The taste of her still lingered tantalizingly in his mouth. Greg threw open the car door and stepped out. "I'll talk to you later."

Wondering if her body would ever stop trembling, Diana stared at him as he walked away. She took several deep breaths. It had been a mistake to kiss him, but she couldn't honestly work up any regret. The forces drawing them together were as powerful as any in nature. Logic was a poor defense against love.

As she strode through the doors of the shop, she smiled at Anita. "How's everything here?"

Anita's gaze strayed over her, and a knowing look charged her expression. "You're late."

"We had some trouble." She recounted the events with Arnie. "I've never seen sketches like the ones I picked up on that table." She pulled them out of her purse.

Anita glanced at them and cringed. "You should turn these over to Don as soon as possible." Anita watched Diana as she returned the drawings to her purse. "But more than that happened today, didn't it?"

Diana felt her cheeks grow hot. "I'm not sure what you mean."

"You've assumed that these drawings prove that Greg is innocent." Anita glowered at her and clicked her tongue in disapproval. "You've lowered your guard around him, and he's taken advantage. I can see it on your face."

"He's not using me, and I haven't made any unwarranted assumptions," she defended. "The only thing I'm doing is not taking his guilt for granted as everyone else seems to be."

Before Anita could answer, they heard a man's heavy footsteps approaching the door. "Diana!" Don's voice boomed inside the small print shop.

"What's wrong?" she rushed out to meet him.

Don's face was flushed, though it was hard to tell whether it was due to anger, exertion, or both. "I was on my way here when I saw Marten driving away. Has he been bothering you?"

"This is one conversation I don't want to be part of," Anita muttered, leaving the room.

Don gazed at Diana for a second, his expression changing into one of shrewd recognition. "Diana, after all I've told you, how can you be gullible enough to trust him?"

Diana led Don to her office area. "Calm down. Everything's fine. In fact, I've got something interesting to tell you."

Don listened to her story about Arnie and took possession of the pictures. "You should have come to me right away. That kid sounds unstable. And taking Marten along with you for protection is like expecting one rattlesnake to protect you from another."

"I don't see it that way," Diana replied coldly.

"That's what worries me the most," Don countered. He glanced at his watch. "I have to get going, but I'll follow up on this. If anything develops I'll let you know. In the meantime, be careful."

Anita and Diana spent the rest of the afternoon taking inventory and ordering materials. It was close to five by the time they could sit down with a soft drink and take a break. As Diana took her first sip, the phone began to ring. Wearily she picked up the receiver.

"How was your afternoon?" Greg's voice seemed rich with a gentle emotion she didn't dare define.

"Busy, but fine," she replied. Diana glanced at Anita, who was shaking her head. How had she figured out that Greg was the caller? Was it possible that her tone of voice also changed when she spoke to him?

"I've come up with an idea I'd like to talk over with you," he said.

"I'll be locking up in another half hour. Would you stop by and meet me here?"

"Sure. By the way, I saw Detective Clark when I was driving away from your shop. Did you talk to him about Arnie?"

"Yes, I did, and he promised to follow it up," she answered, "but he wasn't too thrilled to hear you and I were still working together."

"You're very special. He wants to make sure nothing happens to you," Greg said in a rich, mellow voice. "You can't fault people for loving you."

Her heart, her breath, everything including time seemed to stop. His words had woven a spell around her, and she was afraid to do anything that would unravel it. For several seconds she was at a loss for words. Then, as her gaze locked with Anita's, reality came rushing back. "I can watch out for myself," she answered staunchly. "I'm not a trained detective, but I know a great deal about surviving. That'll see me through whatever lies ahead."

"We all know you can look after yourself," he admitted after a brief pause. "But watching out for you makes us feel as if you need us. And that's more important than you know."

Although he hadn't said it directly, her heart understood his meaning. A wonderful awareness of the power of her own femininity swept through her. Diana hung up the receiver carefully. Afraid that Anita would sense her feelings, she made a show of returning to the paperwork before her.

Anita waited several minutes before speaking. "You're seeing Marten tonight?" she asked.

"Yes. He's come up with another idea for us to pursue."

Anita exhaled softly. "You're young and you've been alone for too long. Be sure that you go past the surface when you make up your mind about him. Judge him on his actions, not his words."

"I'm trying my best to do just that, believe me." Diana smiled slowly. "He's good for me, Anita. Whenever I'm around I feel terrific inside and more alive than I have in years. I respond to him in ways I'd almost forgotten about." She met her friend's gaze. "And no, I'm not hopelessly in love. But the attraction is there, and it could grow."

"That's exactly what I'm disturbed about." Anita picked up her purse. "I've got a few errands to run tonight, but I'll be home after eight if you need anything." She paused. "I could be home earlier if you'd like."

"I'll be fine," Diana assured her.

After Anita left the shop, Diana began straightening up her office. Fifteen minutes later she heard the jingle that signaled someone's entry into the store. As her gaze focused on Greg, her heart leapt and her body began to tingle with awareness.

"Did I get here too early?" he asked.

"No, not at all. I'm almost ready to go. While I'm clearing off my desk, why don't you tell me about this idea of yours?"

"I've been thinking about the school that's next to where we found the trail of blood. It's time we checked out that place."

"They're closed for summer," Diana answered. "No one could get in. The killer might have gone by there, but that's all he could have done."

"Isn't there a caretaker or someone who comes in to watch the place?"

"I don't know, I hadn't thought about it. If there is I'm sure the police have already spoken to him."

"It couldn't hurt for us to go talk with him, too."

"I suppose not. We could go over there now and see if there's anyone around."

"Let's take my van. I parked right out front," he said.

They arrived minutes later. As Greg pulled into a parking space across the street from the church, Diana gave him a puzzled look. "Why are you stopping here?" she asked. "The school's got a parking lot."

"I'd like to scout out the area before our presence becomes obvious. There might be a reason why the killer chose the escape route he did."

"We should find out if anyone is at the school first," Diana cautioned. "We don't want a caretaker or security guard to spot us and report us to the police."

"You're right. Neither one of us needs to spend the night in jail." As they approached the school, Greg glanced up at an open window on the second floor. "There's music coming from inside, hear it?" Seeing her nod, he gestured ahead. "There's also a pickup parked near the side exit."

As they drew closer to the building, Diana began to feel as if dozens of tiny spiders were crawling over her body. A shiver ran up her spine, and she had to fight an almost overwhelming desire to turn back. She shook herself mentally, determined not to let Greg know anything was amiss. The last thing she needed was for him to think the investigation was getting to her.

They'd almost reached the main doors when she caught a glimpse of someone walking past a first-floor window. By the time her senses registered the cowboy hat, the person was gone.

Greg, who'd turned to follow her gaze, shot forward. He pressed his face against the glass, but the classroom inside was empty. Without waiting, he ran toward the front of the building.

Diana followed less than half a step behind and helped him pound on the doors. "That's not the caretaker. Not unless he's working in a costume," she said loudly, striving to be heard over the din they were making.

"I agree," he answered. "But if there is a caretaker inside, why doesn't he come to the door?"

"Maybe I should call the police."

A split second later they heard the click of locks being opened. "Wait a minute," a voice bellowed from inside.

Diana and Greg exchanged glances. "Coincidence?" Diana mouthed.

"Probably," Greg replied in a soft voice.

The door swung open. A short, middle-aged man with thinning dark hair stood before them. "Have you been out here long?" he asked with a smile. "I was changing the radio station when I heard the pounding. Is there a problem?"

"Who's the other man in the building with you?" Diana asked quickly. "The one wearing the cowboy hat."

The caretaker laughed. "Don't tell me. This is a joke, right?"

"I assure you, there's someone else in the building. If you think you're alone in there, you're wrong," Greg replied.

The man glanced out toward the parking lot. "My pickup's still the only one there," he said with a skeptical half grin. "Would you like to come inside? I've been busy washing walls in one of the upstairs classrooms, but I'm finished now." He wiped his hand on a handkerchief, then extended it toward Greg. "I'm Ralph Harper, the custodian."

Diana introduced herself and Greg quickly. "We're not kidding. There really is someone else in here. We both saw him."

"Let me guess. You saw an outline, maybe nothing more than a vague shadow. Then, when you looked again, it was gone."

The accounting, so close to the truth, took her by surprise. "Yes, but how do you know that?"

"Come on in." He smiled at both of them. "My office is just around the corner. During the summer, I work every evening and do the major cleaning jobs we don't have time for during the school year. In the daytime there are painters and work crews doing other jobs. Kids are hard on the old place, you know.''

"Mr. Harper, I think we should take a look around the building right now. You may be in danger," Diana insisted. "Don't you know that there was a murder committed in the church right next door a few days ago?"

"Yes, I know, the police came over to talk to me," he answered, ignoring her request to search. "They wanted to find out if I'd seen anything unusual lately, like prowlers, or people lurking about." He shrugged. "To be honest, I haven't seen anyone, but then again, I never do. I'm always busy, and I like to keep the radio on for company. It gets lonely here at night. I'm not worried about break-ins since all the outside doors except the one you came through are locked and chained from the inside. The one you came through is heavy gauge steel, and it's double locked." He poured them each a paper cup of black coffee, then handed them packets of sugar and cream. "Now, if this had happened in the spring, the kids would have kept the cops running in circles. They're always seeing somebody lurking in the halls, or in empty classrooms. I'm really not sure how much of it is imagination, but the history of this place really lends itself to those kind of stories."

"I don't understand," Greg answered.

"Come on. Haven't you heard about this school?" He laughed. "When the place was first built neither the school board nor the contractor knew they were digging up an old burial site. When they began to unearth coffins, the archbishop gave permission to have those found reinterred in a nearby cemetery. Only coffins that hampered construction were moved. The others remained where they were and the building and adjacent structures were erected over them." He gave Greg and Diana a playful smile. "As you can imagine, ghost stories have abounded ever since." He paused, then grew serious. "Most of them are nothing except kids playing around trying to scare each other. But there are other times..."

Greg gave Diana a playful wink, then glanced at the custodian. "Don't stop there, tell us the rest."

"I play the radio as loud as I can stand it, just so I don't have to hear the other sounds." He lowered his voice as if someone might be listening. "Someone walks these halls at night. I know, I've heard their footsteps, only there's never anyone around that you can see. I finally decided that if I made noise of my own, it wouldn't bother me as much."

Diana's eyes narrowed. "How long has this been happening? I mean, when did you start hearing someone walking around?"

"It started my second week on the job. That's been," his eyebrows furrowed thoughtfully, "about twenty years now, I guess."

Diana's shoulders slumped slightly, and Harper was quick to pick up on it.

"Listen, there's no way a flesh-and-blood intruder could have sneaked in here without my knowing about him. Would it set your mind at ease if I proved it to you? I can give you a tour of the school right now."

"Yes, definitely," she admitted, "but let's do it quietly. It would be better to take the person we saw by surprise."

The custodian chuckled softly. "Let me give you a piece of advice first. If you see anyone who vanishes into thin air, keep it to yourself. If you don't, people are liable to think you're crazy."

"I'll keep that in mind," Diana answered.

The tour of the building took almost thirty minutes. Ralph Harper took the key ring, dangling from his belt, and unlocked the door to each classroom, then ushered them inside. Only a few whispered words passed between them. Diana listened to the silence, hoping for some sound that would confirm the cowboy's presence. Finally they returned to Harper's tiny office.

"What did I tell you?" he said with a chuckle. "There's no one else here. Maybe what you really saw was the reflection of someone moving around outside on the grounds.

Reflected images are tricky, and you said that all you got was a glimpse.''

Greg stared at the floor, his expression remote. "I suppose that's one way to explain it," he said, unconvinced.

"We'd better get going and let you get back to work," Diana said. "We've kept you long enough."

Harper walked them to the door. "Stop by anytime. It's nice to be able to talk to someone during my break."

As the door was closed and locked behind them Diana and Greg began walking toward the van.

"Harper sure tried hard to confuse the issue with all that nonsense about ghosts," Diana said as they ambled across the parking lot. "Do you think he's having friends visit him at night and doesn't want anyone to know about it?"

"It's very possible. Something like that could cost him his job. But he did give us a very complete guided tour."

"Harper knows every nook and cranny of that building, so he could easily help someone hide in there. And remember how long it took for him to answer the door? The cowboy might be one of Harper's buddies. He could also be the killer, and Harper, either knowingly or unknowingly, is helping him to stay out of sight."

"It's a theory, but we don't have enough evidence to support or refute it."

Acutely aware of Greg's presence close beside her, Diana lapsed into a pensive silence. It was such a beautiful moonlit night. Under different circumstances a stroll like this might have been an exciting and pleasant interlude. A man and woman together, enjoying the evening and the thrill found in each other's company.

Yet, instead of soft, whispered words of love, their conversation was focused on the ugliest subject of all—murder. Diana suppressed a shiver and wondered when things would return to normal in her life.

Greg stopped abruptly and turned around slowly. Before she could say anything he held one finger to his lips. The nighttime shadows had lengthened. Tree limbs dappled the ground with dark images that moved slightly as the breeze shook the leaves. "There," he whispered urgently. "Did you see it?"

"What? Is someone there?"

"No. It looks like there's an extra shadow among the trees."

She stood rock still for a moment. "I don't see anything."

"It was there," he insisted. "I think someone's following us."

"The cowboy?"

"I'm not sure, but we're going to find out," he said resolutely. "Let's turn the tables on him." He hurried her forward. "We'll head down the pathway between the rectory and the church, then duck behind the shrubbery. As soon as he goes past us, I'll grab him from behind."

# Chapter Nine

Diana huddled behind the juniper hedge, scarcely breathing. The minutes ticked by with agonizing slowness until her knees began to throb with a dull ache.

Greg seemed frozen to the spot, his eyes glued ahead. Finally he shifted and offered her his hand to lead her out. "Maybe he caught on to us."

As Diana stepped out to the sidewalk, she detected a faint, but familiar scent. Her skin went cold, and she shuddered. "There's that pipe tobacco again," she whispered.

"Like cinnamon and piñon wood." He glanced around, his eyes peering through the shadows. "Let's go. We shouldn't hang around here. For whatever reason, he's playing cat and mouse with us."

Greg walked with her to the van. Once they were on their way, he spoke again. "Do you want to stop somewhere for a bite to eat?"

"Let me take a rain check. I'm bushed," Diana managed with a yawn.

He took her back to the print shop and parked next to her car. "I'll follow you home," he said, walking to Diana's car with her. "We want to be very careful with a killer out there somewhere."

His words filled her with apprehension, but she tried not to show it. "Call me when you get to your studio, okay?"

"Are you worried about me?" He stood by her open car door, a cocky grin playing at the edges of his mouth. "If you are, I could arrange for you to keep an eye on me all night long."

Heat sizzled through her, making her tingle in a most disturbing way. "We don't need distractions right now Greg," she admonished in the sternest tone she could muster.

"Yes, we do," he answered seriously. "Look at it this way. You were frightened before, but now I've given you something else to think about tonight. Hopefully it's something far more pleasant for you." His palm grazed her cheek in a light caress, then he moved away.

Diana's hand trembled as she started the engine. Her body simmered with yearnings that would not be argued away. As she pulled out into the street she saw Greg's headlights appear behind her. Now more than ever, with danger dogging their footsteps, she needed to keep her thinking clear.

When she arrived home she saw Greg wait for her to get safely inside. With a wave, she opened the side door and entered her kitchen, glad to be home.

The first thing that struck her was the stark silence inside her house. She turned on the radio and walked to the living room sofa. Funny how she'd never really noticed that every song had something to do with love or lovers. Her eyes drifted around the room as she sat there waiting for Greg's call. Her home, normally the dearest place to her in the whole earth, suddenly felt empty.

The telephone rang and she picked it up quickly. Greg's voice greeted her. "It doesn't look like either of us were tailed."

"I think the cowboy gave up when we tried to trap him." She paused for a moment. "For the time being let's forget about him and concentrate on Harper. He's someone we can check out. A friend of mine is a guidance counselor at his school. I thought I'd pay her a visit tomorrow."

"Is there any way you can arrange to have me along? I could meet or pick you up anytime."

"I don't think that'll be a problem. Just come by the shop at noon."

"I'll be there," he assured her. "Sleep well." His voice caressed her over the wire.

"Good night." As she hung up the phone, nerves tingling, she figured she wouldn't be getting much rest that night. Yet, only minutes after her head hit the pillow, she drifted to sleep. Her dreams, unhampered by the burden of logic, were filled with whispered promises and forays into forbidden pleasures.

She woke up the next morning before the alarm rang. Without thinking, she reached out to the empty spot on the other side of the bed. The memory of her husband was no longer enough. She needed more. Diana took a deep breath as she remembered the fulfillment that had come from traveling through life as part of a pair. She missed that sense of companionship, and friendship.

The shrill ring of the alarm made her jump. Fully awake now, and realizing the danger of indulging in fantasies, she shook herself mentally. Closeness and togetherness were appealing. But like everything else in life they ended, and the aftermath was worse than never having had them at all.

Two hours later, at the print shop, Diana stood behind one of the presses running off an order. Although her job normally took her mind off everything else, today it was different. She checked her watch often, eagerly anticipating Greg's arrival.

Greg walked through the doors a few minutes after twelve. Knowing Anita was watching, Diana forced her expression to remain noncommittal. "Give me a minute," she told him. "I'll be right with you."

"I'll take over," Anita said, approaching. "When will you be back?"

"In an hour, I promise. We're just going over to talk to Anne Wilson." She quickly filled Anita in on the details.

As they left the print shop, Greg walked alongside Diana. His gaze traveled over her smooth flowing cotton shirt-dress. "That lilac color looks good on you."

"Thanks," she answered, her gaze averted.

He noticed the flush that had colored her cheeks when he'd complimented her. She responded to him with her entire body. The knowledge pleased him. He wanted to matter to her.

"When we get to Anne's," she said, "let me take the lead and handle this. Anne is easy to talk to providing you go about it the right way."

"No problem," Greg agreed. He hadn't slept much last night. Diana had stayed on his mind constantly. There was a vibrancy and subtle sexuality about her that made the blood thunder through his veins. It was hard for him to force his gaze away.

"Anne prides herself on being well-informed about staff and students alike," she continued. "But if she thinks we're being nosy, she won't tell us a thing. That's why I've decided to be completely honest with her."

"While you're concentrating on what you want to ask, I'll watch her expression as she answers. It might be useful to see how her feelings match up to her words." They were opposites in many ways. Her unpredictability and off-the-cuff approaches were in direct contrast to his own penchant for planning. Yet their techniques blended well.

Diana drove to a nearby residential area and parked in front of a modest adobe home. A short, middle-aged woman came to the door and invited them in.

Diana introduced Greg to Anne, then told her about their recent investigative efforts. "We're trying to find leads the police might be able to use. That's why we went to visit Ralph Harper, the custodian at your school. He seemed very nice, offering us coffee and giving us a tour."

"Even with all the problems he has, poor man, he's always done a good job. He's been under a lot of pressure because of his family..." Anne shrugged. "But the kids love him. He always has a few minutes to stop and talk."

"What happened to his family?" Diana asked.

Anne looked at Diana in surprise. "You mean you don't know? Good grief, I thought everyone in Santa Fe knew by now, the way the police have been carrying on." Anne leaned back in the easy chair, relaxing comfortably. "His brother escaped from the State Penitentiary about two months ago."

"What was he in for?" Greg asked, sitting up straighter.

"Eric Harper is bad news. He was convicted for armed robbery and murder."

Diana's mouth dropped open. "Do the police think Ralph was helping him hide out?"

"They suspected he might be, at first. They questioned him repeatedly and followed him, too, from what I understand. Then, after four weeks they finally concluded he didn't know anything about his brother's whereabouts."

"The school authorities must have been horrified," Diana said.

"You don't know the half of it," Anne answered. "Detectives came and questioned some of the teachers. They described Eric Harper to each of us and even showed us a photograph in case we ever happened to see him around."

Diana leaned forward in her seat. "What does Eric Harper look like?"

Anne smiled. "I don't blame you for wanting to know. But you don't have to worry. We have our own security guard. And when Father John Denning was killed the police really started patrolling, too. If Eric Harper had been in the area, they'd have caught him for sure."

"I'd still like to be able to keep an eye out for him," Diana said hesitantly.

"Eric Harper's very tall and thin. He has black hair, which of course he could have dyed by now, and dark eyes. One of the detectives suggested he might have also grown a mustache or beard."

"Thanks for everything, Anne," Diana said, standing up. "If we do uncover any leads, I'll let you know."

"I'd appreciate that," Anne answered, walking them to the door. "I really liked Father Denning. But don't be too hard on Ralph, Diana. He works hard to make a living, and, believe me, his salary isn't that great."

"It's not my intention to make his life difficult. I can sympathize with anyone who has to work hard just to get by. I know what it's like, I've been there."

Greg felt the emotions behind her words. Her life had been harsh. Maybe that was the reason she was so determined to live each day to the fullest. And it was her exuberance that had triggered a change in him. She'd brought him a very special and unexpected gift. With her, he could see everything again as if for the first time. She filled his heart with the joy of living without the burden of having to analyze and evaluate. He didn't want to ever lose her. She was rapidly becoming a cherished part of his soul. But the more they delved into the murder case, the more the danger increased.

"I'm going to tell Don that the cowboy we've seen is Eric Harper. He has to know about this right away," Diana said, cutting into Greg's thoughts.

"I'm not convinced of that," Greg warned, getting back into the car. "At first I thought the cowboy might have chosen his costume to divert attention from his identity. But an escaped convict would want to blend with a crowd, not stand out in any way."

Diana pulled out into the lunch-hour traffic and started back to the print shop. "You may be right. So the questions we have to answer are, how does the cowboy fit in with Ralph Harper, and what part, if any, does Eric play in this?"

Greg said nothing for a while. "We need to find the security guard responsible for patrolling the school and grounds. It's possible we might be able to learn something more from him."

"How are we going to track him down? I can't just call the main office and ask what time the guard makes his rounds."

"I remember the night I was arrested. There was a security guard there who responded almost immediately. I don't know if he came from the school, but it seems likely. Even though I doubt he follows a precise schedule, we could try to go there tonight at about the time I was arrested. Then, if we see him, we can strike up a conversation."

"Do you think he'll recognize you from the night of the murder?"

"I doubt it. He never got that close to me. But just in case, I'll hang back while you do the talking. You're prettier than I am, and his attention is bound to stay on you." Seeing the color that rose to her cheeks again, he grinned.

"I have to work later than usual this evening," she said as she parked beside the shop. "I won't be ready to leave the shop before six-thirty, but we should still be able to make it to the school in plenty of time."

"Sounds fine. The way I figure it, we should be in the area by seven-thirty. We might have a long wait, but if we want to catch the guard, I don't see any other way to do it."

She leaned over and gave Greg's hand a quick squeeze. "I'll see you later then," she said, heading inside.

The afternoon passed slowly. Balancing the books was a never-ending challenge. She remembered the classes she'd taken at night school and recalled that that was another debt she owed Father John. He'd been the one who'd anticipated the need to attend business school. He'd even arranged for her to enroll tuition-free in exchange for printing the vocational school's fall catalog. As the adding machine tape spilled out over the back of Diana's desk, her resolve to find Father John's killer grew stronger.

It was five-thirty by the time Anita approached the desk. "I'm giving a lecture on bonsai at the garden club this evening. Why don't you call it quits and come with me?"

"I'd love to, but I can't. I've got to finish these accounts, then I'm going to do a little more investigating." She told Anita of their plans.

Anita picked up her purse. "Be careful, and if you need anything, call me. You know where I'll be."

After Anita left, Diana locked the door and returned to her desk. Determined to complete the job, she began working with renewed energy.

It was after six when a knock at the door reminded her of the task that still lay ahead. As she let Greg in, a look of concern flashed over his features. "You look tired. Are you sure you're up to this tonight?"

She rubbed her eyes. "I'll be fine. I've just been staring at numbers all afternoon." She grabbed her purse and walked outside with him.

"Let's go in my van," he suggested. "That way you can unwind on the way over instead of having to concentrate on the road."

She climbed into his van, then with a quiet sigh, leaned back against the seat. Moments later they were underway.

"I hope we get some answers tonight. We sure do need a break on this," he muttered softly.

As they neared the corner Greg flipped on the turn signal and started to slow down. As he began a right-hand turn onto a side street, he caught a glimpse of movement on the far edge of his headlights.

"Look out!" Diana shouted, stomping on the floorboard instinctively for the nonexistent brake. A running man had suddenly appeared from behind a hedge and he was on a collision course with their van.

Greg slammed on the brakes and swerved, trying desperately to avoid an accident.

Diana saw the surprised look on the jogger's face, but knew he wouldn't be able to stop in time. She felt the dull thump as the person impacted against the right front fender.

The van screeched to a halt. In a heartbeat Greg and Diana were out of the van and running back toward the victim. He was struggling to his feet. "No, stay down!" Greg warned. "We'll call the rescue unit."

The tall, slender man in the blue jogging suit stared at them wild-eyed. Before they could get close, the man finished scrambling to his feet and broke into a limping run.

The man headed off the street and onto a residential lawn. Rushing past a house, he dodged into an alley and then disappeared into the darkness.

"Let's go after him," Greg yelled, his heart pumping wildly.

Diana grasped his arm. "No, we'll never find him now. It's almost dark."

"I don't understand why he'd take off like that! I wonder if he bumped his head?" Greg's gaze turned to the spot where the man had fallen to the pavement. "It looks like he left something behind."

Diana bent down to retrieve the items. "It's a paperback book of crossword puzzles and a package of chocolate bars. He must have just come from the supermarket on the next block. See the price tag on the wrapper?"

"Let's go there right now," Greg said. "We can use their telephone to report the accident and at the same time check if anyone there knows the man. Everything happened so fast, I don't even have a good description to give the police. All I noticed was that he's tall, and has dark hair and a mustache. Can you add anything to that?"

"Just what he was wearing." She headed back to the van with Greg.

Fifteen minutes later, they were standing outside the supermarket answering a patrol officer's questions. A clerk had remembered seeing a man who fit the description, but had been certain he hadn't purchased anything. The officer filled out his report, taking what information Greg and Diana were able to give him.

"I wouldn't worry too much," the officer told them when they were finished. "From the looks of it, I'd say he shoplifted the items, and took off after the accident because he didn't want to get involved with the police right now. If he was able to get back up and run, then the chances are he wasn't badly hurt. You did say you'd slowed down to make the turn." Seeing Greg nod, he continued. "You've reported the accident, and we know where to find you if we need anything else. Meanwhile, my sergeant will be checking the scene and I'll be making my rounds in that section next, so if we turn up anything we'll be in touch."

Greg watched as the patrolman drove off. "We've done all we can," he said wearily. "Do you want me to take you home?"

Diana's first impulse was to say yes, but then she shook her head. She'd made a commitment to the investigation and she'd see it through. "We still have time to go to the school. Unless you just don't feel up to it, I think we should go ahead with our original plans."

"Agreed." Greg traversed the city streets slowly, his shoulders rigid with tension. Parking the van about half a block from the school, he leaned back and tried to force himself to unwind. "How can so much go wrong on such a beautiful evening," he commented, then walked around to help Diana out. "What would you have been doing on a night like this, under ordinary circumstances?"

The question made her face her life as it had been. In retrospect it seemed lacking some vital element that would have given it greater dimension and direction. "I would have probably been at home. I like to read mysteries, and I do quite a bit of that in the evenings after work. Or sometimes I watch television." Even as she spoke, she compared the old times to the present. With Greg she'd rediscovered the pleasure of being wanted by someone she found desirable and doing things with that person. She enjoyed the attraction, but it was more than that. She liked the sense of companionship between them.

They'd just reached the parking area that surrounded the school when Greg gestured ahead. "There's the security guard. We're too late. It looks like he's finished his patrol and is ready to leave."

"Wait here."

Diana quickened her pace as the guard pulled out into the street and started to speed up. She'd have to get his attention fast. In another second he'd be gone. Taking her wallet out of her purse, she ran out to the curb and flapped it open like a cop holding up a badge.

The car slowed abruptly and pulled to the side. Flashing him her best smile, Diana stepped out into the street. "I'm sorry, I'm not a cop, but I needed to talk to you. I figured this was my best chance of getting your attention fast."

"It's one way," he conceded, his eyes lingering on her in a thorough and appreciative gaze. "What can I do for you?"

"My name's Diana Clark and I've been hoping for a chance to talk to you. Have you noticed anyone hanging around the school grounds lately, or the church?"

"Why do you ask?" the man asked, regarding her suspiciously.

"I'd been helping Father Denning work with the youth gangs in the area and his murder really stirred up trouble among the kids," she said, stretching the truth just a bit. "I'm worried that if any of the gangs are implicated, there's going to be more violence. I've been asking around, hoping to find something the police can use. The sooner Father's murder is solved, the better it will be for everyone."

"I've been worried about gang violence myself. The kids are itching to find whoever did this, and they're starting to get restless."

"That's the problem. Please, won't you help me out?"

He nodded. "I was here the night of the murder, making my rounds. I saw Harper, the school's night janitor, upstairs near one of the windows and waved at him, then continued my check. Everything was in order, so I went back to my car to take a break. I'd just poured myself a cup of coffee from the thermos when the police band radio came on.

I heard the patrol unit at the church call for backup so I went over to see if I could help."

He shrugged, perplexed. "I still don't understand what happened. The man who was initially arrested had a valid reason for being there. That means that the real murderer must have made his escape right under all of our noses. The coroner established the time of death as no more than ten minutes prior to the arrival of the police on the scene."

"All we seem to come up with are more questions," Diana said wearily, stepping away from the car. "Thanks for your help," she said and watched as the man drove off.

Greg, who'd remained out of sight behind some trees, came up to meet her. "Well, we know now that Harper couldn't have been directly involved in the murder. There's no way he could have been in two places at the same time."

"His brother is still a possibility," Diana pointed out, "but I don't think Eric Harper would risk coming here. Surely he would know that this is one of the first places the police would look for him."

"We need to review everything we've learned and see if we're missing something that's right in front of us," Greg said as he started heading back to his van. "Let's stop somewhere and have a working dinner."

"There's a coffee shop a few blocks away. Father John used to go there almost every night for one of their special cinnamon rolls," she smiled sadly. "I met him there many times myself. They've got the best food around."

They walked through the doors of the small corner coffee shop five minutes later. The waitress recognized Diana and ushered her to a quiet table in the back. "We're going to miss Father John around here," she commented, bringing them menus.

Diana and Greg each ordered a sandwich, then waited. "This is a nice little coffee shop, but I don't think I'll come back here again," Diana commented sadly.

"I can understand the way you feel. Once a place becomes associated with a person or event, it's nearly impossible to separate the two."

Their waitress returned moments later and set the plates before them. "It's strange how things work out. Father came here practically every evening for three years. Yet, what sticks in my mind the most is the time he and Francisco Ortega got into an argument here."

"When was this?" Diana asked, instantly recognizing the name.

"About a week before Father died," the woman said, crossing herself. "Ortega was furious, but so was Father. That was the only time I ever heard him raise his voice to anyone. Father wanted Ortega to close down the tile plant. He threatened to go to the police if Ortega didn't do as he asked."

"Did Father say why he wanted Ortega to do that?" Greg asked.

"No, but he made it plain that he was going to put Ortega out of business."

"How did Ortega take Father John's interference?" Greg asked, his half-eaten sandwich all but forgotten.

"Not well," she dropped her voice. "Even if you don't agree with a priest, you should still show some respect, but Ortega was in a rage. Father didn't let up. Finally Ortega threatened to get Father John if he didn't stop meddling in his affairs."

"What do you think he meant by that?" Diana asked, sitting up.

"I know what you're thinking, but I just don't think Ortega killed Father, or had him killed, either."

"What makes you so sure?" Greg prodded.

"Ortega's not stupid. He does a great deal of business with the Hispanic community. He knows they'd turn on anyone linked to the murder of a priest."

"I see your point," Diana agreed.

As the waitress moved away, Greg stared pensively at the worn, checkered tablecloth. "People are capable of many things if the stakes are high enough, Diana," he countered softly. "Murdering a priest may not have been something Ortega would have considered under ordinary circumstances, but we don't know what he was up against."

"You're right. But we need to find out more about Ortega before we talk to him. We should take a look at that tile plant and find out what Father was so upset about. Ortega's an influential man. Don's going to need something to go on before he can go up against him. Maybe we can help out."

The waitress approached and picked up the money Greg had placed on the table. "Did I hear you talking about going to the plant?"

Greg nodded. "It's probably all locked up by now, Diana. It's eight o'clock."

"That won't matter," the waitress said. "I've heard the plant's working double shifts to keep up with orders."

"Well then, it looks like we don't have a problem," Diana said.

"Look, it's none of my business, but you shouldn't go over there," the waitress warned in a whisper. "It's dangerous. Ortega's security people have a reputation for being no better than thugs."

"We'll be careful," Diana said.

"By the way, have you told the police about the argument Father John had with Ortega?" Greg asked gently.

The woman's eyes widened. "No, I didn't think it was important enough. Besides, they never asked me."

"They should know," he insisted.

"You tell them then," she answered shakily. "I can't afford any trouble."

"It would be better if you told them yourself," Diana interjected. "You don't even have to go down to the station. Call Detective Don Clark," she scribbled both the name and telephone number on the back of a piece of paper. "He's my brother-in-law. Say I suggested you speak with him."

The waitress took the paper and looked at it uncertainly. "I'll think about it."

Diana led the way out of the restaurant. As soon as they were outside, Greg placed a hand on her shoulder and pulled her to one side of the sidewalk. "If you're determined to have the plant checked, then I have a suggestion. I'll go alone. It'll be much less dangerous that way, especially if there's a physical confrontation. You can go home and if I don't return, call the police."

"But taking me will minimize the risk for you. They won't be expecting trouble from a couple who, let's say, is having car trouble. While, if they catch a man lurking about, that's going to put them on the defensive right away."

Greg considered it for a moment. "I don't like it. I'd rather turn this over to Detective Clark than have you exposed to any more risks."

"If you don't want to go, I'll do it myself. I can leave a note for Anita and if I'm not back by a certain time, she can call the cavalry."

Greg threw his hands up in the air. "All right, we'll go together. At least then I won't have to sit around worrying."

They returned to the van and Greg followed Diana's directions to the outskirts of the city. "I wish I could get you to plan your moves more carefully. There's a great deal to be said for weighing things before acting."

"True, but being unpredictable gives us the advantage of surprise," she countered.

"We're not professionals, Diana. Our only chance is to rely on our wits, stay sharp and make sure we don't miss a trick."

Diana gestured to the long stretch of gravel road that led to the plant. "There it is." Ahead, in a compound about the size of a baseball field, were several adobe buildings clustered together. The isolated mesa was lit by powerful electric lights.

"It looks like that's the only way to approach," Greg commented. "Ortega picked a great location. No one could sneak up on his operation. They'll know we're coming a good five minutes before we get there."

"Not necessarily. If we're going to claim we had car trouble, it might be better to walk up."

"Nothing doing," he answered flatly. "What if we need to leave fast? It'll probably work better if we drive in and tell them we're lost. I've got Texas license plates, so that should cover us."

"I'll ask to use their telephone to contact some friends in Santa Fe who are expecting us. That'll give us an excuse to go inside," she gestured ahead. "There're two battered pickups starting down the gravel road. Why don't you follow them in? The van's in the same state of disrepair so we might just blend in, at least for awhile."

"My van and I will pretend we never heard that," Greg muttered, staying about three car lengths behind the second truck.

As they reached the end of the drive, he parked in a section away from the floodlights. "Wait until all those people go inside the building, then we'll get out."

Diana felt her heart hammering against her sides. "Let's use the same door they did," she whispered. "We might get even further before we're stopped."

# Chapter Ten

"It sure looks like Ortega's up to something," Greg said. "There were at least a dozen people crowded inside each of those two small trucks. It's obvious they're being bused in here."

"We'll just play dumb about what we see. We're lost tourists, remember?" Trying to sound fearless and encouraging, Diana opened the van door. "Come on. Let's see what we can find out."

"Diana, wait. Let's get the license numbers on those trucks first, in case—" He muttered an oath as he realized that he was talking to himself.

Diana glanced back and saw him jogging to catch up to her. "Hurry up," she said, entering through the sliding wooden door at the rear of the closest building. As she stepped into the room, Diana glanced around. Several men and women were standing around a table, glazing and painting tiles. With boxes and packing material everywhere, the large area resembled a garage. A few workers glanced up momentarily, then went right back to their work.

Greg joined her a moment later. The workers once again glanced up. This time, however, their gazes stayed on him, worried expressions on their faces. Greg gave them a reassuring smile, and they shifted their attention back to the tasks before them.

Diana walked up to a woman hand painting tiles. "Excuse me, can you help me?"

The woman smiled, but shook her head. *"No entiendo, señora. Solamente hablo español,"* she said.

Diana nodded, wishing she understood more Spanish, then she asked the man beside her. "Do you speak English?"

*"¿Que?"*

"Who the hell are you, and what are you doing in here?" a burly man appeared in the doorway and bellowed at them. "This is private property."

"We're lost," Diana explained with a smile. "We thought we'd stop and ask for directions."

"Try again," he sneered. The man looked like a vending machine with a head. Greg was big, but this man outweighed him by at least forty pounds. Diana knew she had to defuse the situation fast. "I know my way around Santa Fe really well, but once I left town I got disoriented. I know Mr. Ortega," she bluffed, "and I thought someone here at his factory could help us. Is Francisco around, by the way?" she glanced around. "I'd like to talk to him."

"If you knew Ortega at all, you'd know he never comes here himself." The man flashed them a predatory smile. "You just screwed up, lady."

Greg came up to stand by her side. "Chill out. We're not looking for trouble."

The man grabbed a hammer from one of the tables. "You're about to find it, man."

Greg stood his ground as the man advanced. "You don't want a fight. Put the hammer down," he ordered in a low, deadly cold voice.

"Get out," the man ordered, giving Greg a clear path to the door.

Greg angled sideways, moving toward the exit. Diana remained by Greg, but then began to slow down as the workers, fearing a fight, moved toward the exits. "We didn't mean to create any problems for anyone," she started.

"Out!" The man reached out and shoved Diana toward the door.

Diana recaptured her balance quickly and, reacting instinctively, kicked him in the shins. "Don't you *ever* touch me!"

Swearing, the man raised the hammer just as Greg jumped forward. Grabbing his adversary's wrist, Greg jerked the man's arm backward in an arc, slamming the hammer against a massive support beam. With a loud crack, the handle smashed in two. "Your arm's next," Greg warned in a whisper soft voice as he forced the groaning man to his knees.

Diana stared in shock at the hammer which lay on the floor in two uneven pieces. When Greg released the man's wrist and reached for her shoulder, she practically jumped out of her skin.

Without taking his eyes off his opponent, Greg began to back out of the building, taking her with him. They emerged a moment later. "Don't run, but move it," he said, hurrying her toward the van.

Her mouth was as dry as the desert landscape that surrounded them, her hands clammy. That display of force and violence had taken her totally by surprise. She'd never expected it from Greg. "Would you have really broken his arm the way you did the hammer?" she asked in an awed whisper.

He exhaled softly. "If that's what it would have taken to keep him from hurting you." He glanced at her as they sped down the gravel road. "You're afraid of me now," he observed, shaking his head, his lips pursed in a tight line. "You shouldn't be. You should know better by this time."

"I do," she said, then took a deep breath. "But that was an impressive show back there."

"It was meant to be," Greg admitted. "Sometimes the best way to avoid a fight is to show 'em what you've got." He gave her a gentle smile. "I still can't believe you actually kicked him when he pushed you. You took me totally off guard.''

"I shouldn't have done that," she admitted apologetically. "But I was just so angry!" She sighed. "My temper can be a problem, since, unlike you, I don't have much to back it up with."

He smiled. "If you'd been alone, you'd have been able to get away. You surprised the heck out of him."

Only a few minutes had passed when a set of flashing red lights appeared in the darkness behind them. "Great," Greg muttered sarcastically, automatically slowing down and pulling over. "Just what we needed. More trouble with the police."

"Were you speeding?" Diana asked.

"No, I was only going forty-five." Greg glanced in his rearview mirror. "That's strange. It's a plainclothes officer."

A second later Don appeared and stood about two feet behind the driver's side door. "Get out of the car, Marten," he ordered.

"Don, what in the world...?" Diana began.

Don ignored her. "Out, Marten, then up against the van, your hands flat against the sides."

Diana scrambled out of the van. "Don, what's going on?" she asked in confusion.

"Stay out of this, Diana," he growled. "Marten, I thought you and I had an understanding." Don frisked him for weapons, then kept his hand on Greg's back, ensuring he held the position.

"You were the one who did all the talking," Greg shot back.

"I don't know what you two are talking about, but there's something you should know, Don. Greg just risked his life to protect me. Unless you have enough evidence to arrest him for a crime, this is harassment."

"I don't think Marten's going to report me," he said in a menacing voice.

"Up to now, you've been a fair man, Don. Unless there's a very good reason for the way you're acting, this is beneath you."

Don took a step back, moving away from Greg, who turned around slowly. "We have a man watching that place and he radioed me the moment you arrived. Which one of you came up with the idea of going to visit Ortega's factory?"

"I did," Diana answered. "Greg didn't want any part of it. In fact, he suggested we take our new information to you, instead." Diana told him about their conversation with the waitress. Greg turned around and leaned back against the van, arms crossed over his chest, watching Don intently.

Don stared at the ground for several moments. As he moved his lips silently, Diana thought she saw him mouth a *one*, then a *two*. Eight seconds later, he glanced up. "Let me try and explain this to you, Diana. You're *not* helping. You're actually getting in our way. That's not a good idea," he said enunciating every syllable. "Our department has been giving Immigration a hand. They need proof that Ortega is hiring undocumented workers. We've spent over five hundred man hours on this case so far, hoping to catch the man in the act of hiring illegal aliens. Now your meddling could have cost us our investigation. The workers have all run off. They can smell trouble a mile off and aren't about to stick around."

"They'll be back," Diana said a bit uncertainly.

"Maybe or maybe not," he answered, then looking uncomfortable, jammed one hand inside his pocket. "I know you don't have much faith in the department, Diana, but we are trained professionals. Interfering with us isn't going to accomplish anything," he admonished gruffly.

Don fixed his gaze on Greg, his glare lethal. "You, on the other hand, are nothing but bad news." His voice held an angry undercurrent that was impossible to miss. "You have no idea how much trouble you've just bought yourself. Keep

out of police business. Take Diana home, and then keep
away from her, too."

He started back to his car, then stopped and gave Diana
a long look. "You've made enough of a mess for one night.
Go home."

Diana watched Don get into his car. Her heart felt leaden.
Don could be abrasive and hard, but he was only doing his
best to fulfill a commitment he'd made on behalf of his
brother. Having her look into Father John's murder only
reopened the wound that had been left by Bob's death and
the bungled investigation that followed.

"He'd have hauled me into jail on some trumped up
charge if you hadn't been around. Then our investigation
would have ground to a halt. Thanks."

"Believe me, I didn't do any favors," she said, returning
to the van. "Don's furious now. He can make things very
difficult for us if he chooses to. I'm his sister-in-law, so he'll
go easier on me. But I wouldn't want to be in your shoes.
Are you still willing to work with me?"

Greg gave her a brief nod. "I'm aware of what I'm up
against, but I can't just give up on this."

They remained silent as they headed back to the print
shop. Greg watched Diana out of the corner of his eye. Despite his assurances and his failure to react to Don's harassment, was she still afraid of him? The possibility made his
gut clench. He wanted her love, but knew he couldn't win
the heart of someone who feared him.

"I don't think we should continue to look for Arnie or
investigate Ortega anymore," he said. "You can bet Don's
going to stay on top of those leads. The police have infor-
mants and contacts who can help them deal with those types
of suspects. Instead, let's concentrate on the custodian and
see if he leads us to the cowboy."

"How about going over there right now?"

He nodded. "We can watch to see if Harper goes to meet
anyone during his shift or if there are any signs that another person is with him."

As they walked toward the school grounds a few minutes later, the only sound they heard was the hum of the cicadas. "If there's trouble, we leave. No more confrontations tonight," he said.

Diana was about to reply when she suddenly stopped and yanked Greg behind a pine tree. "Harper's outside," she whispered urgently. "What's he doing hanging around in the parking lot?"

Greg peered around the trunk. "I'm going in for a closer look. It's too dark, and from here I can't really see what he's doing."

He crept toward the school noiselessly, staying in the shadows and blending with the grayness that surrounded him. Diana waited a moment then, taking a parallel course, also moved forward to watch.

Her gaze was fixed on Harper as he moved a long-handled object back and forth over the ground in what seemed an endless cycle. Puzzled, she tried to figure out what he was doing. Suddenly she felt someone clasp her shoulder. A soft, startled cry barely escaped her lips when a hand clamped down hard over her mouth. Fighting to get loose, she slammed her elbow back into the person's midsection.

"It's me," Greg whispered with a groan. "Relax, will you?"

"You scared the daylights out of me," she mumbled angrily, then with a relieved sigh, she leaned back, taking comfort in the solid warmth of his body.

His arms wrapped around her waist and settled her more firmly against him. "You feel good," his voice was no more than a rumble from his chest. "Too good." He released her.

Disciplining her thoughts, Diana focused her attention back on Harper. "What's he doing?" she whispered.

"He's using a metal detector, so he must be looking for something. From the way he's sweeping the area, I'd say he's determined not to miss one square inch."

"Now what?"

"We watch." His fingers entwined around hers. "Don't even think of rushing out there. If you try, I'm going to catch up to you, throw you over my shoulder, and carry you back to the van."

"Just what I need, a real caveman," Diana muttered, wondering if he really would carry out his threat. Under different circumstances she might have been tempted to put it to a test, but this wasn't the time.

They remained nearly motionless and silent for almost forty-five minutes. Diana's patience was sorely tested, but Greg scarcely moved, his gaze fixed on Harper. Finally, Harper removed his headset and placed the detector down on the ground.

"It looks like he's either stopping, or taking a break," Diana said quietly.

"Let's head back to the sidewalk and then go talk to him. We'll pretend we were taking a stroll in the moonlight and just happened to pass by."

Diana felt Greg entwine his arm around her waist. The warmth from his body seeped into her, touching and caressing her skin. She struggled to concentrate on the task ahead, but her heart was making demands of its own. If only Father's murderer had already been caught and she and Greg really were just out on a carefree stroll! But if the case were over, Greg would probably have gone. A man content to live the life of a drifter would find her need for permanency and roots stifling.

"Hello!" Harper greeted them warmly. "Don't you two make a nice picture, walking together on such a beautiful night!"

"Mr. Harper," Diana smiled, feigning surprise. "What are you doing out here?"

He gave her a sheepish look. "Once I catch up on my work, I sometimes take a break by coming out with the metal detector. It's my hobby. You'd be surprised at all the things I find. Kids drop about everything. I've discovered bracelets, coins, and even rings."

"How are you doing with it tonight?" Greg asked.

He reached into his pocket, and extracted some change. "I've got about a dollar in change and a key chain. Some nights are better than others," he admitted with a shrug. "Why don't you come inside and have some coffee with me?" he invited, a hopeful expression on his face. "I've only got a little bit of work left to do and the hours get long when you're by yourself."

Greg glanced at Diana and, seeing her nod, accepted for both of them. "That sounds fine."

Ralph glanced around before locking the doors after they entered the building. "I've got to keep these closed tight. The gangs are getting active in this area again. In fact, now that I think about it, you really shouldn't go walking alone around here after it gets completely dark. The kids can get rough after a few hours of drinking."

"They won't give me any trouble," Diana admitted reluctantly. "My brother Frankie used to be in the Diablo Locos, so they don't hassle me."

"Frankie Clark?" Harper asked, then seeing her nod, smiled. "I remember him. He'd come by after high school let out and ask me to hide him from Father John. The priest was always after him to go do something." He laughed. "He was a pretty good kid. Whatever happened to him?"

"He joined the Navy and is stationed on a sub."

"Well, things have sure changed around here since his day. The kids used to concentrate on things like shoplifting and vandalism. Now, they've got burglary rings working all around this area and have taken up extortion too. The local merchants have been complaining about kids shaking down customers on the street."

As he finished his coffee, Greg went to stand near the office door. Diana watched him out of the corner of her eye and realized he was listening for sounds in the building. She'd tried to do the same herself, but so far hadn't heard or seen anything that would indicate there was anyone else there.

Fifteen minutes later, Harper walked them to the main door. "I'm glad you guys stopped by. Come again, okay?"

The moment they emerged from the building, Greg glanced around checking for trouble. "If there was anyone with him, I didn't get any indication of it."

"Do you think we're wrong and the cowboy has nothing to do with Father John's murder or Harper?" Diana asked, as they returned to the van.

"It's too hard to say. We'll have to wait until we get more information. In the meantime, we should take another look at our original theory. If the murder was the result of an art theft turned sour, then maybe a clue lies in what was stolen. I think we should research every item. Even the police can't object to that."

"The church keeps extensive records in what Father John used to jokingly call the catacombs. Let me give the secretary a call tomorrow and see if they'll let us take a look down there."

Greg pulled the van into a parking space next to the print shop. "Do you want to go out and have a drink somewhere? We don't have to end the evening now."

Diana wanted to say yes. Her desire to be with Greg was almost overpowering. Taking that as a warning, she shook her head. "Greg, I'm not sure that what's happening between us is right," she admitted. "Until I am, I want..." her voice trailed off.

"That's the problem, Diana," Greg's voice was whisper soft as he shifted and faced her. "We both want, and it's getting harder to deny it. You've brought so many different things into my life. You've opened my heart..."

"Don't, please." She touched his lips lightly with her fingertips to still them, but the feel of his mouth became a temptation that sent her pulse soaring. She pulled her hand away, afraid he'd feel it trembling. "I've got to go. Call me and we'll go over to the parish office together tomorrow, providing they say yes."

Greg helped Diana out of the van, then watched her as she slid behind the wheel of her own car. "Good night," he said, his tone as taut as he felt.

He stood on the sidewalk and watched her pull away. More than the mystery they were trying to unravel, he wanted to find the key that would unlock the secrets to her heart. Diana was like a rare painting hidden beneath the brush strokes of another. Glimpses of what lay beyond enticed him to continue his pursuit.

Greg got back into his van and drove home. As he entered the tiny studio, he was immediately struck by the stark, impersonal feel of the place. His thoughts drifted, and he found himself wondering what it might be like to have a wife, children and a place to really call home. The idea tugged at his imagination and the pull became so strong he groaned out loud in frustration. He realized then, with absolute certainty, that he'd never view his life in the same light again.

THE FOLLOWING MORNING Greg telephoned Diana twenty minutes after the shop opened. He hadn't really expected her to have any answers for him, he'd just wanted to hear her voice. To his surprise, she'd already made all the arrangements. Like him, she seemed filled with restless energy.

It was a bit past nine when Greg left his studio and drove to the church. By the time he arrived, Diana was already there, waiting. "Good morning," he said, glad to be with her again. "It looks like you're as eager to get started as I am."

"We're going to need lots of patience," she said, walking through the door that led to the parish offices.

"Were they reluctant to have me come along with you?" he asked.

"Not really. I spoke to Marie, she runs everything here. As long as I was willing to vouch for you, they had no problem with it." After making a quick stop to pick up the keys, Diana led Greg downstairs. "Brace yourself," she said as she unlocked the door. "This room hasn't been used in a long while."

The interior was even worse than she'd expected. There were no windows, and the musty smell of dust and old papers made it difficult to breathe. "Leave the door open for now," she said, coughing.

"What a wonderful place," he said gazing around. "Look at the binding on some of those volumes on the top shelf."

At first she'd thought he was being sarcastic, but one glance at him convinced her differently. He had the same look of wonder and excitement she'd seen on children standing near the puppies in a pet store window. "This is the section we have to look through," she said, pointing to the cartons stacked against the wall. "The information inside the other stacks has already been cataloged and entered in the computer upstairs."

"Were you able to pull up any information on the items we're interested in?"

"Yes. In fact, with the list you gave me I found out the basics on most of them. Marie was nice enough to give me that information over the telephone this morning." She bent over one of the boxes and began to work it open. "The jeweled cross was a gift from one of the founding families of Santa Fe. It hung in their private chapel for decades, but was given to the church fifty years ago as a result of a promise made to a saint."

"There's a possibility. Maybe an heir changed his mind and hired someone to get it back."

She shook her head. "Marie said that the last surviving member of that family died a decade ago." She paused, glancing at some notes she'd made on a pad. "The chalice is made of pure gold, and was cast about twelve years ago. The smaller gold crosses are not antiques, in fact they date back only a few years. The small gold statue of St. Francis and the one of St. Joseph are also fairly new, crafted by one of our local goldsmiths. The only historic question seems to surround the silver candlesticks. A vague reference in the records upstairs suggests that they've been here almost as long as the church. That means we have to check the records dating back to the 1800s."

"Do you have any idea about the condition of the books? If they haven't been treated or preserved in any way, they might just disintegrate in our hands."

"They've been looked after somewhat." Diana picked up a volume from the box and handed the book to him. "Most of the pages aren't bound, but they are all enclosed in loose cellophane envelopes. We're not to take them out of those for any reason." She took a seat next to a small desk.

"These are in remarkably good condition for their age. The desert air really helps preserve them." Greg pulled up a chair next to Diana. "They must really trust you to allow you to search through these."

"Marie knows me very well, and I've worked with Father John on many projects through the years. It also doesn't hurt that my shop donates its services to the church on a regular basis," she added with a playful smile.

Hours ticked by and neither of them found any mention of the candlesticks. "We're in the right year, I think," Diana commented, squinting at the page before her. "It's hard to make out these numbers at the top. The ink has faded badly."

"This is the last volume in here," Greg said, taking it from the box. "It's not even a book this time. The pages have been pressed inside this legal folder." Greg studied the sheets. "They seem to be miscellaneous daily records. For instance, someone donated four goats to the church, and they were traded for other food supplies." Greg lapsed into silence. "Wait, I think I've got something here." He placed the cellophane-covered sheet on the table between them.

"Candlesticks," she read, leaning forward until she was about twelve inches from the paper. "They were donated by Josiah Blackburn, a silversmith. He crafted them as a gift for the church. There's an entry here that lists them as never having arrived."

Greg carefully extracted several more sheets and placed them before Diana. "Let's split the rest. There have got to be other entries. If they're the same candlesticks, and from what we know that seems to be a logical assumption, then they must have arrived at the church at one point or another."

"Here's another entry," Diana said. "Henry Blackburn, listed as Josiah Blackburn's father, paid for the funeral of his son, daughter-in-law, two granddaughters, and for that of a Sheriff Samuel Givens."

"That's interesting, but I'm not sure what it means in terms of what we're looking for. Is there any mention of the candlesticks arriving at the church?"

"Not on this page," she said, continuing the search.

"I've got something here," Greg said. "It's a page from a journal, I think. It's signed by a Father Paul something. I can't make out the last name. It tells about the candlesticks. Apparently Josiah Blackburn, his wife and family were killed by three thieves who broke into their home. The men took the silver candlesticks as well as other valuables. Sheriff Samuel Givens caught up to the gang and killed them in a gunfight. Knowing he was mortally wounded as well, Givens went to the church instead of seeking medical help. He delivered the candlesticks to the padre who gave him his last rites."

Greg leaned forward, trying to make out the rest. "The priest apparently didn't want to take the candlesticks for the church because of the blood that had been spilled for them. The Blackburn family insisted, however, and the priest complied out of respect for the loss they'd suffered."

"That's fascinating, but I doubt whoever killed Father John knew about all this. We had a tough enough time finding the information ourselves."

"It's strange, though, how things work out. The candlesticks now have even more blood on them." Greg helped

Diana return everything to its proper place. "I'm just not sure how any of this fits in with my theory."

"You've been thinking all along that this was a well-planned art heist that went sour. But maybe what we're dealing with is just a common thief who figured the church was a good place to rob. He did get away with some valuable things."

"But why take the hide *Madonna?* That's not flashy, nor easily sold, nor valuable for what it's made of. It represents folk art at its best, but the market for that is limited."

"Didn't you say it was all wrapped up?" Seeing him nod, she continued. "Maybe the thief ducked back into the sacristy to hide when you moved into the church and took it on the chance it might be valuable."

"I don't think we have the right handle on this yet. The way you've described, it sounds too random. I still believe this was well planned. Look at how the thief managed to elude everyone when he made his escape, and the way he hid his trail. That's got to be more than just luck."

Diana led the way out of the room and locked the door behind them. "Well, let's mull it over some more then. Maybe we'll come up with another theory." She glanced at her watch. "Meanwhile, I've got to walk to a shop near here and deliver an order. It's a special favor for one of my best customers. Would you like to come along? We can do some more brainstorming along the way."

"Sure." He watched Diana as she dropped off the key at the church office and exchanged a few words with the secretary. Diana tried so hard to appear confident and self-possessed, but everyone had needs no matter how deep they buried them inside themselves. He wondered when she'd realize that around him she didn't need the tough front she put on for the rest of the world. With him she'd be safe, his feelings for her would wrap around her and protect her, if she'd only allow it.

A short time later they were headed down the street together. Greg carried the small package of stationery under one arm for her. "It looks like the street gang's out early today." He gestured ahead. "They're harassing that guy, but it looks like he can handle it."

Diana searched for Petey, but he was nowhere in sight. "I don't know any of those guys," she said, studying their faces. "From the looks of it, I'd say they're asking people for money."

"Keep an eye on that little guy, the one with the black T-shirt," he pointed out. "He's putting on a show for the others."

As they started past the group, the boy Greg had mentioned came up, reaching toward Diana's purse. "How about a few bucks, lady? You look like you can spare it."

"Why don't you get a job, kid," she said sharply.

"Aw, come on! Be nice to us, and we'll be nice to you."

"Let her go," one of the younger boys ordered. "She's a friend of Petey's."

"Tough," the kid shot back.

"You're Belinda Martinez's kid, aren't you?" Diana said facing him.

"What's it to you?" he spat out.

The gang member they knew as Carlos came up and joined them. "You still panhandling?" He shook his head at the younger boy. "You better knock it off, man. There's two cops driving this way."

"So what? I ain't afraid of them," the kid in the black T-shirt countered with a cocky grin.

Carlos laughed mirthlessly. "You would be if they ever found out who put our plaque on their squad car."

While the boys were busy arguing, Greg placed his hand on Diana's back and hurried her on. Annoyed at being propelled that way, Diana moved away from him as soon as they reached the corner. "Will you stop that? What did you think I was going to do to him?"

"It wasn't that," he answered quickly. "When Carlos mentioned the squad car being spray painted, I suddenly remembered something important. The night I was arrested, the cops had their vehicle's logo defaced while they were busy with me. If the boy panhandling is the one who did that, then he must have been in the area the night of the murder. It's possible he could have seen something that might lead us to the killer."

"Or he could have seen the killer himself sneaking out of the church," Diana commented thoughtfully. "Everyone else's attention was focused on you that night, but his undoubtedly wouldn't have been." She paused. "That boy's a real hard case. I recognized him once I saw him up close. He came into the print shop one time with his mother and was trying to hustle some money from her. I'm not sure how we're going to get him to talk to us. I do know it'll be impossible around the other boys."

"We could try to catch him at home," Greg suggested.

"His mother complained that he only comes home to eat dinner and sleep. I suppose we could go over at around dinnertime and see if he's there," Diana said doubtfully. She led the way into a small law office and delivered the package.

As they came back out, she continued. "Why don't you meet me at the shop at six? We can go together," she suggested, heading back toward the church.

"I'd like that. In the meantime, I'll make some more calls. Maybe some of the missing items have surfaced by now."

Alone, twenty minutes later, Greg drove back to his studio. He spent the rest of the afternoon telephoning pawn shops and art dealers, but managed to turn up no new leads. It was five-thirty by the time he could drive back to the print shop. Despite the wasted day, he felt his spirits lifting at the prospect of seeing Diana. He cursed softly. His business was at a standstill. With potential charges of murder and art theft hanging over him, his career was going down the chute. Yet, despite all that, knowing that he was on his way to meet Diana made him want to whistle. Questioning his sanity, he zigzagged through the evening traffic. As he pulled up, he saw Diana outside the shop, waiting.

"I've asked Anita to lock up for me," she explained, approaching his van and climbing inside. "I got hold of Belinda and she said it's okay with her if we ask Joe a few questions. She told me that he'd probably be home early today since he knows it's her payday."

"This kid sounds like a real winner," Greg muttered, putting the van in gear.

Twenty minutes later they entered what was reputed to be the roughest area of town. Greg's van, in its dilapidated condition, seemed to fit right in, and scarcely anyone paid attention to them as they parked and got out.

Belinda was bending over the lock on her front door as they approached. Diana called the woman's name and waved, trying to get her attention, but Belinda didn't react. Rushing forward, Diana caught up to her as she started to go down the porch steps. "Hello! I guess you didn't hear me."

Giving Diana a glazed look, Belinda Martinez started to hurry past her. "I can't talk right now. I've got to get down to the police station. They arrested my Joe."

## Chapter Eleven

Diana stood behind Belinda at the visitors desk of the Juvenile Detention center. After signing several forms, they were allowed into a small windowless room. A few minutes later Joe was escorted in, a guard at his side.

"I didn't do nothin', Ma, so don't hassle me," Joe said sullenly.

"*Hijo*, I didn't come here for that. You don't ever listen to what I have to say. I just can't believe you would stab anyone!"

"It was self-defense! We were just asking the guy for a few dollars when he freaked out and attacked *us*!" He stared defiantly at Diana and Greg. "Who are you? I've seen you before someplace."

"They're friends, Joe. If you answer some questions for them, maybe they can help you. They think you might have seen something going on the night of Father John's murder."

"Oh, great! You think I had something to do with that, too?" The boy stared at them, a trace of fear beginning to show in his eyes.

"No, not at all," Diana assured him. "Joe, don't you remember us from this afternoon? I'm Petey's friend. Carlos mentioned something about a car that you'd worked on near the church," she said obliquely, motioning with her eyes at the guard. "And I thought that after you finished up for the evening, you might have seen someone wandering around or someone going in or out of the neighboring buildings."

The boy's expression lost some of its harshness. "No, I didn't, and believe me, I've been thinking about it, too. I wish I could help but I just don't have any information you can use—" he paused and shrugged "—not about that, anyway."

"But there's something else?" Greg prodded.

"Forget it, it's nothing."

"Then tell us," Greg insisted.

"I know who trashed your studio. It was payback time for some of my friends. But you're not getting any names," he stated flatly.

"Joe, they might be able to help you," Belinda pleaded.

The boy shook his head. "Forget it, Ma. I'm on my own now."

Joe's face mirrored a grim acceptance that surprised Greg. He had the distinct impression Joe was regarding what was happening to him as a test of his manhood. Greg continued to hold the boy's eyes for a moment, then glanced at Diana. "Let's go. There's nothing more we can do here."

As they left the room, they could hear Belinda pleading with him to cooperate with the police instead of remaining silent.

Diana shuddered. "I've seen them like that before. Belinda's not going to get anywhere with him. Joe's caught up in the act he puts on to convince everyone how tough he is."

Greg drove back to the print shop and parked next to Diana's car. "I was really counting on a lead from that boy," he said quietly.

"We're back to the cowboy, I guess." Diana sighed. "I'm going home. I need time to think and get things back into perspective." She couldn't tell Greg that just being with him made their discouraging lack of progress easier to take. It was becoming increasingly difficult to walk away from the warmth and caring he offered her.

As she pulled out into the street, she saw his van in her rearview mirror. Longing cut through her like shards of broken glass. There was no future for them, and she couldn't accept a relationship that offered her nothing more than a few fleeting moments. She owed herself more than that.

Ten minutes later she entered the driveway of her home. Don's car was there, and the lights in her kitchen were on. She exhaled softly. Bob had given Don a set of keys years ago, and she hadn't wanted to hurt his feelings by asking for them back. Still, she'd never become used to his unannounced visits.

Diana walked inside and found Don sitting at the kitchen table, a can of soda in his hand. "Make yourself at home, Don," she said, unable to resist the tiny barb.

He smiled at her. "We've got to talk. Pull up a chair."

She placed her purse on the counter, then sat across from him. "Sounds serious."

"It is." Don leaned forward and regarded her intently. "I was leaving the detention center this evening when you arrived with Marten."

"We went to see the Martinez boy." She went on to explain their reason for the visit. "We'd hoped he'd seen someone sneaking out of the church."

"There's more than that to what's been going on." Don held up a hand. "Wait, let me finish." He rubbed the back of his neck. "I know you haven't dated since Bob died, and that's your business. But Marten is using your need for companionship to his own advantage. You need to have more people around you, and not Marten's type, either. Let me introduce you to some of the guys in the department. You're a beautiful woman, you don't have to settle for anything less than the best. Marten's just a rich bum who's never worked an honest day in his life."

"First of all, you're making me sound desperate, and I resent that," Diana countered angrily. She began pacing, trying to hold her temper in check. "And your facts about

Greg are wrong, *as usual*. He works hard at what he does, even if you don't think much of art restoration.''

"Come on, Diana. Wake up and smell the coffee! I don't know what kind of line he fed you, but look at the guy. He's perfectly happy living the life of a drifter because he knows he's got a wealthy family that'll back him up if things get rough. You're too proud to live off somebody else and too practical to accept a life-style like his. You've known what it's like to go hungry. People like Marten don't understand people like us who have to plan for our own futures and live on budgets. We've never taken financial security for granted, so our mind-set is totally different.''

"I know very little about his family, but I'm aware of everything else you've mentioned,'' she replied. She took a deep breath and let it out slowly. Don meant well, he was only trying to keep her from getting hurt. She couldn't fault him for being loyal. Love of any kind was too rare a commodity nowadays to discard casually. "I shouldn't explain myself to you, but I don't want you to keep worrying.'' She managed a thin smile. "There's nothing going on between Greg and me, except for the investigation.''

Don's shoulders lost some of their tension. "I know that you think I'm always butting in, but Bob was my kid brother, and I loved him. When he died, I did what he would have expected me to do—watch over you.''

"I understand you very well, Don,'' she said coming up from behind and giving him a quick hug.

He watched Diana as she went over to the counter to make some coffee. "Someday I know you'll get married again. I'd like to think that whoever you pick will be a worthy successor to my brother. Someone he would have approved of, you know what I mean?'' Don glanced up, a faraway expression on his face. As his gaze drifted over the clock on the far wall, he suddenly jerked upright. "Look at the time! I didn't realize it was so late!'' He grabbed his jacket from the back of the chair. "I'm on duty in another fifteen minutes. I've got to go. Thanks for the soda.''

Diana saw him shoot out the door, then a moment later heard the roar of a car engine. Shaking her head, she poured the contents of her coffee pot down the sink. All she felt like doing now was crawling between the sheets and going to sleep. She walked to the bedroom and slipped on her nightgown. She had just reached out to turn the lights off when she heard a knock at her side door. "Wait a sec," she called out, scowling. Slipping her robe on, she returned to the kitchen and peered out the tiny curtained window. "Greg! Is something wrong?" she asked, opening the door quickly.

"No, everything's fine," he assured her. "I decided on the spur of the moment to go back to the school to do an all-night stakeout. Only I realized that unless I told someone about my plans, I'd be leaving myself wide open to trouble. Since I was only about a block from here, I thought I'd stop by just long enough to tell you. I'm sorry if I disturbed you."

"You're going to watch Harper? But why? We've seen what he does with his time and it's led us nowhere."

"I can't shake the feeling that we're missing something. Harper's a nice guy, but the clues we've found all lead to the school. I'm going to give it one last try."

She sighed softly. "All right, I'm in."

"You don't have to come along," he countered. "You were about to go to bed. I'll call you in the morning and let you know if I found out anything."

"Not a chance. If you're going, so am I. I'll leave a message on Anita's answering machine. She disconnects the telephone at night, but if anything happens the message will let her know where we're at." She walked back to the bedroom, and emerged five minutes later. Her jeans fit snugly, but were comfortable. Her favorite old sweater, which clung to her softly, was perfect for a cool desert night.

Greg's eyes lingered over her appreciatively. "You look terrific in those," he commented. "You should wear jeans more often."

"Thanks, but these are so old half of the fabric is worn away."

"I know," he answered, giving her a wink.

Diana felt her cheeks burn. "Let's get going," she said, hurrying to the door.

In the van Greg glanced over at her again. "I'm glad you're here with me, but why were you so insistent about coming along? Don't you trust me to tell you what happened?"

"No, that has nothing to do with it. I didn't think it was safe for you to go alone. I would have been—" She clamped her mouth shut.

"Worried?" he finished.

"That doesn't change anything between us," she insisted quietly. "I still know very little about you, Greg, and what I have learned makes you appear to be a mass of contradictions."

"If that's so, it's because you're not asking the right questions. What is it that's bothering you?"

"Don came by tonight. He mentioned that you come from a wealthy family. I've tried to figure it out, but I can't imagine why you live like you're barely making ends meet."

"My family is wealthy, but I'm not. Traveling takes a considerable portion of my earnings as a conservator. But I'm convinced I made the right move leaving Houston. I was a disappointment to my father, and trying to work in the family business was the biggest mistake I ever made."

"Sounds like you hated it."

"At first I had only one reason for being at the firm. My father had financed my education in exchange for my spending three years working there. He was convinced that once I got a taste of it, I'd never be able to leave. I learned the ropes, but I never did learn to love it like he did."

"So you left to pursue your own career," she finished.

"I left, but the circumstances weren't that simple. Halfway through my second year, my father started to buy out a rival investment firm. The deal was they'd continue to operate, but under our ownership. Then I found out that a very different scenario had been worked out behind the scenes. The C.E.O. and top management were to be paid handsomely to resign after the sale, but two hundred others would also have lost their jobs. My father planned to sell all the company's assets, basically gutting it, and then take over their client list."

"What did you do?"

"I was supposed to buy out one of the owners on behalf of our firm. That would have given my father, together with their management, a majority on the board of directors. With that they would have controlled any vote and ensured the sale. Well, I bought out the owner all right, but with my own money, not my father's. The whole deal fell through because I wouldn't sell to my father." Greg parked about a block from the school and helped her out of the van.

"Very clever." She chuckled softly. "But your father probably didn't think much of it," she said, as they cut across the church grounds.

"He was furious when he found out I was the one who stood in his way. He accused me of being disloyal and letting sentiment interfere with a legitimate business deal. He fired me, saying that I lacked the 'killer instinct.' Seems ironic now, in view of the problems I'm facing."

"Do you keep in touch with other members of your family?" she asked.

"My mother died eight years ago, so the only person I talk to is my stepsister Celia. My father and I have very little to say to each other."

As they approached the school Greg spotted Harper near one of the upstairs windows washing the walls of a classroom. Selecting a vantage point by the church, they sat behind a low juniper hedge and waited.

"Don't you ever worry about the future? Your profession doesn't have a great deal of security attached to it."

"My business fluctuates with the economy, that's true, but I make a good living. I've also invested some of my earnings, so I do have something to fall back on if I need it."

She was about to ask him why he'd never found another place to call home when all of a sudden she noticed the temperature around them had begun to drop. Uneasy and cold, Diana shuddered and crossed her arms. As Greg rose to his feet and stepped back into the shadows, she shifted to look at him. "What's wrong?" she asked.

"Nothing, I just wanted to move around a bit," he said, his tone not at all convincing.

Diana rose and glanced around warily. Despite the quiet of the evening, she couldn't shake the sensation. It was more than a sixth sense. She sensed it with the acute certainty that came from actual knowledge. "We're being watched," she whispered.

Greg scanned the area immediately ahead of them, then glanced from side to side and behind them. "Do you see anyone?"

"No," she answered. Aware of the puzzled look he gave her, she added, "For heaven's sake, don't you *feel* it?"

"The weather's a little strange," he observed after a pause. "There seems to be peculiar pressure in the air. It reminds me of the way it gets right before a tornado," he commented pensively.

"Oppressive is the word you're looking for," Diana ventured. It was as if a shadow had settled over them. She tried to argue away the feeling, but she could still feel the watcher's eyes on them. As she studied the surrounding grounds and found no one, she began to sink into uncertainty.

Diana glanced at the upstairs window and saw Harper still there, working. Ready to find a comfortable place to sit again, she turned around. Suddenly her breath caught in her throat. "There!" she managed.

The cowboy stood off to one side of them. His features were obscured by the gray shadows of night, but the glow of his pipe was unmistakable. Diana fought the urge to run as far from there as possible. Why did this man fill her with such terror? This was the break they'd hoped to find! It was no time to lose her nerve.

The cowboy remained motionless for a few seconds, then he cut across a flower bed and started toward the far side of the school building. As he disappeared from view, Diana followed. "I think he's leading us somewhere," she said breathlessly.

"It could be a trap," Greg said, catching up and then moving ahead of her. "Stay sharp!"

A few feet behind Greg she cut across the soft earth of the small flower garden and ducked behind the playground's jungle gym following the cowboy's path. As she emerged on the other side, she caught a glimpse of the cowboy just ahead. He stood in the parking lot, near the front corner of the building, waiting. Then, just as Greg was about to catch up, he slipped around the corner.

Greg's long legs had made it easy for him to match the cowboy's pace, but Diana's legs ached with the strain. As she turned the corner, she saw Greg standing a dozen feet further ahead, looking around. "Where did he go?" she asked.

"He came this way, I saw him," Greg muttered. "I was just a few seconds behind him. He's got to be around here someplace." Staying close to the building in order to avoid being seen by Harper, Greg walked along the front wall. "There are no open doors or windows, except the one on the second floor where Harper is, and he would have had to fly up there," Greg whispered, not wanting Harper to hear. "How did he get away?"

Diana walked across to the other side of the building. "He must have ducked inside using an entry we know nothing about. That's the only answer that makes sense."

"Let's backtrack. Maybe we'll find something we missed before."

They retraced their steps slowly, alert for danger. As they reached the flower bed, Greg stopped and studied the ground. "I don't get it," he said, staring at the soft earth beneath his feet. "I can see my footprints here, and yours, but where are his?" He crouched down angling for a better look as the soft rays of moonlight bathed the ground. "I could have sworn that this was where he went through."

"He did. I saw him, too," Diana protested.

"Maybe the darkness distorted our perceptions. He must have stayed to one side of the flower bed," Greg insisted.

"I suppose," Diana answered, not at all convinced. Perplexed, she stared at the ground. She was certain the cowboy had walked across here. But she had no explanation for the missing footprints. At least none that she cared to say out loud.

# Chapter Twelve

The following morning Diana stood next to one of the lay-out tables, her mind on the events of the evening before.

"You look like you're miles away." Don's voice came from behind her, jolting her back to reality.

She jumped and turned around. "I didn't hear you come in," she said. "Have you been standing there long?"

"No, I just got here. Anita showed me where you were. I wanted to talk to you about Arnie Walker." He met her eyes. "We've searched everywhere for that kid, but he knows he's in trouble and has gone underground. Depending on how mixed up he is, there's a chance he might blame you for his problems and come to even the score. Stay on your guard."

"What about the lead we gave you on Ortega?"

"It fizzled out. Ortega was at Don Diego's Cantina the night of the murder. He was watching a baseball game on the large screen there. Several people, including the bartender, remember seeing him. Of course, he could have hired someone to do the hit, but a professional killer would have used a faster, more efficient way to eliminate someone."

"So once again, we have absolutely nothing."

"Not quite. We've turned up something interesting about Joe Martinez. The knife he used when he attacked that guy on the street turned out to be the murder weapon."

Diana's mouth fell open. "So he killed Father John?"

"We're not sure yet. The boy claims he found the knife on the street where the gang hangs out. We questioned a few of the kids and they confirmed his story. Of course it stands to reason they'd stick together."

"I'm not sure that the gang would back him on something like this unless it was true."

"The forensics team is going over the details again to see if Martinez fits the other evidence they have. But these things take time. As soon as I hear anything else, I'll pass it along to you."

Diana watched Don leave. If Joe Martinez turned out to be the murderer, then the case would be closed. Justice would be served, but nothing would ever bring back her friend. Another selfish thought occurred to her immediately. She stared at the printing press and wondered when Greg would be moving on.

Hearing rapid footsteps behind her, Diana turned her head. "You better come out here," Anita said, rushing to where Diana was working. "We've got trouble. Some of the gang members are coming this way, and they look like they mean business."

Diana walked to the front and saw Petey, Carlos and five other boys coming toward the shop. People on the sidewalk were scattering to either side as the hostile-looking young men took their share of the path from the middle. The three youngest were glancing around nervously, as if being pursued, but Diana didn't worry about them. It was Petey and Carlos she was concerned about. Both had their hands in their pockets, and she wondered if they were concealing weapons of some kind. "Hello, boys. What can I do for you?"

"We've been waiting for the cop to leave. I didn't want to run into him." Petey gave Anita a suspicious glance. "Is it okay to talk?"

"You bet. Whatever you say to me, you can say in front of her."

Petey nodded somberly. "We hear the police still don't have any suspects in Father John's murder. That's why they're so eager to blame Joe and the Diablo Locos. To take the heat off our guys, we're going to have to find the scum who did this ourselves. We know you've been looking into this for a while without having any luck, so we figured you could use our help."

Diana regarded the boys thoughtfully for several moments, then told them about Arnie Walker. "The police haven't been able to find him and neither have we. Can you check around and find out where he lives or where he might be hiding?"

"I know that dude," Carlos replied with a nod. "He's crazy enough to do something like this. He hangs out in my cousin Manuel's neighborhood. The home boys there will help us on this. They'll be able to find him if anyone can."

"You can count on us," Petey assured her. "We'll have something for you in a few days."

"Wait a minute, Petey. Remember that what I've told you doesn't mean Arnie's guilty," she warned. "All we're trying to do is find him so we can talk to him. Go easy. Don't scare him off."

Diana watched the boys leave, then returned to the back to finish the order she'd interrupted. It was nearly five o'clock by the time Anita came in and sat down near the sorting table. "I've been thinking about the conversation you had with the boys earlier this afternoon. Are you sure it's wise to involve them? I overheard Don say that there's a possibility some of them were responsible for Father John's death."

"They wouldn't have hurt a priest. Don doesn't know as much about that gang as I do."

"Maybe you see the Diablo Locos in a better light because Frankie used to be one of them."

"No, that's not it," Diana said slowly. "I just understand them more. Father was their friend, they'd have done anything for him. Right now they're on the defensive because the police arrested one of their own. Putting them to work finding Arnie will channel their energies into something constructive. It's also a job they might be able to accomplish faster than the police.''

"I hope, for everyone's sake, that you're not making a mistake.'' Anita stood, and began to put things away. "Come on. We've both worked hard today. Let's get out of here on time for once.''

Diana followed Anita out to the parking lot five minutes later. She'd just switched on the ignition when Greg pulled in beside her.

"You must have had a rushed day,'' he said, getting out and coming toward her. "Every time I called I got a busy signal.''

"We were busy, but I'm glad you came by. There're some new developments I need to tell you about.'' She filled him in. "The way I see it, we should keep looking until the police are sure about their facts. Don wasn't convinced that Joe's the killer, and I have a tough time believing that the gang is involved.''

"From the sound of it, there's only one lead left for us to pursue. We still need to find the cowboy, but I don't know where else to look for him.''

"I do. We need to sneak inside the school and look around when Harper's not there to direct our search.''

"That sounds like breaking and entering, Diana,'' Greg said warily. "I'm already in enough trouble with the police. If we get caught, your brother-in-law is going to do everything he can to keep me in jail.''

"We won't be breaking in, the door will be open,'' she answered. "According to what Ralph himself told us, he comes out once a night to search with the metal detector. Since he's within view of the door, he leaves it open. Remember how he just walked back inside? What I'm counting on is that his metal detector will keep him busy enough for us to sneak past him. Keep in mind that he uses a headset, so we won't have to worry about him hearing us.''

"We'd have to time it just right. And what happens if we get caught?"

"I'll do my best to charm Harper and talk him out of calling the police."

Greg leaned against Diana's car and stared off into the distance. "We should turn this over to Don. He has the clout to get in that building and turn it upside down if necessary."

"He's going to need more evidence than we have in order to get a search warrant."

"Ours would be an illegal search and anything we found would be inadmissible anyway."

"But it might just give us a lead that we can turn over to them. At the moment, we don't know a thing about that cowboy. The man hasn't even left footprints or said a word. What we have on him is purely circumstantial."

Greg turned his palm upward in a gesture of resignation. "Do you want to go over there now?"

"No, it's too early. Come by my house in a couple of hours. We'll take my car. It can really accelerate if we have to make a fast exit."

"What comfort!" he muttered sarcastically.

Diana said goodbye and drove home quickly. She'd have to talk to Anita and let her know where she'd be. Although she'd tried to minimize the risks in front of Greg, she was quite aware that they were high.

Still trying to figure out how to tell Anita without worrying her, Diana walked to the kitchen and fixed herself a sandwich. Dinner in hand, she went to the bedroom. An hour later, showered and ready, she emerged wearing an old windbreaker, black jeans and a faded gray cotton sweater. After a brief search through the kitchen cupboards, she found her flashlight and stuffed it into her pocket.

As she started out the door, she practically collided with Anita. "Where are you going in that outfit?" Anita demanded. "You up to something?"

"Come in. I was just on my way over to see you." Joining Anita at the kitchen table, she explained her plans.

"I'll stay at home and wait for you. The way I see it, the best that can happen is that Harper will catch you and call the police."

"We won't get caught, at least I hope not."

"I still don't understand what you plan to do with the cowboy even if you find him. The man obviously doesn't want to talk, and for all you know he might be armed."

"I don't think he's going to hurt me. He could have done so before, yet he's never even come close."

"Do you think that'll change if you go after him?"

"I'm not sure, but I have no intention of cornering him. All I want is a few answers."

Anita remained silent for a few moments. "If you're not back by ten, I'm calling the police."

"Okay, that's fair enough," Diana agreed, seeing Anita out.

Not long afterward Greg arrived. "We better get going," Diana said, grabbing her keys from the counter. "It was about this time when we saw Harper making his search."

Diana drove to the school quickly and parked just down the street. As they padded silently across the grounds, staying in the shadows, Diana glanced at Greg. "What's on your mind?"

"I'm trying to figure out a contingency plan in case we can't use the front door when we're ready to leave."

"If that's the case, we have other options. For example, we can find an unlocked room and duck out a window."

"What if the only ones we can get to happen to be on the second floor?"

"Then we'll go out that way, and walk around the ledge until we reach the tall maple that's next to the building. From there, we can climb down."

DIANA SAT DOWN by the edge of the school's property and waited. The minutes ticked by slowly. "Greg, maybe you should reconsider going inside with me. You've got much more to lose than I have."

He crouched beside her. "We stand a better chance together than separately." He tilted her chin up with one finger and met her gaze. "You may not need me," he said softly, "but I'd like to think that you do. There's no harm in that, is there?"

Diana didn't know what to say. Her heart was pounding against her sides as his eyes burned into hers. "You're letting your feelings for me place you in danger, and I wouldn't be much of a friend if I allowed that to happen."

"You don't have a choice. I intend to stay right by you, lady," he answered, his voice husky. "We're in this together." He traced the outline of her lips with the pad of his thumb.

Ribbons of warmth started where he caressed and blazed a trail down her body. She took a deep, uneven breath, and with effort stood and moved away. "Harper should have been out by now," she said, fighting to keep her mind on what they'd set out to do.

"A light just came on by the door," he said, "and here comes Harper now."

Diana kept her eyes glued on the custodian. "He didn't lock the door. We're in business."

"Wait until he moves a little farther away from the entrance. We need every advantage we can get." Greg watched as Harper put on the headset and started sweeping the area.

Using the bushes for cover, they moved until they were about ten feet from the doors. It took several more minutes before Harper reached the corner. "It doesn't look like he's going any further than that," Greg said, "but his back's to us." The custodian stopped and pressed his hand against one side of the headset as if listening for a sound. "Now's our chance. Go!"

Diana rushed forward, staying in the shadows as much as possible. As Harper leaned down to pick up something from the ground, they slipped inside the building.

Diána moved quickly down the hall. "Come on," she said in a harsh whisper. "We'll search all the rooms that are unlocked."

Greg glanced at his watch. "Last time he took about forty-five minutes, but that doesn't mean he'll do the same today. Let's move quickly and keep it to fifteen minutes."

Diana listened for sounds as Greg tried each door. The opened rooms they examined were large, empty classrooms full of desks that wouldn't have given anyone a place to hide. Moving to the second floor, they wound their way around the corridors. Almost all the rooms were locked, and the place echoed with an eerie silence.

"It's time to go," he whispered. "If there's anyone hiding in here, then they're either asleep or in a coma."

They went down the stairs and headed toward the entrance to check on Harper's progress. "With any luck, we'll still be able to use the front door," Greg said.

They crept down an unlit corridor and were halfway to the door when they heard the metal front door swing open. Harper came in and stood the metal detector against the wall. As he pulled the door shut and locked it, he glanced casually their way down the hall.

Diana pressed her back against the wall, scarcely breathing. Only a miracle could save them now. She could feel the tension that held Greg immobile. For what seemed an eternity no one moved. Finally they heard Harper curse loudly and start toward them.

With the flick of a wrist, he switched on the lights, exposing them. "Greg Marten and Diana Clark! What the hell do you think you're doing?"

To run seemed pointless, Harper could see them as clearly as they could see him. Their only hope was to talk Harper out of calling the police.

"This is what I get for being nice to you," Harper said as he strode toward them, metal detector in one hand. "We're going to go through the building together right now. If anything's missing, I'm holding you both responsible." His glare was cold, but his face was red with anger. "And if you try anything, Marten, one of you is going to get it across the head with this metal detector. Now get going," he ordered.

Diana started to offer an explanation, but Harper held up one hand. "Save it."

As they worked their way down the corridors, Greg made sure he remained between Harper and Diana. Finally, after a careful search, Harper escorted them back to the front. "Okay, you've had your fun. Nothing's missing, so get out of here. I never want to see either of you two sneaking around here again. And I'm calling the police about this, you can count on that." Harper unlocked the door, then held it open. "Now get out."

Greg hurried Diana away from the building. "I wonder what the cops will do when he calls. We didn't leave any evidence that we were there, and we didn't take anything."

"All they'll really have is Harper's word for it," she said. "I don't think they'll be able to take us in on just that."

"Don's been itching for an excuse to hassle me. He's not going to pass up this opportunity."

"Come over to my place. We'll have some coffee and try to relax. You'll feel better once you unwind."

Diana returned to the car with Greg and quickly got underway. Her nerves felt taut, but her concerns were for him. He was right about Don. He wouldn't make it easy on Greg. By the time they walked into her kitchen, silence hung oppressively in the air.

Diana led the way to her living room, and gestured for Greg to have a seat. After a quick call to Anita she joined him. "I don't know where else to look for the cowboy," she said at last. "That man should really hire himself out as an undercover agent. Trying to find him is like chasing a shadow. Maybe he's a magician or a former member of one of those elite commando units."

"Let's not talk about it anymore," Greg said wearily, as his gaze wandered around the room. "You know, it's nice in here. It's an easy place to relax in." He stood and walked to a wooden carving that was set in a recessed area within the wall. "Did you have this space built just for the carving?"

"No, it was already here. A lot of the older houses around here have those," she explained. "They're called *nichos* and they serve as a place to put *santos,* carvings of saints, or Indian kachinas."

He crossed over to a small table and ran his hand over a small wooden carving of a cowboy carrying a calf in his arms. "This is a good piece of work, but I don't recognize the artist."

"I have no idea who it is. All I know is that I fell in love with the sculpture." She picked the figure up and handed it to him. "The man looks tough and weathered, but I love the gentle expression on his face."

He smiled, then joined her on the couch. "I like your tastes. You've created a comfortable home."

"How does it compare to your carefree life-style?" Diana asked, tucking one foot beneath her and watching him intently.

"Living in my van and traveling around has suited my needs. I've been searching for something I can't quite define, and moving from place to place seemed the best way to look for answers. But lately, as my feelings for you grew, I've realized what was missing in my life." He weaved his fingers beneath the curtain of her hair and smiled gently when she shivered at his touch. "We bring out the best in each other, Diana. We belong together," he whispered.

He gathered her into his arms and was glad when she made no effort to resist. "I need to hear you say what I know is in your heart. I need to know that I matter to the woman who matters most to me."

Greg made Diana feel beautiful and every inch a woman. The love in his eyes made her feel dazed with longing, but her survival instincts were too strong. If this continued, they would make love, and once she welcomed him into her body, he'd find a permanent place in her soul.

She felt his lips brush a kiss over her forehead and her resolve teetered precariously. "How I feel doesn't matter. There's no future for us," she answered, her voice shaky. She knew she should move away, but couldn't quite find the will to resist him. "I spent most of my life going from one town to the next. As migrant workers, my parents hired out and went wherever there was work. I never felt like I belonged anywhere. Finally I have a place to call my own, and I love it here."

She tore herself from his embrace and stood. Restless, she paced, unable to risk even looking directly at him. "Your job requires that you travel, and you enjoy the life-style it's given you. You haven't felt deprived at all. I can't believe that just because you've met me, you're going to change all that and be perfectly happy staying in one place."

Diana's throat tightened as she struggled between what her heart yearned for and the truth that would keep them separated. "You don't share my need to surround yourself with possessions that define you. You don't require a sense of permanence and continuity to be happy. If anything, you've thrived on the opposite."

Greg closed the distance between them and cupped her face in his hands. "I don't have to feel exactly the same way you do. All I have to do is respect and understand that need in you." He pulled her against him and held her. "You can't just ignore what's been happening, Diana," he whispered, his lips brushing her ear. "Love is too precious an emotion to waste. Problems can be worked out when people care enough."

He took her mouth with his own, his tenderness doing more to melt her resistance than anything else could have. As her lips parted, his tongue came forward to mate with hers. Soft and warm, it explored and stroked, making her body turn languid. She felt her mind slip away, and a need powerful as it was urgent began to thrum inside her. Instinctively she moved her hips against him, rubbing and seeking a joining she knew shouldn't be.

With a groan he angled his head, deepening his kiss. Tenderness gave way to hunger as his body ached with the need to take her.

"I... want you," she managed, her breathing coming in fast and shallow gasps.

He'd told himself he could stop and pull back if that's what she wanted. But her words made a fire start in his loins. His mouth slid down her throat as he pushed the fabric of her blouse away from her shoulders. With deft movements, he bared her breasts and lowered his mouth to one nipple.

Her legs threatened to buckle. She tried to hold on to him, and as she felt her body sway, his arms tightened their hold. Heartbeats later, she felt him move one hand between their bodies and unfasten her jeans. He slid them down, trailing hot kisses down the length of her.

Breathless, she clung to his shoulders, fighting for balance. An instant later, he lifted her easily into his arms. "Where's your bedroom?"

"Down the hall to the right," she managed to reply, her words a whisper close by his ear.

Her warm breath and the soft sound fueled his need. He wanted to make love to her slowly and very thoroughly, but his body was so taut he felt ready to explode.

He set her down gently on top of the quilted bedspread and gazed lovingly at her body. Most of her clothing had remained in the living room, and now only tiny lavender panties shielded her from him. Lying beside her, he pulled them gently down her legs, then slipped his hand behind her back and pressed her to him. "Honey, you feel so good."

Soon his own clothing became an intolerable aggravation separating her from him, and he moved away. Greg stood by the side of the bed and pulled off his shirt. He could feel her gaze searing over him as his fingers undid the buckle of his belt and he removed the rest of his clothing.

Diana's eyes widened. She stretched out her arms in a silent invitation to his manhood.

Greg lowered himself to lie beside her. He stroked her gently, loving the way she sighed his name over and over again. He'd never have enough of this lady, a lifetime would still leave him hungry for more.

He kissed her hungrily, his tongue swirling boldly in her mouth. He heard her whimper and felt her straining toward him. The passion inside him was raging out of control, but still he held back needing one more thing from her. "Tell me you're mine," he demanded, his voice ragged. Making love to her would mean taking her into his heart. As she drew him into her body, he had to hear her say the words.

A part of her resisted, but the words slipped out, needing to be expressed. "I am yours," she whispered, wanting him to understand why he'd become the only man she'd wanted to welcome into herself. There were other words she wanted to say, but as he moved over her an unquenchable fire engulfed her.

Unable to stand it any longer, he entered her warmth. "You're so small I was afraid I might hurt you. Yet even in this, we're right for each other," he gasped. She was hot and tight around him. The pleasure was so intense his control snapped.

She dug her fingers into his back, pressing him to her with each thrust. They remained locked together for what seemed a blissful eternity.

Afterward, she laid her head on his shoulder. "It's been a long day," she whispered. "But at least it ended wonderfully." She rested peacefully against him. "I love it when it's so quiet outside that all you can hear is the breeze through the pines."

He brushed the hair from her forehead. "As long as I could have you like this in my arms, I wouldn't care if there was a freeway right outside the window." He nuzzled her neck gently.

"Everything's going our way," she said, smiling happily. As her gaze drifted lazily to the telephone on her nightstand, she tensed. "We never did hear anything from the police, and it's been hours since we left the school."

He stole a lazy glance at the clock on her nightstand. "You're right. Maybe Harper never called them, though as angry as he was, I fully expected he would."

"He *must* be hiding something. That would explain why he didn't call them while we were still there." Diana shifted away and reluctantly started to get up. "We should probably go back ..."

Greg snaked his arm around her, preventing her from getting up. "It'll wait until later," he said, raining tiny kisses down her back. "Rest here with me for a while."

Diana shivered. "I won't want to rest if you keep doing that."

"Then I'll have to tire you out some more," Greg answered, pulling her over him again.

Diana drifted off to sleep, and for a while she was at peace. Then unbidden images began to intrude into her dreams. Luminous eyes watched her, penetrating the semiconscious void between wakefulness and oblivion. A face began to form through a thin haze, and suddenly the dream became a nightmare. She was alone, unable to move, and the cowboy was standing by the side of the bed. The unnamed terror that accompanied him hurled her over the brink, and she awoke with a terrifying start.

As her eyes sprang open she *saw* the cowboy, pipe clenched in his teeth, leaning over her. As in the dream, a cloudlike vapor crept along the ceiling above. Diana yelped and grabbed the covers, holding them tightly against her throat.

Greg shot up into a sitting position, saw the man and instantly leapt out of bed. He lunged at the intruder, but the cowboy eluded him easily, ducking into the living room.

Greg disappeared after him, but returned a heartbeat later. "There's a fire. Get up." He grabbed his pants from the floor and slipped them on in one fluid motion. Smoke curled through the doorway in thin wisps.

Diana jumped out of bed, slipped on a shirt and pants, then ran into the living room. Yellow and red flames were quickly invading the area beneath the window, illuminating the room in flickering shadows. The cowboy was nowhere to be seen. She coughed in the thick air, the acrid scent of smoke assaulting her lungs.

## Chapter Thirteen

With a great clattering rip, Greg yanked the burning curtains from the wall, then turned to shove the sofa and the coffee table away from the fire.

Diana rushed out of the room and returned a few seconds later with the kitchen fire extinguisher. She handed it to Greg and ran to the kitchen again.

Seconds later she returned, bucket in hand. She worked methodically. First she doused the wall and curtains, then rolled up the rug to stop further spread of the fire.

As she smothered more flames with the damp curtains, she admitted to herself that the cowboy had probably saved their lives by waking them. Yet his unexpected entry into her home had filled her with apprehension. Her thoughts were diverted suddenly as she saw flying embers leap across the room and ignite surfaces there. Diana made a dash for the linen closet. She'd saturate some towels and smother those spots before they could become a problem.

When she returned with the dripping towels, she realized how much darker the room had become now that the fire was almost out. Struggling to see, she switched on the corner reading lamp. She was grateful when it still worked. At least one part of the room had survived relatively intact.

Greg pointed the fire extinguisher at the wooden trim above the window, spraying the powdery chemical on the glowing pine. "We need to make sure that there's nothing left smoldering," he said, coughing.

Diana handed him a wet towel to place over his mouth and nose and opened the living room door halfway to help vent the room. "I'll finish," she said, taking the fire extinguisher from him. She noticed the reddened skin on his hands immediately. "You've been hurt."

"No, the fire never touched me. Don't worry. It's just a reaction from the heat." He looked around. "By the way, the cowboy got away before I could catch him."

"I figured as much." The aerosol chemical from the extinguisher fizzled to a trickle and Diana placed the container on the floor.

Greg stepped into the kitchen and turned on the light switch. "I didn't have enough time to catch him," he said, walking to a chair. "Just a few more seconds..."

Before he completed the sentence, the door flew open and Anita rushed inside, keys in hand. "I heard noise and got up to take a look. That's when I saw smoke coming out of your window. I called the fire department right away. What on earth happened?" Her eyes were wide and her face pale in the overhead light.

"Did you see anyone leaving the house?" Diana asked, glancing out the door, not really expecting to see anyone.

"No one was around as I came up," Anita answered, then walked to the doorway to the living room. "How did the fire get started?"

"I really don't know," Diana said as she went to the telephone, "but I'm calling the police right now."

It was less than three minutes before a fire truck pulled up in the drive. Close on its tail was a patrol car. The firemen walked into the living room, the police officer a few steps behind them. As they surveyed the damage, the police officer glanced at the senior fireman for an opinion.

"I smell fumes—kerosene I think," the fireman said. "I'll radio in and request the arson investigator. He'll be able to tell us more."

Greg walked to the window frame, calling one of the firemen's attention to it. "I believe the fire started here. That's where the most extensive damage is."

"Did you hear anyone trying to break in?" the policeman asked.

Greg and Diana exchanged glances, but neither was quick to answer. Finally Diana spoke. "No, but a man somehow got in and woke us." She explained about seeing the cowboy, including the fact that he'd fled through the kitchen while Greg was warning her about the fire. "I don't know how he knew about the fire, but I doubt he was the one who started it. If he had, he sure as heck wouldn't have stuck around to warn us about it."

"There are some sick people who set fires just so they can be heroes and take part in a rescue, ma'am," one of the firemen said.

Just as Diana was about to refute that notion, the arson team arrived. A captain in the fire department, serving as the arson investigator, took a quick look around, then went directly to the window. He called over an assistant, and they began gathering samples of the wood and ash.

Diana went into the kitchen with Anita and prepared a pot of tea. Just as Greg decided to join them, a portly detective appeared at the doorway.

"I need to ask you both some questions," he said, glancing at Greg and then at her. "Is there some place we can talk in private?"

"Your people seem to be everywhere," Diana replied, "but we could try the den."

Diana led the way and gestured for the men to have a seat. She made herself comfortable on the love seat against the wall and waited.

The detective cleared his throat. "By the way, I know you're Don Clark's sister-in-law. I've had a message relayed to him, but he's in Albuquerque on police business." He pulled a small notepad from his shirt pocket. "We're aware that you've been investigating Father Denning's murder on your own. Do you think that's related to what happened here?''

"It's very possible. Don warned me about a kid named Arnie Walker," she said, then explained, "but there are others who might have done this, too."

The detective glanced at Greg. "You look as if you've got something on your mind."

"It's this cowboy," Greg explained, and quickly gave him a rundown of what they'd told the last officer. "The only place we've ever seen him is around the church and the school. Yet he came inside to warn us tonight. I'm wondering if he saw either Ralph Harper or his brother start the fire."

"Ralph Harper has no criminal record, so I doubt he'd do something like this. We checked him out when his brother escaped from prison. He's just what he appears to be. Eric Harper, on the other hand, is likely out of state by now. Either way he has no connection with either of you, right?" Seeing them nod, he continued. "So what makes you think either of them is responsible?"

Diana glanced at Greg. Answering that question would undoubtedly create even more problems for them. "We don't *know* it's them, but they're the most likely pair that comes to mind," she interjected. "And while we're on the subject, I'd sure like to see a photo of Eric Harper. We've spent a great deal of time looking around the area, and it's possible we might have seen him."

"I've got a mug shot in my car, I'll get it for you." The officer walked out and returned a short time later. "This is the most recent one on record," he said, and handed it to Diana.

She looked at it for a long time, then handed it to Greg. "He reminds me of the jogger who ran into the side of the van the other day. What do you think?"

"It could be, I suppose, except our man has a mustache." He studied it a short time, then returned it to the officer. "I'm sorry, but I can't be certain it's the same person. I just didn't get a good enough look."

Accurately guessing the detective's next question, Diana and Greg explained about the accident and mentioned the report they'd filed with the police.

The detective took some notes, then continued. "By the way, had you locked the kitchen door tonight?"

"Yes. As a matter of fact, I keep that door locked all the time," Diana answered flatly. "I didn't unlock it tonight until after the fire was out. I really can't explain how the cowboy got in."

"Besides yourself, who's got keys to your home?"

"Don and Anita. That's it."

"And all those are accounted for?"

"Anita has hers and Don would have told me immediately if he'd lost his."

"Then you must have thought you locked it, got sidetracked and forgot." He studied the kitchen door mechanism carefully, noting it was a dead bolt, not a spring lock. "This shows no sign of tampering. But you still might want to consider changing locks anyway as a safety precaution."

"If I did leave it open, then what happened tonight is my own fault," Diana said glumly.

The arson investigator came into the room and approached them. "The fire was set by someone standing outside the living room window. My opinion is they slit the screen, poured kerosene inside, then tossed in a lighted match. We found a book of matches from a place called Coin's Realm in the driveway a few feet from the window."

Diana looked startled but said nothing. Coin's Realm was an arcade located on the Diablo Locos's favorite street corner. As she glanced at Greg, she saw that he'd recognized the name too.

They remained silent until the men filed out through the back. "Someone's working awfully hard to pin everything on the kids," she commented.

"It could be other kids trying to implicate the gang. The Diablo Locos have made enemies, you can be sure of that. Or maybe it's one of the Diablo Locos working alone."

"I doubt it. Petey has to be aware of everything that goes on with his gang. That's how he remains their leader. If he thought one of his guys killed Father John or was a threat to me, he'd have handled it."

"Maybe Arnie decided we were getting too close, so he started the fire," Greg suggested.

"Then how did the cowboy know about it?" she countered. "We haven't seen the remotest connection between them."

Diana stood up. "Well, for the time being, I have more immediate problems to worry about."

Diana walked to the living room and ran one finger over the charred end table that had been beneath the window. "The dump's the only place for this now." She picked up the incinerated remains of the cowboy sculpture she'd so loved. "I'll never be able to replace some of these things."

"You'll find other things to treasure," Greg said softly.

"Get your things," Anita said to Diana. "You can move into my place until we get your home organized again. It's not safe for you to stay here alone."

Diana stuck her chin out and glanced around the room defiantly. "No one is going to displace me from my own home, especially not the snake who did this."

"She won't be alone," Greg assured Anita. "I'll move into the spare bedroom and stay here."

Anita glared at Greg. "So far your help hasn't done her much good." Approaching him, she dropped her voice to a harsh whisper. "If anything happens to Diana, even by accident, I'll never forgive you. I'll do whatever it takes to turn your life into a nightmare."

Staring down at her, Greg said nothing.

Anita turned and headed out. "I'll open up the shop tomorrow, so don't you worry about that." She stopped and glanced back at Diana. "Bolt the door."

Diana turned the latch and as she did, she felt certain that she'd done it earlier too, when Greg had entered. If nothing else, it was habit. But of course that didn't make sense. The cowboy couldn't have gotten in or out any other way. "Let me get you some sheets," she said, glancing at Greg.

"You look beat. Why don't you tell me where they are, and I'll take care of it myself?" he suggested, his voice gentle.

"All right. Everything you'll need is in the linen closet down the hall."

He reached for her hand and gave it a reassuring squeeze. "I'll help you get everything back to normal in no time, you'll see."

She managed a thin smile. "I don't feel like talking anymore. If you don't mind, I'm going back to my bedroom. All I want to do is get some sleep."

She felt Greg's eyes on her as she shuffled down the hall. Someone had tried to *kill* her. It didn't make sense. She didn't know anything that could have made her a threat. Obviously, however, the murderer thought differently.

She sat on the edge of the bed and folded her arms. She felt vulnerable and exposed. Tonight she'd been loved and had loved in return. Yet those emotions had not protected either of them from the world and in fact had almost cost them their lives. Their feelings for each other had been turned into an additional tool in the hands of an enemy bent on destroying them. Still dressed, she crawled between the sheets.

Diana didn't emerge from her room until eight the following morning. She was in the living room taking a look at the damage when Greg came up to greet her.

"I can help you fix this. It's mostly a matter of a lot of scrubbing and maybe a little plastering and repainting. You're lucky most of the house is adobe. There's also some carpentry work that needs to be done, and the locks will have to be changed." He saw her nod, but continue to stare at the burned rug. "There's some Mexican tiles beneath there, so it'll probably look just as good if you roll the rug up and take it out of here.''

The damage to her home made her heart constrict. Her sanctuary, the place she'd created as a haven had been violated. She struggled to keep her voice steady. ''The one job I can do right away, I guess, is washing the ash and soot residue off the walls. I have everything I'll need on hand for that. Once it's all clean in here, we'll have a better idea of what should be done next.'' Diana started to say more when the telephone rang. Diana walked to the kitchen and picked up the receiver.

She listened to Anita's voice and said, ''It's awfully early, for them *and* for you. Is Petey there?'' A moment later, she placed the telephone back on the hook.

''What's going on?'' Greg asked.

''Anita went to the shop early and found the boys waiting for her. Petey's insisting on talking to me in person. Anita didn't want to give them my address, but wasn't sure how to deal with them, either. I told her I'd be right over.''

''Maybe they've found Arnie.'' Greg's expression grew dark. ''Or maybe they have something to tell us about the fire. I can't get those matches out of my mind.'' He followed her to the door.

''Trust my instincts on this. No matter how it looks, the boys didn't do this to my home.'' Diana went directly to the car with Greg and hurried out of the driveway.

They arrived at the print shop fifteen minutes later. Petey and a group of about five boys sat on the window ledge, waiting. ''Hello, guys,'' Diana greeted. ''What's up?''

Petey walked up to her, a smug grin on his face. ''We've got some good news. Once we let the word out we were looking for Arnie and why, some of the other gangs got into the act, too. Last night a lookout spotted him going into Joe Green's Food Stop near the edge of town. He followed Arnie and found that he's been holed up in an old abandoned house just west of Santa Fe. He was still there this morning when the dudes watching him finally went home.''

"What time was Arnie spotted?" Diana asked quickly.

"About seven. Why? Does it matter?" Petey asked.

"I was just trying to find out if he was responsible for setting the fire at my place last night," she answered, watching the boys' expressions.

"Someone burned you out?" Petey's shock was evident.

"They tried, but we got it under control." She met his gaze. "Someone tried to kill us, Petey, so if you're going to keep looking into Father John's murder be very aware of the danger involved," Diana said.

Petey nodded, jaw clenched. "Well, it couldn't have been Arnie. The Dark Lords had their eyes on him all night."

"Did you get the exact location of Arnie's hideout?" Diana asked.

Petey gave her directions. "We're going with you," he insisted. "You might need help."

"Petey, you guys have done a terrific job, but going over there in a large group is the worst thing we can do right now. The only way we're going to be able to talk to Arnie is to sneak up on him. If he sees us coming, he's going to bolt. This is one of those situations where the fewer people we have along, the better it'll be."

"Let us know if you change your mind," Petey said, gesturing to the others, and starting them down the street.

Diana watched them go, then turned to Greg. "Let's go out there right now."

Anita emerged from inside. "I heard everything," she said. "I was eavesdropping in case of trouble. Before you go anywhere, don't you think you should call the police? What if this Arnie is waiting for you, or what if the gang is setting you up?"

"We'll have to take that chance. The directions Petey gave me lead right outside the city limits. That means that it's in the jurisdictional haze between city and county law enforcement agencies. By the time the cops get rolling on this, Arnie could have moved on. We've seen how skittish he is.

We can't afford to blow this chance." Diana started walking back to the car.

"If we're not back by noon," Greg said glancing at Anita, "call the police and tell them everything."

"You've got it," Anita replied.

"I'd originally thought we'd find the murderer if we could find out who set the fire, but now I'm wondering if maybe we're dealing with two separate things," Diana said as they walked to the car.

"We've managed to make more than one person really angry, so I guess it's possible the two are unconnected."

Diana followed Petey's directions. The house, set along an abandoned stretch of road, was nothing more than a shell. Its walls showed signs of the fire that had gutted it. "There's plenty of brush and rocks to provide us with cover," she said. "We should be able to get close without being seen."

"I don't think he's there right now," Greg said. "Arnie must have transportation of some sort—a bicycle at least. How else would he get this far out?" Greg checked the rocky ground for tire tracks before continuing. "But there's nothing parked near the house now. Of course, it's possible he's hiding it inside somewhere."

Diana considered the matter for several seconds. "Why would he bother? I'm sure he thinks no one's found him."

"Could be a safety precaution. Or maybe he's already moved on." Greg glanced around. "Let's leave your car around the bend of that arroyo. It won't be visible from the road there. Then we'll hike in for a closer look."

They cut across the rocky canyon, staying behind cover as much as possible. The massive boulders that dotted the landscape provided stopping points as they moved toward the house.

While Greg worked his way around the back, Diana angled forward in line with a hole that she surmised had once been a window. Noiselessly she crept toward it and peered inside.

This one section of the house had survived fairly intact. Inside, she could see a small table and wooden crate beside it that served as a chair. She listened for sounds, but only silence greeted her.

Greg appeared from around the corner and joined her. "He's not in there, so this is our chance. We'll wait and ambush him when he returns." He cocked his head toward the rear of the house. "We can go in through the back without leaving tracks by the doorway. There's a portion of the wall that's crumbled away." He led her to the spot. "Let me go in first."

"Some gentleman," she baited.

"You want to take the lead in case there's trouble? Go ahead. Make sure you let me know when it's all clear," he answered easily.

"On second thought, you go in first."

Greg slipped inside and studied the small room Arnie seemed to have selected as his living quarters. Diana came in behind him, took one look around and shuddered. "Cripes, look at the artwork on the walls. This guy's sick!" Violence of almost every sort was depicted in the sketches that covered the walls. Knife slashings and shootings seemed to have received particular attention and were portrayed in graphic detail.

"His reading material isn't much better," Greg said, leafing through the magazines that littered the small table. "I've heard of these, but I'd never seen one. They're horror comic books. You have to be over twenty-one to buy them."

"Arnie didn't look that old to me." Diana walked over to where Greg stood and picked up one. "These are disgusting! Why would anyone read these?"

"It's a matter of taste, I suppose," Greg commented. "But it does say something about Arnie." He glanced around the room. "Start looking for a place to hide. I'll stay by the door with my back to the wall and the second he steps in, I'll grab him."

"I can duck into the next room. The portion of the wall that's still standing will be enough to hide me."

Hearing the faint roar of a motorcycle, Greg peered outside. "Unless I miss my guess, that's him coming now."

## Chapter Fourteen

Greg stood immobile as he heard the motorcycle being switched off and the soft crunch of approaching footsteps. He scarcely breathed. He'd have to be fast. Arnie had an uncanny ability to elude anyone who cornered him.

Listening intently, he heard the boy stop just outside. Greg wondered if the boy suspected a trap. He waited, not daring to move. Arnie stepped through the doorway a second later. Reacting instantly, Greg lunged forward and locked his arms firmly around the boy's midsection. Arnie cursed bitterly as he thrashed and kicked, trying to break Greg's hold.

Just to let Arnie know he meant business, Greg lifted the boy off the ground and squeezed, forcing the air out of his lungs. "Calm down," he ordered.

Diana stepped into the room, making sure she stayed well away from the pair. "Arnie, we don't want to hurt you. All we want you to do is answer a few questions."

"I *know* what you guys want. You think I had something to do with that priest's murder!"

"No one's accusing you of anything. We just want to know why you're so interested in the murder. You tore the article out of the newspaper and made all these sketches of it." She waved her hand around the room.

"I get lots of ideas from the papers," Arnie argued, still firmly in Greg's grip. "I'm an artist. All the stuff on the wall is mine. Check out the signature."

Greg tried to remain nonjudgmental. "Well, let's say we agree to call it art, are you in the market for models?"

"Man, you're sick!" Arnie shouted. "Look at the comic books. It's all right there in front of you. I'm a cartoonist, or trying to be. I'd like to get a job with one of the houses that publish horror comic books. That's why I have to work up sketches. I mail them in as samples of my work."

Greg glanced at Diana and saw her shrug. He released the boy, but kept the doorway blocked. "So where were you the night Father Denning was killed?"

"At the main library. Ask the librarian. She helped me find the addresses and submission requirements of several publishing houses I wanted to contact." He walked to the table and showed them a handwritten letter. "This is the letter I'm sending them. I haven't mailed this one yet since I'm trying to figure out which drawing to send the publisher."

"If that's true, then why have you been hiding out all this time?" Diana asked, raising one eyebrow.

"People are *always* singling me out. All through school, whenever anything went wrong, I was the first person accused. I've learned that when someone comes looking for me, there's going to be trouble." Arnie turned to face them. "I'm not lying. You can check."

"We will," Greg assured, catching Diana's eye and motioning toward the door.

"Wait a minute," Diana protested when she realized Greg was ready to leave.

He pulled her close so the teenager wouldn't hear. "Let's go. We've done what we set out to do," he said quietly.

As she followed Greg from the house, Diana stared at him aghast. "We can't just let him go! If he's lying, he's not going to stick around here waiting for us to come back."

"We can't do anything else at this point. Even the police can't detain a suspect without reasonable cause, and he does have a good explanation for what he's been doing."

"I hate to admit that his story, in an odd way, seemed to fit," Diana said as they reached the car. "To be honest, I felt sorry for him. I know what it's like when you're different from the rest. Being the daughter of migrant workers made it rough at times. Kids can be unbelievably cruel."

"But you took those experiences and let them make you stronger," he said. "I hope Arnie sticks it out and comes out on top, too. He's chosen a hard profession."

Diana drove back to Santa Fe. With the sun shining brightly overhead, the desert seemed filled with life. Prairie dogs scurried about, peering from their burrows. An occasional jackrabbit would stop at the edge of the road and watch the car pass by. Overhead, a prairie hawk drifted easily with the currents.

She stole a glance at Greg and realized he was also looking at her. Her pulse quickened and an enticing warmth rippled through her. They were allies and friends, but as much as she yearned for his love, the time was not right for them. Perhaps it never would be.

"If you don't mind, I'm going to go directly to the main library," Diana said, fighting the heaviness of spirit she felt. "I'll call Anita from there and let her know we're both okay."

Thirty minutes later they stood by the reference desk in the library. The young woman who'd been working the evening shift that night was there and remembered Arnie. "He seemed so at ease in the library. I helped him find a reference book for artists that listed publishers and contacts. After that he sat down at the corner table, and studied it for hours. I know it was either late afternoon or evening because I was working with the computer terminal on the desk by the window. I avoid that location if the sun's still out because it's like sitting in an oven."

It was shortly after two when they descended the library steps and returned to the car. "Where do you want me to drop you? I was thinking of working at the shop for the rest of the afternoon. I've got tons of work piled on my desk."

"If you'd like, I can start doing some of the cleanup work that's needed at your house."

"That would be great. I can call the home center and arrange to have them charge my account and deliver whatever you need." As she approached her driveway, she saw a car already parked there. She muttered under her breath. "Don's here and by now he's got all the details of the fire. He's probably inside looking at the damage. Stay out here and let me deal with him alone."

Greg shook his head. "I'd rather face him, Diana. I want to be included in your life, but I can't do that unless you're willing to let me."

"This was your idea, remember that," she sighed softly. "If you want to come in, then let's go."

Diana walked to the back door, realized it was unlocked and strode inside. Don sat beside the kitchen table, staring at the cup of coffee before him. Glancing up, he transfixed Greg with a lethal stare. "I want to talk to Diana alone."

"Don," she replied quietly, "Greg is a guest in my home. I'd appreciate it if you'd show him a little respect."

"Any man who takes advantage of a widow isn't worthy of respect." He stood and pushed his chair back angrily. "Marten, I want you and your stuff out of this house."

Diana's eyes widened. "Wait one minute. This is *my* house. You don't dictate who comes here," she managed.

"Diana needs to have someone with her," Greg explained. "She's placed herself in the middle of an investigation and could still become a target."

"Diana might be in danger, all right, particularly now that we're about to release the suspect we had. But I don't know what good you're going to do her. You've been part of this case from the very beginning. Diana would be safe now if you hadn't involved her in the murder."

"You're going to release Joe Martinez?" Diana asked.

"The medical examiner has ruled out the Martinez kid as a suspect—he's left-handed and the throat wound was made by a right-handed person."

"More reason for me to stay with Diana. Forget the insults for a minute, Clark, and take a look at what's happened," Greg said. "So far, I've done more to protect Diana than you have, despite all your good intentions."

Don's eyes blazed with a rage that shocked Diana. He stepped away from the table and moved slowly toward Greg. "I don't have to take that from you," he growled.

Greg moved sideways, his tall frame poised in a defensive stance. The air practically vibrated with tension, and neither man was about to back down.

Moving quickly, Diana grabbed a broom from the corner and stepped between them. She looked from one to the other. "I've had it with both of you. This is my home, not a downtown bar. You'll treat it and me with respect." Seeing Don take a step forward, she raised the broom high over her head. "Don't tempt me, Don. I'll clobber you, I mean it."

Greg started toward her. "Diana, be careful with that thing."

She turned the broom toward him, and he froze. "Sit," she said, glancing at one, then the other and waiting until they complied. "Now stay!" she ordered. Both men were seated at her kitchen table, and she fought hard to suppress a smile. She'd won this round at least.

"Diana, I could take that broom away from you in a second," Don said patiently. "But I don't want to hurt you."

"You might grab it, and you're right, you could hurt me. But you'd be picking splinters out of your forehead for a week, I guarantee it." She turned and looked at Greg. "You too, in case you're interested."

"Forget it, I've seen you in action," Greg muttered. "Now what?"

"I want a promise from both of you that you'll show some consideration, if not for each other, then for me."

"Diana, that's exactly what I'm trying to—" Don said, but seeing her raise the broom, clamped his mouth shut.

"Now, do we have a deal?" she asked and saw Greg and Don exchange leery glances. "Someone tried to kill me last night. I can use all the help I can get." She glanced at Don. "There's no way Greg could have been responsible for the fire. Kerosene was poured in through a slit in the screen."

Don shrugged. "You have a right to make your own mistakes, Diana," he said, staring at Greg. "Besides, I'll have plenty of time later to even out the score." He leaned back. "I'm off duty for the rest of the day, so I can help you with whatever repairs have to be done. There won't be any need for anyone else to hang around."

"There's more than enough for everyone, believe me." She handed Don a bucket. "Fill this up with water, grab a sponge from under the sink, and start scrubbing the walls in the living room." She turned to Greg. "Make a list of everything you'll need, then take the other bucket and get to work."

Diana ordered the supplies from the store and called Anita to let her know she wouldn't be in that afternoon. Then she joined the two men in the living room. The work was difficult and tiring, but neither man seemed willing to admit they needed a break. An hour later Anita arrived. She explained she'd closed the shop early to come out to help.

In a hushed tone, Diana explained her plan. "Let them do the hard part. It's taking the fight right out of them."

The two women began cleaning the upholstery that hadn't been damaged. It was nearly four o'clock before the walls were finished. Sweat had trickled down Greg's forehead leaving shiny trails. Don's face was reddened with exertion, and his hair was slick and pasted to his scalp.

"The walls look great, guys. I think you can both call it a day," Diana said, taking pity on them.

"Yeah, I have to go bowling with some of the guys this evening," Don said. "I better go home and shower."

"I'm going to head to the studio, pick up my basketball and get some exercise."

Diana watched them as they walked silently down the driveway to their respective vehicles. "There's no way either of those guys are going to do anything but soak in a hot tub."

Anita laughed. "That was their pride talking," she said with a chuckle. "I must say you handled the situation beautifully. They were too tired to even argue. Where Don's concerned, that's nothing short of a full-scale miracle."

Diana smiled wearily. "By the way, I'm sorry I wasn't more help at the shop today. This investigation is taking more of my time, and my life," she added thoughtfully, "than I ever expected." She told Anita about Arnie, and what they'd learned from Don about Joe Martinez.

"Diana, someone tried to kill you here, in your own home. That should prove that you're outmatched against this killer."

"But I wasn't hurt, his plans failed."

"You've got people watching over you, that's for sure, including that strange cowboy. Have you made any more progress at finding him?"

"I'm going to have to wait until he comes to us again, if he will," she said, shrugging. "I don't have a choice."

Anita shuddered. "I'm glad Greg's going to be with you," she said, then smiled, seeing the surprised look on Diana's face. "I've changed my mind about him. I've seen the way he looks at you when he thinks no one is watching. His feelings for you are real."

"Do you finally agree with me that he had nothing to do with the murder?"

She nodded. "He's too kind and patient. Anyone who can work with Don for a whole afternoon without getting violent is a better person than I am," she teased half-seriously.

IT WAS SHORTLY after eight by the time Greg returned. He seemed completely relaxed and back to normal. Diana, who'd bathed, was ready for nothing more than a good night's sleep. "There's food in the fridge, if you're hungry."

"I'll get the lock changed, then I'll watch some television."

"I'm going to bed," she said.

Greg stepped toward her, then stopped in mid-stride. His fingers curled tightly over the back of one of the chairs. "I better say good-night to you from here," he explained quietly. "I said I'd look after you, and I can do that better this way."

Diana smiled. She felt herself surrounded in the tenderness that emanated from him. A lump formed at her throat. Wordlessly, she walked down the hall.

SHE MET GREG in the kitchen the next morning. He sat by the table, a copy of the Sunday paper before him. "There's supposed to be a religious procession passing by just north of the plaza today. The statue they carry of the Virgin is a historical piece dating back to the conquest of Santa Fe. I'd love to see it, and I think it would do us both some good to get away for a few hours. What do you say?"

"I think it's a great idea. Let's get started. It's bound to get crowded very fast."

The drive to the plaza took longer than usual as the streets seemed to overflow with cars. Finding a parking spot proved another challenge. Diana managed to squeeze in between two pickups, then walked with Greg north toward the plaza.

As they walked, Greg asked, "Do you know what the procession is about?"

"*La Conquistadora* is the oldest depiction of the Madonna in North America. She's taken from the cathedral to Rosario Chapel. The location is thought to be the site of the encampment of General De Vargas, his troops and colonists during the Spanish Reconquest of Santa Fe in 1693. They have a thanksgiving service to the Madonna at that location to fulfill General De Vargas's vow to honor her for her aid in retaking the Palace of the Governors.'' She smiled. ''The annual thanksgiving mass is held in September and that's also the time of the Santa Fe Fiesta. What you'll see today is the procession and people and merchants who come out to commemorate Santa Fe's heritage.''

He gestured ahead. ''I think the procession is just about to reach Lincoln Avenue. Let's hurry and see if we can get a better look.''

''If we get separated, I'll meet you at the obelisk in the plaza after the procession,'' she managed to say as the press of people moving north with them seemed likely to force them apart.

She lost sight of Greg as everyone gathered at the edge of the sidewalk, trying to angle for the best view of *La Conquistadora*. It was impossible for her to see over the heads that towered above her. Everyone jostled against each other. Diana worked her way to the fringes of the crowd trying not to feel apprehensive as a sea of chests and shoulders pressed in around her. Suddenly and quite inexplicably, she had the strong sensation that someone nearby was watching her. She glanced around, but could see no one who appeared particularly interested in her.

She shook herself mentally. Lately she seemed to have developed a vivid and overactive imagination. As the people began to move farther down following the procession, she searched for Greg. Unable to find him, she set out for the park. Mariachi music echoed from the radio of a young man sitting on one of the many cement *bancos* or benches constructed in Old Mexico style. People still clustered in groups on the sidewalks, planning where to have breakfast or where to shop. Now that *La Conquistadora* had passed, a more relaxed, vibrant feeling seemed to fill the downtown area.

Slipping through a group gathered by the front of an ice-cream shop, she decided to go east and then down Washington Street. There she hoped it would be less crowded, and she'd make better time getting to the plaza.

On San Francisco Street, the city seemed almost back to normal. A steady flow of traffic filtered through the narrow streets. Diana was waiting at the curb for a chance to cross when suddenly someone behind her shoved her forward hard. As she stumbled out into the street, she caught a glimpse of a car nearly upon her. A rush of hot air engulfed her and she shut her eyes tightly, knowing there was no time to get away. Her last impression was of sunlight reflecting off a bright, chrome bumper.

# Chapter Fifteen

Diana trembled at the terrible squeal of skidding tires, and someone screamed. But the collision never came. Dazed, she opened her eyes and looked around. The smell of burning rubber stung her nostrils, and skid marks were clear on the pavement. They stopped a few feet away from where she was. Blinking, she saw the car that had almost hit her. It was four feet away, front wheel touching the curb, but otherwise intact. She started to get up, intending to thank the driver. His alert response and skill behind the wheel had saved her life.

A man suddenly burst through the crowd that had gathered around her. "Lady, where the hell is that guy who was with you? There was no way I could have missed him! By the time I saw him step in front of my car, it was too late. I tried to swerve, but I knew it wouldn't do any good. Then when I got out of the car and rushed to see if I could help him, *there was no one there!* What's going on? Is this some kind of magic trick?" the shaky driver demanded.

"There was no one with me. What are you talking about? I was pushed out into the road, then before I knew what happened, I saw your car. I shut my eyes and prayed! If you hadn't been so alert—"

"I had no choice! That cowboy just showed up out of nowhere! He was inches from my front bumper when I saw him." He ran a hand through his hair in exasperation. "I still don't know how I managed to miss him!"

"Cowboy?" Diana shook her head trying to clear her thoughts. "He was here?" her voice was whisper thin. A second later she saw Greg rushing toward her, a look of concern etched on his face.

As Diana struggled to her feet and started toward the sidewalk, Greg reached her side. Placing his arm around her waist he steadied her. "I went to the park," he said, "but when you weren't there, I decided to double back. I was about a block away when I heard the commotion. I came in for a closer look and there you were, sitting in the middle of the street! What happened?"

Diana took a deep breath. As a familiar scent reached her, she grabbed Greg by the arm. "Do you smell it? He really was here!" She looked at the driver. "You never saw the cowboy leave?"

"Lady, he was there one second and gone the next."

Understanding dawned on Greg's face as he inhaled slowly. "Will you *please* tell me what happened?"

As Diana tried to gather her thoughts, the driver of the car answered for her.

Greg saw Diana shrug. "I had my eyes closed. I thought for sure I was about to be hit!"

The driver shook his head. "I wasn't worried about her. In fact, I didn't even see her until later. It was that other guy who scared ten years off my life."

"Did anyone see where he went?" Greg asked, glancing at the crowd.

"I saw someone rushing back to the plaza, but I'm not sure if it was the person you're talking about or not," one woman offered.

"Someone pushed me deliberately out into the path of a car!" Diana repeated softly, trying to come to terms with it. "If only I'd seen who did it!" She bit her lip, afraid it would quiver and she'd start crying. She was so scared she could scarcely breathe. All she wanted to do was collapse against

Greg's warm chest and be comforted, but there was no time. Both her assailant and rescuer were still out there. If they moved now, maybe they could get some answers.

"I'm calling the police," the driver said.

Diana shook her head. "There's no need for that. There's been no accident. No one's been injured and your car's just fine."

The driver turned and said loudly to the curious onlookers. "You all heard that. My car never touched anyone."

An old man laughed derisively, then people began to disperse, their curiosity sated for the moment. With one last look at Diana, the driver walked away, muttering something inaudible.

After the panic of a few moments ago, Diana felt washed out and weary. Yet she called upon energy reserves she didn't even know she had, and started toward the plaza. "If the cowboy's around here, we have to find him. I think he probably saw the person who shoved me, and that's why he reacted so quickly."

"That guy always seems to be right there to help," Greg observed thoughtfully. "Maybe we are dealing with someone who sets up situations so he can play hero. Remember what the fireman said?"

Diana turned around, searching the faces of people crossing the plaza. "Look directly ahead. That's Francisco Ortega. I recognize him from newspaper photos."

"There's another man with him. Any idea who he is?" Greg asked, quickening his steps to keep up with her.

"It looks like Al Contreras, his partner." As the distance between them narrowed, she saw them go inside Don Diego's Cantina. "That's where he claimed he was the night of the murder."

They followed the men inside the darkened restaurant. It took a few moments for their eyes to adjust, but finally Diana gestured to a table in the corner. "There they are, by the back door."

Diana and Greg seated themselves where they both had an unobstructed view. Ortega hadn't taken more than a sip of his drink when he glanced around, dropped some bills on the table, and headed for the rear exit. His friend remained behind and watched the baseball game about to begin on the large-screen television.

Greg and Diana exchanged glances, then followed Ortega out the back door. "Be ready to reverse directions or look occupied if he turns around," Greg warned as they started down the street after Ortega.

Ortega cut through a narrow alleyway and crossed the footbridge over the *Acequia,* an irrigation ditch that provided Santa Fe residents with water. As he reached the other side, he stopped and looked behind him.

Using the afternoon shadows, Greg leaned against the wall and faced Diana. "Stay still. With luck we'll pass for two people who stopped to talk in the shade."

Seconds dragged on, but then Ortega turned and entered the courtyard of a large residential complex. As he knocked on the door of one of the townhouses, Greg and Diana angled for a better look.

"Wow," Greg muttered under his breath, when a young woman appeared momentarily at the door wearing nothing but a lace teddy. "Now we know why he's lost interest in baseball."

"That's *definitely* not his wife. She's pretty, but at least twenty years older."

"Unless I miss my guess, this is a regular routine for Ortega. I think we should go back and talk to his friend. Maybe Ortega's alibi for the day of the murder isn't as ironclad as the police think."

When they returned to Don Diego's, Ortega's friend was nursing a drink, his gaze still on the baseball game. Diana walked over to the table, and pulled out a seat directly beside the man. Greg grabbed a chair from one of the adjoining tables and set it on the other side of him.

"What's going on?" Contreras demanded, a touch of fear in his voice. "Am I going to have to call over some help?"

"Lighten up, Al," Greg suggested. "We followed Ortega all the way to the young lady's place. You don't want any trouble right now, or your little alibi scheme is liable to become public knowledge."

"What do you want from me?" Contreras's voice was a harsh whisper.

"We'd like to ask you a few questions. Ortega claimed to be here the night of Father Denning's murder, but now we've learned that sometimes he ducks out. Was he here that night or not?"

The man squirmed uncomfortably. "Francisco had nothing to do with the priest's death. He wouldn't touch a man of the cloth, not even Denning."

"That doesn't answer the question, does it?" Diana prodded.

Contreras stared at his drink. "Francisco can ruin my life. Why should I talk to you?"

"If you prefer, you can make your statement along with Ortega for the public record when we bring in the police," Diana answered pleasantly.

"No!" he said, then lowered his voice immediately. "Look, Francisco and I come here twice a week. We provide alibis for each other in case our wives get suspicious. First, we make sure the bartender sees us, and at least one of the waitresses. Then, we alternate walking out through the back to be with our women for a few hours."

"And no one ever notices?" Diana asked incredulously.

"If they do, they keep it to themselves. Francisco's uncle owns this place, and the employees know not to make things difficult for the owner's nephew."

"So which one of you was gone the night Father John was killed?" Diana asked insistently, her disgust obvious in her tone.

"Francisco was with Mercedes. Ask her if you want. But don't get the police involved. It won't help and it will only hurt our families."

"Fine time for you to think of that," Diana muttered, rising from her chair.

"What are you going to do?" Al asked as Greg stood also.

Greg said nothing, walking with Diana to the door instead.

As soon as they stepped outside, he took a deep breath, then let it out again. "That's still not much of an alibi. His girlfriend is bound to corroborate the story, don't you think?"

"Sure, and that means Ortega's back on the suspect list," she said, heading back to her car.

"When we get to your house, I think you should telephone Don and tell him everything that's happened," Greg said.

"I will, but he's going to be impossible after that. First, he'll probably try to blame you for what happened to me with the car. Then, when I tell him about Ortega, he's going to be furious that we managed to find a crack in Ortega's alibi. It's not the department's fault Ortega covered himself well, but it'll make Don feel that they've been played for fools."

They were a block from the courthouse when Greg spotted the police cars gathered near the corner. "There's Petey, right in the middle of that group of police officers."

"Let's go see what's going on," she said.

Spotting them, Petey waved. "Yo, guys, over here! You won't believe this," he said approaching them. "We found this tall, thin guy wearing a cowboy hat, just like you described. He was near the school and looked kind of nervous, so we followed him. Carlos thought he saw a pipe in his hand, so we decided to find out who he was. Only the pipe turned out to be a knife, and he made a move on us with it."

"Did any of you get hurt?" Diana asked quickly.

"Naw, we know how to fight. Bullfrog kicked the knife away from him, then some of our guys pinned him down while Carlos called the cops."

"Do the police know who he is yet?"

"Yeah. He's some escaped convict."

Carlos sauntered up to them, a cocky grin plastered over his face. "It's Eric Harper. He's the brother of that school janitor, Ralph Harper. The cops have really got him talking now. He's been living in a storage building near the gasoline station and stealing food from gardens and stores. He said he was going to contact his brother when some of the heat wore off."

"Did he have anything to say about Father Denning's murder?" Greg asked.

"He swears he didn't do it, and wants the cops to give him a lie detector test."

"Lie detector tests aren't conclusive, but if he's willing to risk one, then maybe he *is* telling the truth," Greg ventured, looking at Diana.

Congratulating the boys for a job well done and thanking them for their help, Diana walked with Greg back to the car. The silence between them remained unbroken until they were on the way to her home.

"There's something bothering you. What is it?" he prodded gently.

"When Father John was murdered, I had to face the passing of someone else I cared about. I got involved with the investigation because I needed to see justice done. But despite our best efforts and all our successes we still aren't getting the one answer we need."

As they drove by the dinner theater, Greg's eyes fastened on the actors gathered in the back alley. "The case is far from over, Diana. What we have to do is keep eliminating possibilities and narrowing down the field of suspects. The way I see it, our biggest problem is that there are too many loose ends. For instance, we still don't know who the cowboy is or how he fits into this. At least we know he's not Eric Harper. Harper's face is thinner and his eyes are closer together, not as broad and chiseled as the cowboy's."

"I have a theory about him. Are you aware that we've never actually *seen* him before six in the evening?"

Greg turned his head back toward the dinner theater. "If the cowboy has a role as an extra, or maybe just a walk-on part in the play, that could explain why he's free later at night, and also why he's dressed up."

"Let's check right now. It's possible that the waitress we spoke to initially really didn't know as much about the actors as she suggested." Diana turned and headed toward the theater.

When they went inside, the manager took one look at them and rolled his eyes. "I told you before, pay the cover charges, have a nice dinner, then you can talk to the actors. They work the room after the performance." He strode into the office.

Diana followed him, unwilling to be put off. "This isn't an arbitrary request. We're looking into the murder of a priest, and we have a lead that points directly to your dinner theater. The way I see it, you can deal with us or you can deal with the police. Keep in mind that if the cops come and start questioning everyone, the publicity is going to damage your business. Our way is much simpler and far less costly."

There was venom in the man's gaze as he looked at her, then at Greg. "Go backstage," he said in a taut voice, "talk to whomever you please, then get out. You've got ninety minutes before the play starts."

Diana walked out of the office, Greg behind her, then led the way through the curtained section. Working together they spoke to as many people as they saw backstage, but no one knew any extras who matched the cowboy's description. The director, they learned, didn't hire anyone above average height, since that meant spending money on costumes others wouldn't be able to wear.

Finally, fifty minutes after their arrival, they headed back to the car. Diana remained quiet, frustration tearing at her patience.

Wordlessly Greg reached for her hand and gave it a squeeze. "We're not out yet. I've got another idea. We've tried the largest tobacco store in the area, but there are others. There's one in a hotel gift shop near the plaza. I found them in the yellow pages when I was shopping for my brand. Their ad says they're open eight to eight every day, and they also custom blend tobaccos."

"It's worth a try," she said, getting the name of the hotel from him. Greg was a friend when she needed one, and so much more. Her body reacted with a warm flush of pleasure as she remembered.

Fifteen minutes later, they walked through the doors of the hotel. Diana saw the shop's sign and headed down the long corridor. As they entered, a young shopkeeper came out to greet them. "How may I help you today?"

"We're looking for a particular blend, but we're having a very difficult time finding it," Greg answered.

Diana described it for the man, then saw the thoughtful look that crossed his face. "Do you have anything like that?" she asked hopefully.

"My grandfather used to smoke a blend he described the same way. I tried to find it once, but found it hadn't been available for over fifty years. I don't know of anything currently on the market that even comes close to that description." He gave them a knowing look. "I bet you're trying to find this for an old-timer."

"No, the man who smokes this isn't that old."

"Really?" he said surprised. "Well, either the old blend's been reissued, or he managed to get some from a collector. If you want to try to identify the brand and composition so we can try to order or duplicate it, you might visit a friend of mine. He's got a collection of old pipes and tobacco tins, and I'm sure he'd love to show them to you. Some of those tins might still retain the scent."

"How do we get hold of him?" Diana asked quickly.

"I can give him a call right now, if you'd like. He runs a little private museum filled with Old West memorabilia. He's open until ten every day, but you have to call ahead and make an appointment."

"Would you ask if it's possible for us to come over now? We'd like to go straight from here," Diana said.

The shopkeeper left the room and returned a moment later holding a small piece of paper. "You're all set. I've drawn you a map. He's located in a residential section near here. There's a sign beside the driveway. Just honk your horn twice when you get there."

Greg took the paper. "Thanks for the help."

"I'd like to ask a favor in return. If you find out that the old blend has been reissued, come back and tell me, okay? I take pride in having the latest for my customers and I'd be happy to special order it for you."

"We'll do that," Greg answered.

Diana followed the directions on the map and drove to an old section of the city. There were no sidewalks here. The adobe walls bordering the houses seemed to define the boundaries of the street.

As the car's headlights cut through the twilight, Greg leaned forward. "There's a sign on the wall up ahead. Maybe that's it."

Diana slowed to a stop by a hand painted sign that read: Jorge Rodriguez Museum. By appointment only.

Diana honked twice. A minute later a teenager appeared and opened the gate. "There's an admission fee," he said. After he collected the money from Greg he said, "Go straight down. You can't miss it."

As Diana parked, a middle-aged, muscular Hispanic man came toward the car. "Come in! Charlie said you were interested in my collection of old tobacco tins. I'll be glad to show it to you, but you really should take time to see the rest of the displays as well. I have what I modestly consider the best private museum around."

His enthusiasm seemed boundless as he led them through sections filled with old photographs and early firearms. "This display coming up is my pride and joy," he said leading them down the aisle. "The articles of clothing in there are all genuine. They date back to the 1800s. Take a look at those cowboy boots. Inside there's a slot that hides a boot pistol. The suspenders next to it are an early hideaway rig, and as you can see by the pockets in the linings, they can hold two percussion pistols."

Diana stared at the long vest and dark trousers also displayed inside the glass case. "Greg, look at the clothing laid out next to the suspenders. Does it look familiar?"

"Our cowboy's costume is a darned good replica," he muttered.

"The shopkeeper said you also have pipes," Diana said, hoping to lead their host in the direction they were most interested in.

"Oh yes! I've been adding to a collection I inherited from my great grandfather. They're all in the case coming up, along with the tobacco tins." He stood aside, letting them look through the glass.

Diana stared at the briar and clay pipe in the center. "Look familiar?" she asked Greg in a soft voice.

"Interesting," Greg answered.

"Charlie said you're trying to identify a particular tobacco blend. He described it to me, and I've separated the tins and pouches I thought came closest." He reached inside the case. "You're welcome to try them all, though. I've got the most extensive collection in the state."

Greg and Diana checked the ones that had been set aside. Some of the scents were close, but none were an exact match. They began testing those inside the case. Soon, they'd gone through all thirty containers. Their host, disappointed, began to put them away. "If you can't find it here or at Charlie's, I'm not sure you ever will," he said.

"What about that one?" she pointed to a tin that had accidentally been shoved to one side.

His expression brightened. "Give it a try and see what you think," he said, opening it for her.

Taking the tin from him, she sniffed the empty metal container and her heart began to race.

## Chapter Sixteen

"This is it!" She passed the tin to Greg.

"No doubt about it," he agreed.

The man read the writing on the small metal container, then gave them a quizzical look. "You must be mistaken. The key tobacco in this mix was an experimental strain that became too expensive to grow and was replaced by a more common leaf. This blend hasn't been available since the turn of the century."

Diana glanced at Greg. "I'm certain that's it," she insisted.

Greg nodded. Thanking the proprietor, he walked back to the car with her. "Maybe someone came up with another blend that's almost a match."

"Then why don't any of the locals know about it?"

"It could be new, or maybe our cowboy has managed to get hold of a custom blend. We don't know who he is, so there's no way we can know what his connections might be."

Diana pulled out of the driveway and back into the street. "We know one thing. He's playing the cowboy role to the hilt. His clothing, his pipe and even his tobacco fits the time period." She shuddered. "I know he's helped both of us, and I'm grateful, but I can't help it. He just gives me the creeps."

"I can't shake the feeling that there's something he wants to tell us," Greg ventured slowly. "But even that doesn't make sense. All he'd have to do is stick around long enough to talk to us." He ran a hand through his hair in exasperation. "Unless he's a mute."

With a sigh, Diana shifted in her seat. "I need a break. Let's pick up something to eat. There's a little fast-food restaurant near here that has great New Mexican food."

She found a space in the crowded parking lot, then led the way inside. A few minutes later they sat in one of the booths facing the parking lot. Their burritos were smothered in a spicy green chile salsa, which in turn was covered with melted cheddar.

Diana ate greedily for several minutes. Then, as she finished her last bite, she leaned back, her eyes still on the parking area outside. "There's a chance we're being followed," she said, calling Greg's attention to the street. "When we left the museum, I spotted a light-colored sedan about a car length behind us. I'm not sure if it's the same car, but there's one that's circled this block at least three times."

"Let's go find out," Greg said, putting down the remnants of his burrito.

They left the restaurant together, Greg close by Diana's side. As she headed toward the car, he pulled her away gently. "I think I've spotted the car you meant. Let's find out if it's really us they're interested in. The sidewalks have plenty of people walking around. We'll stay out in the open, and see if they try to follow us."

They had walked for about a block when they noticed two kids lagging behind them. "I don't recognize them from this distance," Diana said. "Do you think they were the ones in that old sedan?"

"I don't know, but let's see how persistent they're prepared to be." He gestured at the movie theater ahead. "We'll go in there, wait a few minutes, then duck out the side."

Diana stood at the cashier's window with Greg, and saw the boys hanging back. They didn't look directly at them, but rather seemed more interested in watching some of the girls around the entrance. No one followed them inside as they entered the darkened theater, even though they waited several minutes. "Maybe we're getting paranoid," she said.

"Let's go out the side exit," Greg answered with a shrug. As they emerged into the adjacent parking lot he glanced around, but there was no sign of the kids. "It looks like it's all clear."

Walking at a leisurely pace, they headed back to Diana's car. "Do you think I was wrong about the sedan?" she asked.

"There was one there. I saw it, too. Maybe whoever it was is waiting for us to return to your car."

"That doesn't make me feel a whole lot better."

He placed one arm over her shoulders. "You don't have anything to worry about. I'll be right by you, and I can't think of anyone you'd be safer with," he said quietly.

She remembered the events at Ortega's factory and suppressed a shiver. "I appreciate the thought behind that," she said, trying to act matter-of-fact, "but I'm not driving home until I'm sure the sedan's not tailing us."

Greg's eyes narrowed as he slowed his strides. "I just saw the reflection of two kids behind us in a store window. They're back."

Diana glanced sideways at the kids as they crossed the street. "They're turning away, and two others are tailing us now. I recognize the taller kid as one of Petey's top guys. Come to think of it, that sedan looks like one of the ones those kids go cruising around in. I'm not putting up with this," she said flatly. "Just what in the heck do they think they're doing?" She spun around and jogged after the boys.

Greg rushed after her. She was about to start something she couldn't finish. Being around her sometimes was like trying to hang on to the tail of a tornado. As she confronted the boys, Greg came up and joined her. In a matter of seconds, other gang members quickly appeared to back up their two friends.

Diana glowered at them. "Okay, no more games, guys. What's going on?"

The boys seemed not to even hear her. "Hey man," Carlos challenged Greg, "if you've got nothing to hide, why are you playing cat and mouse with us?"

Bullfrog and three others approached, and began to circle around Greg. "Don't you like our company, or what?"

Diana watched apprehensively as Greg stood his ground, his eyes fastened on Carlos as he moved around him. "Cut it out!" she ordered loudly. "What the heck do you guys think you're doing? I had an agreement with Petey. Where is he?"

"Right here, Diana," a voice came from the shadows. "The boys are just having a little fun. Don't worry."

Greg took Diana's hand and moved until they had a low wall to one side. "Look fellows, I don't want to have a problem with any of you, but the game's getting old."

"There's nine of us, and only one of you," Bullfrog shot back with bravado. "You can't do nothin'."

"Guys, you want to see if the local emergency room will give you group rates or something? Bullfrog, don't your friends know about the free flying lesson you received last time we tangled? You'd do well to remember I've got an extremely long reach," Greg said slowly and calmly.

"He doesn't like our company," one of the taller kids taunted, stepping back a few feet nonetheless. "That's too bad 'cause you're gonna have it everywhere you go from now on."

"Have you guys lost your minds?" Diana demanded. All their attention was focused on Greg. They scarcely looked in her direction. Her temper was beginning to reach the boiling point when she saw a familiar car slowing down as it approached.

Don pulled to a stop and stuck his head out the window. "Boys, you be sure and let me know if this man bothers you. If he does anything illegal, like get violent, I'll have to arrest him."

The realization that Don had instigated the boys' actions infuriated her. Diana strode up to Don's car, prepared to haul him out by any means necessary and have him put a stop to the harassment.

She went to the driver's side, snaked her hand out, and grabbed his necktie before he could react. She yanked on it, pulling a surprised Don toward the window. "Don't you understand that Greg could pick up one of those boys and use him like a fly swatter on the others? He doesn't want to hurt anyone, but if they strike out at him, he'll have to do something to defend himself."

"That's what I'm counting on," Don grinned, gaining the upper hand and gently forcing her to release her grip.

"This serves no purpose," she yelled as Don got out of the car. She could hear the boys taunting Greg. Occasionally one of them would jump forward, trying to goad him into action.

"There's a reason, even if you don't see it," he growled, then walked a little further away, drawing her with him. "I've promised the kids that police pressure on them will ease if they keep close company with Marten. Hopefully this'll force him to make a move. I'm not certain where he fits in, but Marten's got a part in Father Denning's murder, you can bet on that."

"Yes, he's been helping look for answers, which is as much as you and the department have done." She told him what they'd learned about Ortega and what had happened to her after the procession.

"Marten's always there when there's trouble, but he's never fast enough to keep it from happening. I still think he's setting you up." Don gave Greg a long, speculative look. "Stay away from him, Diana, at least for the next few weeks. I'm going to force him to show his true colors. It might become very dangerous for you once he's rattled." He strode up to the boys and interrupted the half circle they'd formed around Greg. "Take the lady home, Marten, then go home yourself. You don't want her around for the trouble you might be seeing the next few days."

The boys dispersed, and Greg returned to Diana's side. "Let's go," he said in a voice too quiet to pass as natural.

"Don's doing his best to unnerve you," she commented softly. "Don't let him win. He's very stubborn and, despite the evidence in your favor, I think he still wants to believe you killed Father Denning. He just doesn't like you."

"I'm glad you're concerned about me." His deep voice held a note of harshness, but the gaze that lingered over her was breathtakingly gentle. "But there's nothing for you to worry about. I've met people like Don before. They resent me on principle. My life-style doesn't fit in with their definition of how things should be, and they don't know how to deal with people who can't be intimidated."

"I've tried talking to him, but I'm not getting through."

As they reached Diana's car, Greg took the keys from her hands and unlocked the driver's side. He waited until she settled behind the wheel, then came around. "I never wanted power or money, Diana. But now that I've met you, I wish I had gone after those things. I would have had more to offer."

"That's not what's important to me," she answered, surprised. How could he not know just how much he had to offer a woman? "A man can't be measured by how much he's accumulated in terms of wealth or how much power he wields," she said, her voice barely audible. "All that really counts is how strong he is inside and how he holds to his ideals." And that was why she'd fallen in love with Greg and why it would be like giving up a part of herself when it came time for him to leave.

"I can't force your heart." The tenderness in his deep, measured voice made her heart melt. "But there are times like right now when I know we can work out whatever problems separate us, if you'll let it happen." He shifted and touched her cheek in a light caress.

She tried to suppress the shiver she felt building, but was only partially successful. "If we were right for each other, neither of us would have to give up anything," she managed, her heart twisting. "We shouldn't be forced to make trade-offs. We should be adding to each other's lives, not taking away."

"It doesn't have to be a matter of giving up anything. It's learning to make room in your life for the other person's needs." He lapsed into silence. "You always find a reason to back away, Diana. There's more involved here—something you're not telling me. You're a person who acts on instinct and emotion, not someone who calculates the odds. I'm not sure why you're holding back, but until you work that out, there really isn't any hope for us."

"There was a time in my life when I wanted a close relationship and family more than anything else in the world," she admitted quietly. "But I can't keep fighting what isn't meant for me. When I met Bob I thought I had everything. But fate stepped in and he was taken from me. In the aftermath I felt emptier and more alone than I'd ever been. Then after Frankie left the gang, he and I grew close and for a while I had a family. But he left, too, and joined the Navy." She struggled to make Greg understand. "For me, loving means people leaving. I'm not sure I've still got the strength to survive the sadness and emptiness that follows."

"No one can live in a vacuum. Sooner or later, we all need someone," he said, his voice deep and gentle. "But I can't force you to see this my way. All I can do is hope your feelings for me grow so strong you'll need to reach out to me. There's so much that's right between us, Diana, that it makes what we have worth fighting for."

Diana pulled into her driveway and began to walk to the door. "It isn't that easy."

"I never claimed it would be," he answered.

Realizing that Greg wasn't following her to the house, she stopped and turned around. "Aren't you coming in?"

He shook his head. "Don's warning was clear. This is something I have to handle on my own without endangering you. I'll call you tomorrow morning. In the meantime why don't you see if you can stay with Anita. I really don't think you should be alone in the house, not after what happened."

Diana nodded, then walked inside.

The vulnerability shining in her eyes made his gut wrench. Maybe he'd been too hard on Diana, but he didn't know how else to get through to her. Greg went to his van and started the drive to his apartment. There was a softness about Diana that made every protective instinct he had come charging to the surface. Around her he'd discovered a side of himself he'd never known existed.

Diana tackled everything with such fervor, from the burrito at lunch to the challenge they'd faced with the boys. By contrast, he'd almost forgotten how to stop planning. He'd always worked to keep an open mind, but Diana had taught him to keep an open heart as well. He wasn't sure how, but he had to make her see that their love was too precious to walk away from.

As he entered his studio minutes later, the stark solitude of the place left him feeling empty. He tossed his keys on the table, then walked to the bed. What had she done to him? The life-style that had suited him before, now seemed pointless. Then again maybe it was. In a way, he'd found that elusive something he'd been searching for, only it still remained just beyond his grasp.

The telephone rang, interrupting his thoughts. He picked it up cradling the receiver between his ear and shoulder. "Hello."

"Listen to me, Marten, because I'm only saying this once," a gravelly voice informed him. "I've got some information on the murder that you're going to be very interested in."

"Who is this?" he demanded.

"You don't need to know that, so shut up and listen. Meet me at De Vargas Park in twenty minutes. Stay on the south side of the river and walk to the corner where the wall ends at the Paseo de Peralta bridge. When you get there look around, you'll know what to do."

"What kind of information—" The dial tone interrupted him. He glanced at his watch. It was a bit past nine. After dark his visibility would be hampered, and there'd be no telling what he'd walk into. Maybe this was part of Don's "plan."

He'd been to that park before, but he consulted a city map just to make sure of the details. Then he reached for the telephone and dialed Diana's number. Briefly he explained the call he'd received. "I want you to follow me there on the parallel road that runs down the north side of the park. The park's only about one hundred yards wide if my memory is correct, so you shouldn't have any trouble seeing me. Don't get out of your car, just watch. If there's trouble, get the cops."

"Maybe I should go with you—" she started.

"No, I need someone who'll be free to get help if there's trouble. Can I count on you?" he asked, already knowing the answer.

"I'll be there," she replied without hesitation.

Greg arrived at the park three minutes late. He parked his van and glanced around. The area seemed totally deserted. He walked to the spot the caller had indicated, then searched with his flashlight for instructions on what to do next. He found nothing, even the city trash bin nearby was empty. Greg waited, alert for trouble, but no one drew near.

He could see Diana's car off in the distance, hidden almost completely in the darkness. Had she been spotted? He found that doubtful. Jamming his hands into his pockets, he paced by the wall. Suddenly he stopped and aimed his light into a crevice in the wall itself. It had been partially obscured by some litter, but now, thanks to a breeze, he could see the newspaper wrapped bundle nestled inside it.

He knew he should call the police before disturbing it but he couldn't risk being accused of crying wolf.

Greg pulled the bundle out and opened it carefully. Inside was a small gold cross and a blood soaked handkerchief. A cold chill crept up his arm and his eyes darted around the park. There was only one reason for this to be here. He was being set up. Picking up the package by the fringes of the paper, and making sure he didn't touch the objects themselves, he started jogging toward Diana's car.

Spotting him, she waved and got out. Greg speeded up, eager to get the bundle to the authorities. The last thing he needed was to be caught with what he was certain was evidence in Father Denning's murder.

As he jogged past a section filled with tall pines, two cops jumped out from behind the trees, pistols drawn. "Police, freeze!" Two other officers suddenly appeared on either side of him. "Put the bundle on the ground in front of you, Marten, and don't even think of trying anything."

Greg bent over, placing the package on the ground. Seconds later, he saw the beam of a flashlight shining over the objects. Someone muttered an oath.

Before he could explain, Greg saw Diana running up. The officers spun around quickly, their aim on her. "Diana. Stay back," Greg warned.

"I'll be fine, Greg. *You* be careful," she cautioned. "I'll explain what's going on."

"Listen to her. She'll verify that I was set up," Greg said.

"We've got plenty of time to talk down at the station, Marten. Just keep your hands where we can see them."

The officer stood rock still with his gun drawn and aimed, as his partner came up behind Greg. "Down on your knees, hands locked behind your head."

"Diana, did you telephone them?" Greg asked, seeing her behind an officer on his far right.

"No, of course not! I was waiting, like we agreed."

One of the officers crouched by the package Greg had placed on the ground. "I'd be willing to bet the blood on this handkerchief is Father Denning's."

"It probably is. I was set up. How else would you guys have known to come here tonight? The only person who could have tipped you is the guy who's trying to frame me!"

"Don't say another word until I read you your rights," the officer ordered brusquely. "No way you're getting off on a technicality."

Greg waited until the officer finished. "The same man who called me about twenty minutes ago must have also telephoned you. He left that stuff here for me to find, and he neatly arranged for you guys to show up, too," Greg insisted. He saw the skepticism on the cops' faces and felt his heart pumping like a steam engine. Diana's word wouldn't substantiate his account, not enough anyway. He was the only one who heard that phone call. Fear and anger swept through him. This time they might not release him. He glanced at Diana, who was arguing with one of the officers. He smiled, proud yet worried about the trouble she might get herself into for him.

He felt the coldness of the metal cuffs on his wrist, then the police officer jerked him to his feet. "With you, it's always the same tune. You're getting boring, buddy."

"He's telling the truth," Diana argued behind him.

He caught her eyes and held them. There were so many things he wanted to say to her, but there was no time. She looked so worried about him that he had to fight the urge to pull away from the hands that held him and go to her. "I'll be okay. Take care," he said in a whisper-soft voice.

Diana nodded, but didn't say anything. She'd fight like the devil on his behalf, he knew that. Only this time, he wasn't sure if anything they could do would be enough.

Greg was taken down to the station and led through the booking procedure. He made his expression into an impenetrable mask and held his shoulders erect. Finally, after it was over, he was allowed to make a call. "Mr. Crowley, I need your help. I'm down at the station..." he began.

DIANA WAS PACING by the door of the station when Don came out. "Marten's not going to be released, so there's no point in your hanging around. What we found was enough to hold him," he said, and considered adding, "until he rots," but seeing Diana's stricken expression made his heart twist inside him. "You never heard that call. Don't you see? He played you for a fool."

"He's not guilty! It doesn't make any sense. You confiscated all his clothing after he came out of the church the night Father John was murdered. He was covered in blood then, how would he have hidden the handkerchief until now? And how did he keep you from discovering it in the first place? There's also the matter of the stolen cross. When would he have had time to hide that?"

"I've always said he could have worked with a partner. Your emotions are too involved in this," he continued softly. "That's why you're shutting your eyes to the facts."

"You're the one who refuses to judge the facts in a fair manner. You want to close this case so badly you're willing to accept circumstantial evidence."

"That's not true," Don bellowed. Then he forced his voice back to a normal tone. "We're still questioning Marten because we're aware of the discrepancies. Only remember, we didn't catch him as he left the church. He was already outside."

"Oh, come on! Why would he call tonight and ask me to go with him to the park if he'd known what was in the package?"

"Maybe he thought that would substantiate his story," he held up one hand. "I know what you're going to say. Why would he get rid of the stuff at the park where anyone might find it, then wait so long to go back?"

"So you do see it's a frame," Diana said, with a tiny satisfied smile.

"I see no such thing," Don roared. "All I know is that we got an anonymous tip late this evening. The man claimed he'd seen the tall redhead linked to Father Denning's murder in the park hiding something."

"Can I see Greg now?"

"No, he's going to be questioned until we're satisfied we have all the facts." Don placed his arm around Diana's shoulders as he walked her to her car. "There's nothing you can do here. Go home and try to get some rest."

Diana felt sick. Greg had taken her along in case of trouble, and she couldn't do a thing to help him.

"Diana, listen to me for once and don't try to investigate on your own. *If* this is a frame," he said cautiously, "then the murderer is still out there. A man who's willing to kill another is a powerful adversary. You don't have the training or ruthlessness needed to play this game."

She nodded slowly, but said nothing. "Does Greg's lawyer know he's in jail?"

"Sure. Marten called him right away. I expect him to be here in another hour or so. Crowley's going to want to talk to Marten, then he'll try to arrange for bail." He leaned over her opened window. "Diana, I want your word you'll sit tight and not try to look into the case by yourself. I buried my brother, and I don't want to bury you, too."

The queasy bubble in Diana's stomach grew. She placed her hand over Don's. "You have my word, so stop worrying."

He stepped away from the car. "I'll keep you informed."

"Please do," she said as she started the engine. "Good night, Don."

Diana drove home slowly, taking the long way. The thought of Greg sitting in a jail cell made her ache all over. There had to be something she could do.

As she passed the corner, she saw Carlos and Petey leaning against the wall of Coin's Realm talking to others in the gang. Diana slowed down, realizing she'd just found her answer.

# Chapter Seventeen

Diana parked in the closest available space and walked to where the boys stood. "Hello, guys," she said. "I need to talk to you."

"If it's about Marten, don't bother. Talk to your brother-in-law. He's the one leaning on us," Carlos answered.

"I didn't come here to tell you what to do. You're old enough to make your own decisions." Just then she noticed one boy was keeping in the background. "Joe, you're out of jail! That's wonderful! Your mother must be relieved."

"Yeah, she bailed me out," he answered, staring at the ground. "I've still got to go to court, but the guy admitted that he started pushing us around. It should go okay for me."

Petey eyed her suspiciously. "What brings you here, Diana?"

She allowed a few moments of silence to drag on, making sure she had their complete attention. "You boys initiated Joe the night of Father John's murder. Joe even spray painted your plaque on the first cop car that arrived at the church."

The boys stared at the ground, avoiding her gaze. "So, what's your point?" Carlos shot back.

"I'm not trying to cause any trouble, so relax. I just wanted you guys to think back to that night again. Did any of you see anything that struck you as out of place? Don't think in terms of a person, concentrate on things or events surrounding Greg's arrest.''

"What difference does it make now? The cops already arrested your boyfriend for the murder. I hear they even caught him with some of the stuff."

"How did you—" she started to say, then shrugged. "Never mind," she continued. "Greg was set up." She told them the story.

"And the cops just showed up, right?" Petey shook his head. "If what you say is true, someone's doing a real number on him."

Joe glanced at her. "I'd like to help you, but all I saw was that Greg guy walking up to the church carrying a big, wrapped package, and..."

"What?" she did a double take. That was the first corroborating evidence that Greg had actually gone inside the church with the hide painting.

"So what? We all know he went inside the church."

"Yes, but you actually saw him carrying a package! That's terribly important. Joe, if you could tell the police—"

Petey straightened up, moving quickly away from the wall. "Hey, you said there would be no trouble. What about your word?"

"I wouldn't betray any confidences, you know that," she answered sharply. "That's why I was *asking*. You see, this verifies Greg's story," she explained.

"I can't help him without putting myself on the line," Joe said shrugging helplessly, "and I'm in enough trouble."

Petey scowled at Joe, then glanced at her. "Don't ask us to sacrifice our own." He stared at the sidewalk, his eyes narrowing in thought. "There is something we can do for you, though. We'll lay off Marten. We can deal with the cops and their harassment."

"Yeah," Carlos agreed, kicking a stone on the sidewalk absently. "And if we hear anything out on the streets, we'll let you know."

Discouraged, Diana returned to her car and drove home. She couldn't help but wonder if, like Joe, she too had overlooked some vital clue.

Diana went inside the house and walked to the bedroom. Slipping out of her clothes, she crawled beneath the covers and listened to the antique clock on her nightstand. There was a dull pain in her heart as she thought of the night Greg had lain beside her. She turned her head and reached out, her fingers grazing the empty spot where he had been. With a ragged sigh, she turned on her side, and stared into the darkness.

DIANA WAS FINISHING a cup of coffee the following morning when she heard a car pull into her driveway. Parting the café curtains, she saw Don walking toward her door. Not waiting for his knock, she opened it. "You're here early. Has something happened?"

"Marten's going to be released. The more we checked, the more convincing his story looked. For example, Marten doesn't use handkerchiefs. We checked every article of clothing he owns without finding any. The cross we found him with was one of the stolen items, but it was the least valuable one. It was a small thing that hung around the neck of one of the *santos*. We figure the murderer was willing to sacrifice that part of the stash to incriminate Marten, but not the rest. Also, there were no traces of fingerprints on it. It had been wiped clean. Marten's lawyer was threatening to go public with all the details if we didn't let him go."

"Good for A. J. Crowley!"

"Marten's van has been impounded, and he won't be able to pick it up until tomorrow." Don gave her a grudging smile. "He'll probably need a ride."

Diana grabbed her purse and keys. "Come on," she urged. "Your car is blocking mine and I need to get to the station."

Diana waited impatiently until Don backed out of the driveway, then followed him down the narrow street. She cursed as she saw how slowly he was going. She couldn't even pass him! She suspected he was doing it to tease her, but it infuriated her just the same. She leaned on her horn and saw him laugh.

By the time they walked into the station, Greg was at the main desk, Crowley beside him. It took all her willpower not to rush up to him and throw her arms around his neck. "Hi!" she managed brightly.

"Hello yourself," he answered softly. "It's good to see you."

Realizing that both Don and A. J. Crowley were staring at them, she tried to stop smiling and look more business-like. Unfortunately she couldn't quite manage it. She felt so good she was about to burst. "I'm glad you're ready to get out of here. It's about time the police realized that you had nothing to do with the murder."

"Marten could still be involved with the theft," Don countered. "This little incident could be part of an elaborate plan he has to throw suspicion off himself."

Diana gave Don a look of utter disbelief. "You never give up!"

"Just making a point," he replied sourly.

"Okay, Marten," the officer behind the desk said, handing over Greg's personal possessions. "Sign here and you're free to go."

"But don't leave Santa Fe without informing the department where you're going," Don added.

Greg's eyes locked with Don's. "Eventually you'll see the light, Clark, I really believe that. I just hope more innocent people won't be hurt by your trial-and-error investigative techniques."

Don took a step toward Greg, but Diana quickly stepped in the way. "Okay, that's it. You've signed the papers, Greg, now let me give you a ride out of here. I'll explain about your van on the way to my car." Entwining her arm around Greg's she quickly ushered him out of the station.

"I'm not a violent man," he managed through clenched teeth, "but there are times—"

"Forget it. They'd stick you back in jail so fast, you wouldn't know what hit you."

"I'm aware of that," he growled. "As you noticed, Don was still standing when we left."

As Diana pulled into the parking area by Greg's studio, she caught him watching her. "You're staring. That's impolite."

"So I'm rude, but I missed you, and damned if I didn't spend more of my time worrying about you than me." He got out of the car, then came around to help her out.

"Good," she replied with a smile. "It's much more equitable that way."

"Is that your way of saying you missed me, too?" he asked, stopping by his door.

She touched his face in a tender caress. "I missed you terribly, and I did worry," she admitted in a whisper-soft voice.

He searched her eyes for one long moment then, as her hands went to his chest, he pulled her against him tightly. "While I was in jail, I kept myself busy thinking what I'd do if you said that to me," he admitted, his voice rough and low. "Now that you have, it's time to make my fantasy real." He lowered his mouth to hers, taking from it a kiss that was deep and tender.

His tongue was warm and knowing, expert. She couldn't seem to stop trembling. As he started to release her, she drew him back down gently and tasted him as he'd done her moments before. Diana felt him shudder, and his breathing came harsh. Emboldened by his response, she pressed herself against him, caressing the moist cavern of his mouth with all the love that was in her heart.

His arms clenched tightly around her, and his kiss deepened. "We've got to go inside, or we're both going to be arrested for what I'm about to do with you."

His words started a fire inside her that made it difficult to breathe or think. He held her against himself with one arm and unlocked the door with the other hand. As the door swung open, she heard him swear.

Diana pulled away from him, the scene registering slowly in her brain. The walls, the curtains, and even some of the furniture were covered with the crimson spray paint. The acrid smell of aerosol and paint burned her nostrils.

She stared at the far wall. "That's the gang's plaque," she said in disbelief. "I'm going to go find them." Her anger rose, bubbling over like a hot cauldron. They'd ruined what would have been a very special moment for her, and had forced Greg to come back home to a disaster. "They did this, so they can undo it." She shot out the door and rushed to her car.

"Let it go," Greg said, going after her. "At least nothing's broken this time. Besides, your brother-in-law shares most of the responsibility for what's happened here."

She got behind the driver's seat. "You don't understand. I spoke to the guys earlier today, and they made an agreement with me." She gave him the details of their conversation. "Considering that Joe won't go to the police and Petey's backing his decision, the least they can do is keep their word. Now are you coming or not?"

Greg climbed in on the passenger's side. "If Joe won't go to the police, then that's that," he said, exhaling softly. "And as for my studio, it's possible they did this before you spoke to them."

"Then Petey should have warned me," she said flatly. "He's playing games now and I'm going to confront him on this. I want to know where he stands." Spotting some of the Diablo Locos on the corner by Coin's Realm, she slowed and pulled into an empty parking space.

Seeing them, Carlos sauntered up. "Hey man, glad you're out," he said to Greg. "Your lady told us how you were set up."

Diana looked around and saw Petey coming out of the arcade. "I need a second of your time, please." She took him aside. "Okay, what gives? Greg's apartment was vandalized again and the plaque of the Diablo Locos was spray painted on the wall. If you'd already trashed his place before I spoke to you, why didn't you tell me?"

"What are you talking about?" Petey stared at her, his confusion too evident to be faked. "We didn't go near Marten's place, not on *my* orders." He cocked his head toward the other boys. "Let's find out who's been getting independent."

Petey challenged the others with a hard glare as he gave them the news. "Bullfrog, you've got quite a talent with the spray cans, and a grudge against the man. Anything you want to tell me?"

"Not me," he said, looking at Petey, and taking a step back.

"Carlos?"

"It couldn't have been any of our guys, man. We would have heard about it by now," Carlos protested.

Petey glanced at Diana. "You sure it's our plaque? Maybe you should take another look."

"I've got a better idea. Pile into my car. I'll take you over and you can judge for yourself."

It was a tight fit. Diana drove while Petey shared the rest of the front seat with Greg. The three other boys were crammed against each other in the back. Shortly afterward they pulled into the parking lot by Greg's building and got out of the car. Greg opened the door, then stood back watching the boys, trying to gauge their reaction.

Petey stepped inside first. His eyes fixed on the plaque on the opposite wall. "None of our guys did that."

Carlos came up and stood beside him. "Yeah, we have our own way of shaping the *D* and the *L* of Diablo Locos. These are way off. And it's nothing like the Dark Lord's plaque either."

"And that's not our color," Bullfrog added. "We only use Indian Red. That's more like—pink," he said with obvious distaste.

"Yeah, but someone is trying to use our logo, Petey," Carlos warned. "We have to put a stop to it."

"Right. This isn't our work, but we'll find out who's responsible," Petey said as he started toward the door. "Later."

As the boys left, Greg looked around. "It's pointless to call the police. They'll just assume it's the boys' work, no matter what the kids say. Not that they could do much anyway. From the looks of it, nothing's been touched. They were too busy spray painting."

"Who could have done this?" She rubbed a finger against the cloth couch and noticed that the paint had already dried there. The sofa would have to be replaced or reupholstered. "Harper's brother is in custody, so it can't be him. There's Ortega. By now he knows we've been meddling in his business. He could have hired someone to do this as a payback for the trouble we've caused him. Don's another possibility, though I doubt he'd stoop this low. Then, there's the cowboy, but he doesn't strike me as the type to do this, either."

"There's also Harper," Greg added. "He could blame us for the arrest of his brother. You know what they say, 'blood's thicker than water.'" He shook his head in exasperation. "Well, for now, I better get this place fixed up before the landlord comes by. He collects the rent himself and it's due tomorrow."

They worked until early evening, stopping only for a quick lunch. As Greg began to work on the last wall, he realized the last bucket of paint was empty. "I'm going to have to go buy some more paint."

"There's a home center not too far from here, just a few blocks past the church. Why don't we walk? We could both use some fresh air," Diana suggested.

"It's getting dark," Greg pointed out. "You should go home. If someone's targeting me, you want to be as far away as possible."

"Wrong." She stuck her chin out and stared at him defiantly. "Shall we go?" she stood by the door and waited.

"I should know better than to try and tell you anything," he said with a rueful smile. There'd been a time when he'd hoped she'd show him the same unflagging loyalty she reserved for her friends. Now, faced with the risk it meant to her safety, he wished it had never happened. How could he keep her safe when he couldn't even manage it for himself?

"It's a perfect evening for a walk," she said as a breeze ruffled her hair.

Greg placed his arm over her shoulders as they walked down the street. "Being with you makes it perfect," he murmured, his hand curving to graze her cheek in a light caress. She was so soft, and if things had been different, she would have given herself to him today. He remembered the way she'd tasted when he'd kissed her, and his body tensed almost painfully.

The lavenders and blues of twilight descended softly around them, and they both drifted along in silence. He was aware of Diana's warmth and the way it touched him despite the coolness of the evening.

"It's so peaceful tonight," she said, sighing contentedly.

They were passing by a narrow alleyway when they heard a loud meow, then the sound of a trash barrel being knocked to the ground. As the cat shot past them, Diana stopped short, then started to laugh. "That silly cat practically gave me a heart attack."

"Don't turn around," a voice said suddenly from behind them.

Greg felt the point of a knife being jabbed into the small of his back and saw Diana's head jerk back as a hand grabbed her hair. "Get into the alley. Now move," the man ordered.

"Let the woman go," Greg answered, "then I'll do what you want."

"You don't have a choice, buddy." The man jabbed the blade lightly against Greg's spine. "Not unless you want this knife to go right through you."

"There's no need to hurt anyone," Diana managed, her voice trembling slightly. "We'll do as you say."

As they stepped into the alley, she tried to turn around. The man reacted instantly, winding his hand even more tightly around her hair and yanking back hard. Diana cried out in pain.

"Don't hurt her," Greg ordered, his voice low but clear.

"You're not in a position to make demands," the man said, maintaining his grip on Diana.

The pain was so sharp it brought tears to her eyes. Diana bit her lip and forced herself to remain still.

"What do you want from us?" Greg asked.

"I'm here to deliver a message," the man said.

"All right, get to it," Greg prodded.

"Mr. Ortega doesn't like it when people nose into his business. I've been told to leave you with a little reminder—" A shadow suddenly cut off light from one end of the alley and, realizing someone was approaching, the man stopped in mid-sentence. "Looks like you just got lucky," he whispered. "Take my warning, or next time things will be a lot rougher." He pushed Diana forward, taking off in the opposite direction, heading down the alley away from the unknown benefactor.

As Diana stumbled to her knees, Greg rushed to her side. He helped her up, worry lining his face. "Are you okay?"

Before she could answer, he took a step forward, placing himself in front of her. His attention was riveted on the end of the alley. Puzzled, she followed his gaze.

The cowboy stood there, illuminated only by the full moon shining into the darkened alley. There was something so sad about the smile he gave them that it wrenched her heart.

The cowboy glanced down at a small object on the ground in front of his feet. For a second, moonlight seemed to catch on it. With slow deliberation, he glanced back up at them, wordlessly calling their attention to the object. Then, his silence unbroken, he turned the corner and disappeared from sight.

## Chapter Eighteen

Greg inhaled sharply, realizing it was the first breath he'd taken since the cowboy appeared. "This guy has some kind of presence. I felt as if I was frozen to the spot." He shook his head in bewilderment. "I'm not a coward, Diana," he said softly, "and I think you know that by now. But there's something odd about this I can't quite get a handle on." He clamped his mouth shut.

Diana nodded, realizing that neither of them had yet made a move toward the object that still lay on the ground. "It's not just you," she whispered. "But we're not being fair. The cowboy's helped us a great deal. He's an ally, not an enemy."

Greg walked over to where the cowboy had stood, then bent down and picked up the object. "It's a key. It's got a number on it, but I have no idea what it unlocks." He handed it to Diana. "Do you?"

Diana studied the key, then shrugged. "He's doing his best to tell us something. I just wish he'd come right out and say it."

"Maybe he *is* mute. You've noticed how he keeps that bandanna around his neck. Maybe it covers a scar." Greg paused. "I don't think he's mentally handicapped. Despite his costume, he strikes me as highly intelligent and alert."

"I agree, but what are we going to do about this key?"

"We've almost always seen him around the church and school. Maybe this fits something there," Greg suggested.

"Do you think this is connected to Ortega?" Seeing Greg shrug, Diana sighed. "Okay, let's walk over to the school. It's only a block from here, and the grounds are well lit so we shouldn't have any problem looking around."

"We'll have to watch out for Harper. He's not going to be happy if he spots us prowling around again. Let's make sure we stay away from the windows."

Protectively, Greg stayed close to her as they approached the school. "If we don't find anything fast, we'll quit. I don't want to stay out in the open tonight. There's been enough trouble for one day."

"Do you think Ortega's thug will come back?"

"No, but I'd rather not take any more chances." Greg pointed to one well-lit window on the second floor as they approached. "Let's search the other three sides and leave that one for another time."

They were halfway down the second side, when Diana stopped. A large metal plate was fastened over a concrete square in the ground. "What on earth is that?"

He crouched before it. "My guess is it's an access point to a utility tunnel."

"Then that would lead underneath the school," she commented pensively. "The latch is padlocked." She tried the key the cowboy had shown them, but although it was the right type, it didn't fit. "Do you know how to break through these things? I think we should find out what's down there."

"Breaking that padlock is going to take some doing, and there's no way we'll be able to mask the noise," he said flatly. "I hope you're not even considering doing that."

"Well, the thought had occurred to me, but there might be another way." She stood up and glanced around. "I'll tell you my idea on the way back to your studio."

IT WAS SHORTLY after noon the following day when Greg came by the print shop. "I'll be back before long, Anita," Diana said, peering into the back room.

"Be nice to John Miles. It took me over twenty minutes to convince him to meet you at the school." Anita gave her a sharp look. "John's a good friend of mine, and I'd like it to stay that way."

"All I'm going to do is ask him a few questions," Diana assured her.

"Let's go in my van," Greg suggested as they left the shop. "I got it back this morning. In the meantime, you can fill me in on who John Miles is, besides Anita's friend."

"He's the district facilities engineer. He's in charge of maintaining the utility systems in each school," she answered as they got underway.

When they arrived at the school, the doors leading to the playground were wide open, and painters and scaffolds seemed to fill the hall. A tall, thin man in his early fifties came out of one of the classrooms. "Diana Clark?"

"You must be John Miles," she said, extending her hand.

He gave her a wary look. "Anita spoke very highly of you, but I'm still not certain what it is you want from me."

"Anita said that we could trust you, so I'm going to be completely honest. We've been watching this area since Father John Denning was murdered. There's a strange looking cowboy who hangs around here. We've wanted to talk to him, but he's always managed to disappear just as we get close. We searched the grounds, but couldn't find anything to explain his successful elusiveness. Then, recently we came across a steel plate on the ground beside the building. It appears to be an access tunnel."

"That's exactly what it is," John Miles answered. "Many of the buildings in the area have them so the maintenance staff can reach the pipes and duct work. Several tunnels interconnect beneath the foundation of the school. There's also a building entrance in the basement."

"Is there more than one outside entrance? We saw only one cover plate," Greg asked.

"There are several openings around the building. Some are behind shrubbery or beneath the lawn edging. But you don't have to worry about anyone sneaking in there, if that's what you're thinking. Only two people have a set of keys, the head of maintenance and the custodian at the school. For security reasons the padlocks on each entrance aren't even keyed alike. If a key is lost, the matching lock is replaced. The school system has a firm rule that *no one* but authorized personnel is ever to go down there."

Diana saw the determined look on the man's face and knew he wasn't about to let them be an exception. "All right, Mr. Miles. We appreciate your time."

As they left the school, Greg gave her a skeptical look. "You gave up much too easily. Why don't you tell me what you really have in mind?"

"Those tunnels could explain how our cowboy appears and disappears so easily. We may not be able to go down there, but the police can. I'm going over to the station."

They arrived a short time later and were informed that Don was in his office. They walked down the corridor to meet him and Diana shared their latest findings.

Don didn't seem impressed, nor particularly interested in the key. "We've already checked out the tunnels at the school because one of the openings wasn't too far from where the blood spots were found. Our crime scene unit searched for traces of blood in there, but the floors had been cleaned and painted recently as part of the regular summer schedule. There was only one thing that was even mildly out of the ordinary down there. Our guys found a place Harper uses to sneak a nap now and then."

"Is there anything new on the anonymous caller who tried to frame me?"

Don glared at Greg and directed his answer to Diana. "No, but I imagine there's lots of people who don't like Marten much."

"Do you think the caller might have been Father John's murderer?" Diana asked.

"No." Don leaned back in his chair. "We believe Eric Harper's lying about his whereabouts the night of the murder, and that he's probably the killer. Our guess is that he was trying to steal enough to be able to finance his getaway, and poor Father John showed up at the wrong time."

"Does this mean I'm finally in the clear?" Greg asked hopefully.

"Not until we have more conclusive evidence," Don shot back. "Look, I have to get back to work." He stood and walked them to the door.

As Greg and Diana started down the hall, Don reached out and held Diana back. "By the way, we found out that Marten pulls in a substantial amount of money from his carvings alone. His last one sold for over twenty thousand. If he is the thief, money certainly isn't a motive," he said, loud enough for Greg to hear.

Greg stared at Don in complete surprise. Before he had a chance to respond, Diana ushered him gently out of the station. "You may not realize it, but that's as close as Don'll ever get to an apology. Regardless of what he said, you are in the clear."

"It's about time," he said, "but I have to admit there are a few things that still bother me about this case. I realize that the police are almost convinced Eric Harper's guilty. But if he is, then there are still more players involved. Someone tried to frame me since Eric Harper's arrest. And we still haven't been able to determine who the cowboy is, or how he fits in."

"Let's take a look around the church grounds this evening," Diana said slowly. "I still have the key we found, since Don wasn't interested in it. Maybe it will fit a lock over there."

"It's worth checking out," Greg agreed.

"I'll call the parish office this afternoon and tell them what we're planning to do. That'll cover us in case we're seen and someone reports us to the police. Can you meet me at the shop at around seven? Anita and I have to work late tonight.''

Greg nodded, lost in thought. ''You might also try to find out if anyone at the church has lost a key, and if so, to what.''

The afternoon seemed endless. Although there was plenty of work to do, Diana's mind remained on the key. By the time seven came around, she was more than ready to go.

Anita watched her prepare to leave. ''When are you going to let go of this? If your brother-in-law thinks Harper's brother did it, then take his word for it.''

''I can't,'' she answered. ''I'm not convinced, and for that matter, I don't think Don is, either. Even if Harper's brother is guilty, we still need more proof. Wish us luck,'' she said, grabbing her jacket from the chair and moving to join Greg at the door.

Restlessness gnawed at her as they drove to the church. ''The church was built a hundred years before the school, so it probably won't have the same kind of access tunnels. I wonder what else this key could fit? I called, and nobody has reported losing any keys lately. It isn't to the door, those keys are of a different type, and all are accounted for.''

Greg parked the van and they crossed the street and walked over to the church. ''Let's search close to the church walls and walk around the entire building slowly. If this key fits anything there, it's bound to be something that's all but forgotten. Otherwise, someone would have reported the key missing.''

They decided to start on the side that faced the school since that was also closest to where they had found the key, and the blood.

''The juniper hedge borders all sides of the church except the area by the front doors,'' Greg observed. ''We'll have to get behind it, and it's bound to be rough going.''

''I hate to volunteer, but I'm smaller and likely to have an easier time back there than you would. Let me leave the key with you so I don't lose it in there," she said, then got down on her hands and knees and angled for a way in. "You can pull the shrubbery away from the wall as I crawl through."

Her progress was slow, but made easier with Greg's help. There was a clearing of about eighteen inches between the base of the hedge and the wall of the building. By hunching her shoulders, she could crawl through.

"Can you see?" Greg asked.

"Sure. We've still got plenty of light and..." She stopped in mid-sentence. The space between the outside wall of the building and the hedge was suddenly about six inches wider. "There's a heavy metal grate here resting over a concrete lined opening in the ground."

"Where does it lead to?" Greg asked, peering over the hedge.

Diana shifted so her body wasn't blocking the light, and peered down through the steel bars. She pulled a small flashlight out of her jacket pocket, and aimed it down. "I can see a brick floor down there. It's like a tiny landing with a half door leading into the basement. I'm not sure, but it could be where they had a coal chute in the old days."

"Is it large enough for a person to go through?"

"Yeah, I think so. But the grate has a padlock holding it down. Can you hand me the key the cowboy found for us?"

She slipped it into the lock, her heart thumping. "It fits! Can you force your way through the hedge? I'm going down."

Diana eased herself into the walled enclosure. Crouching, she studied the half door before her. She pushed at the knob, and the door creaked open. With care, she made her way down a half-dozen steps into a large room, then located a light switch.

Moments later, she heard a grunt, and Greg appeared behind her. "That's a tight fit," he muttered, studying the area around him. "This furnace room must double as the custodian's office." He studied the pegboard filled with old keys. "The one the cowboy gave us must be a new copy of one of these."

Diana studied the large heating unit that took up the center of the room. Massive sheet metal ducts led away from it and, she surmised, made their way through the entire building. She searched for a vent opening, and found one near the doorway to the janitor's office. "I've got an idea," she told Greg. "Bring a chair."

Greg brought one over for her. "What . . ." He followed her gaze and saw the vent. "You're thinking that the killer might have used one of those to make his getaway?"

"It would explain why there was no trail of blood outside any of the church doors. By the time he got here, most of the blood would have either rubbed off on the ducting or dried on his clothes. And if he took off his shoes he wouldn't leave tracks."

Greg nodded, then studied the duct above them. "Let me go in. I think I can fit, and it'll be easier for me to pull myself up into there." Standing on the chair, he lifted the grate out of the way. Then, in one fluid motion, he hoisted himself up and out of her sight.

"I'm going to need a flashlight," he said, his voice echoing oddly in the cavernous interior of the ducts.

"Here," she said, standing on the chair and handing him the one from her jacket pocket.

"I'm not sure exactly where these will lead, so don't worry if it takes me a while."

Greg lay on his stomach and pulled himself forward with his elbows. The beam of the flashlight cut through the blackness, but all he could see was more of the metallic tunnel looming ahead. He moved carefully for about three feet, then stopped and studied a section of pipe on his right. Bringing the flashlight closer, he stared at the marks there.

Immediately he began backing out, careful not to rub up against any more of the marks. Reaching the opening, he jumped out of the duct work and into the basement. The look on Diana's face made him freeze. Her eyes were wide and her mouth had dropped open slightly.

"Look at the front of your shirt," she managed in a taut whisper. "You're covered with red specks." She swallowed, then in a barely audible voice added, "It looks like dried blood."

"I think it is," he said, slipping the shirt off his shoulders, and leaving his T-shirt on. "My shirt can be used as evidence, so I'll leave it here. Let's go. We've got to call the police immediately."

She took a deep breath. "So now we know how the killer evaded the police. The church custodian must be the murderer."

"Do you know who he is?" Greg asked, walking toward the small half door that led to the basement.

"I don't think I've ever seen him," she answered. "But how did the cowboy find out about this?" she asked as she followed Greg back out the grate. "We're going to have to find him again. He's *got* to talk to us."

They emerged by the side of the church and hurried out to the sidewalk. They'd almost reached Greg's van when she saw a patrol car coming down the street. "I'm going to stop them," she said. "The officer can radio Don for us."

Greg tried to shake off a feeling of déjà vu. He could still vividly recall what had happened the last time he'd flagged down a cruising patrol car for help. His gut coiled into a hard knot.

Diana rushed out into the street and strode up to the patrol car that had slowed to a stop. "I'm Diana Clark," she said. Then she explained what they'd found. "Can you radio my brother-in-law, Don Clark?"

The officer contacted the dispatcher, then, with his eyes firmly glued on Greg, waited for his call to be relayed to another unit. "Don Clark is out in the field with the crime scene unit right now. We're getting patched through to his vehicle."

Diana heard Don's voice on the radio speaker after the officer explained the situation. "The crime scene unit is still working out here, but we should be finished shortly. Stay there and protect the scene until we arrive."

"Tell him that the killer must be the church custodian. He would have known about the duct work and had the right keys."

"Give her the microphone," Don ordered, hearing the relayed message. "Diana, go home and wait for me. Our team will arrive there shortly and we'll check out the blood stains you claimed to have seen."

"They're there," she answered angrily. "You've got to arrest the custodian."

"One of the first things we did was check all the church employees. The custodian passed away over three weeks ago and they haven't hired a new one yet. Now give the officer back the mike."

She stared at Greg in confusion as Don finished giving the patrol officer his instructions. "I don't get it," she said. "Who else would have known about the ducts and been able to gain entry?"

Before he could answer, the officer interrupted. "Ms. Clark, Detective Clark wants me to remind you to go home. He'll meet you there as soon as he's free."

As Diana started back toward the school, walking slowly, Greg placed his hand over her shoulders. "My van's back in the other direction."

"I know," she answered, "but I want to make a pass through the school grounds. Maybe we'll see the cowboy." She brushed away a few strands of hair that had blown into her face. "I was so sure the church's custodian was our man!"

"That was my first impression, too, but once I thought it over, I saw there were problems with the theory. For instance, why would the custodian need a duplicate key? He had the original, and all he would have had to do was put it back on the hook when he was done. And even if he hadn't, no one would have suspected him.''

As Diana reached the edge of the parking lot her foot struck a stick lodged into the gravel. "Ow!" She started to stumble, but quickly recaptured her balance. "What the heck was that?"

Greg bent down, and retrieved a small wooden peg with an orange flag attached to the end. "It's a survey stake." He held it between his thumb and forefinger pensively. "You know, I remember seeing a crew out here the day after the murder."

"So do I. They were adding truckloads of gravel and resurfacing the area."

"Harper told us that he was coming out here to search for things lost during the school year. Yet that seems unlikely and pointless since anything lost would have been buried even further down. I wonder if he's been looking for something he buried out here. His marker could have been destroyed by the work crew."

Diana stared at the school, lost in thought, then suddenly jumped back behind cover. "He's coming out now. Let's watch him for a minute."

"He's got a shovel. Maybe he's finally located what he's been searching for."

"That's the same spot we lost sight of the cowboy."

"By the far end of the school," Greg mused. "He led us there, then turned the corner and disappeared."

As Harper began to dig, Greg inched forward. "I'm going in for a closer look. I want to know what he's looking for."

"I'm going too," Diana whispered, then crept forward.

They stayed behind cover and watched from about seven feet away. In breathless silence they waited as Harper dug into the hard-packed earth beneath the gravel.

The minutes dragged on, but Diana managed to keep perfectly still. Then, without warning, her body began to tingle. The air seemed to vibrate with a vitality that made shivers run through her. Something was about to happen.

Fear gripped her as she glanced around. Off in the distance, she saw the cowboy. He stood tall, wearing his Stetson and top coat, just as she'd seen him in the church that day. Illuminated only by the faint rays of a security light on the outside of the school's wall, his body cast a strange, almost ethereal glow. "Cowboy's back," she mouthed.

Greg glanced up. Instinct told him they were being protected, not threatened. His attention was suddenly diverted as Harper grunted and pulled what appeared to be a bulging, dirtstained laundry bag out of the ground.

Greg gestured to Diana and, reaching for her hand, began to lead her slowly back toward the patrol car. They'd just emerged from behind a cluster of pampas grass when Harper stepped out in front of them. His gun trained on Greg.

"You two aren't going anywhere. Not this time."

Diana felt her mouth go dry. "The cops are right next door at the church. We found the path you used to get in and out," she said, checking the accuracy of her guess against his reaction. "They're inspecting the ducts now."

"Then it must have been you two who found my key. I couldn't figure out where I'd lost it!" He glanced at the church, then focused his gaze back on them. "If you'd been sure it was me, the cops would have been here by now. I'm going to have to fix it so neither of you can tell anyone until I'm long gone."

Diana stuck out her chin. "You won't shoot us. The police would be here in moments."

"Maybe, but by then you'd both be dead, and I'd still have time to get away." He gestured for them to start walking along the side of the school.

"You had everyone fooled," Greg admitted. "They thought Eric was responsible."

"That idiot actually came here hoping I'd give him cash to make his getaway. I hid him in the tunnels during the days, and after it got dark, let him visit me at the school. The night I killed Father Denning, Eric was waiting for me in the classroom I'd been cleaning. As it turned out that was the perfect place for him to be. The security guard saw him, assumed it was me and gave me a perfect alibi.''

As they passed the hole he'd dug, Diana casually glanced into it. ''You aren't going to retrieve the rest of what's in there?'' she said, taking a step to one side and peering in. ''Isn't that a cross?''

''It's attached to a coffin, and there's no way I want to touch that. It doesn't concern me.''

''If you feel that way about death,'' she said, noting his revulsion, ''why did you kill Father Denning? Couldn't you just have tied him up?''

''I was about to crawl back into the duct when the old man came into the sacristy. He recognized me because I had been friends with the church custodian. I had to act fast to keep him from running back out. Then I heard you coming in, Marten, so I hid in the duct work. You left your package right there on the chair below the grate, so I helped myself to that, too, when you stepped out.''

''Where are you taking us?'' Diana asked.

''I had a drink with one of the men in the day crew and he told me you were curious about the tunnels that run beneath the school. Well, you're going to have lots of time to study them. This school's going to be shut down for the rest of the summer now that the paint crews are finished. You can yell your heads off in there and no one's going to hear you.''

''You can't leave us in there, we'll die!'' Diana said, stopping to face Harper.

''Keep going, lady, or you'll die right here.''

Greg turned his head for a moment and saw the blank, emotionless stare Harper gave them. He knew then that Harper intended to kill them the minute they were inside the tunnel. Just as it had happened with Father Denning, they had become witnesses he couldn't afford to leave behind. Greg slowed his pace slightly.

"Stop here," Harper ordered, then tossed a set of keys on the ground before Diana. "Find the key that fits the lock, then open it."

Praying that she'd stall as long as she could, Greg turned sideways, and glanced back at Harper. "You were lucky no one saw the trail of blood leading inside the ducts."

"Lucky, hell!" Harper laughed mirthlessly. "It was my shoes, gloves and the bag that had the most blood on them, so I tossed those in first and crawled in after them. I had some on my shirtsleeves too, but I was careful not to touch the metal sides except with my knees and elbows until I was more than twenty feet down the shaft. You would have had to look deep into the duct before seeing any trace of blood."

Diana dropped the key chain, and Harper swore. "Give Marten the keys, you clumsy idiot." He pointed the gun at Greg. "Hurry it up, or I'll shoot you both right here."

Greg crouched by the panel and began trying out keys. "How did you finally get out of the building?"

"I waited until the police were gone, then used the exit point closest to the school. Only I managed to drop my shoe and stain the gravel path with the old guy's blood." He grabbed Diana by the hair and pulled her back against the gun. "Marten, you better hurry. I'm losing my patience."

"Give me a minute to find the right key," he protested. "So after the cops left, you snuck out, took the loot and buried it out here."

"Right, all except the little gold cross. I'd slipped that into my jacket pocket, then forgot all about it. It came in handy later when I set you up with the cops." He stuck the cold gun barrel up against Diana's neck and grinned when she gasped. "Enough talking. Find the key or she's history."

"I've got it," Greg said, shoving one of the keys into the lock. "Now let me turn it. Oops." He held up a key that was missing the bottom portion. "It broke in the lock."

"You big dumb jackass! You jammed the lock with the wrong key. Give me that."

Greg stood and tossed the key ring up into the air. As Harper strained to catch it, Greg swung his leg out, sweeping Harper's feet out from under him, and shouted, "Run, Diana!"

Harper tumbled to the ground hard, still clutching the gun. Greg ran after Diana. As he caught up, he grabbed her hand and pulled her around the corner of the building. "We can't run straight to the church. We have to stay out of Harper's line of fire. He's still got the gun!"

Diana could hear footsteps rushing toward them. "Where the heck is the cowboy? Do you think he went for help?"

"I don't know," Greg said, pulling her forward. "Damn! This is a dead end." He glanced at the large metal doors of the loading dock on the side of the building. Greg tried to force the massive doors, but they wouldn't budge. "They're locked tight."

"There's a ladder up to the roof," Diana said, running toward it.

Just as they reached the old metal ladder, the custodian turned the corner. He fired three shots in rapid succession. The bullets slammed into the wall, sending plaster chips flying into their faces.

"Hurry, but be careful," Diana said. "This old ladder's seen better days."

Greg followed her up hastily. As they reached the roof, he glanced around. "Move as far as you can to the other end and stay down!"

"What are you doing?" she asked, when she realized he wasn't coming with her.

"He won't be able to climb and shoot at the same time. If he tries to follow us, I need to be able to grab him as soon as he reaches the top." Staying low, he crept to the edge of the roof, but as he peered out, a shot forced him back. From below he heard the sound of Harper beginning to climb the ladder. He turned to look at Diana one last time. "I love you."

"Greg, no!"

## Chapter Nineteen

Greg savored the sound of Diana's voice as he moved forward and braced himself for the fight to come. Suddenly he caught a strong whiff of pipe tobacco. Risking a glance over the edge he saw Harper staring at the cowboy a few rungs behind him on the ladder.

Cursing loudly, Harper tried to free a hand for his pistol so he could shoot the man below him. As he shifted his weight, the rung he was standing on gave way with a sharp crack. Harper's feet slipped off the ladder. He dropped his gun and made a desperate grab for the roof parapet, but it was too late. His terrified yell was cut short as his body crashed to the ground with a sickening thud.

Diana rushed to Greg's side. "What happened?" she asked, looking down. Her breath stuck in her throat as she saw the cowboy climbing down the ladder and Harper on the ground below. The cowboy glanced at Harper then looked up at them. Tipping his hat to Greg and Diana, he silently walked away, disappearing into the shadows.

"He just saved both of us," Greg said. "I couldn't have kept Harper from climbing up here without getting shot."

Diana's throat constricted. "I know," she said, her voice taut and tears welling up in her eyes. "I . . ." she stopped as the beam of a powerful flashlight blinded her.

"Police! Nobody move!"

"What timing," she said, half-laughing. "It sounds like Don."

Diana saw two uniformed police officers rush up, guns drawn. Don followed, flanking them. "Are either of you hurt?" he asked, gazing up at them. "We were on the way to the church, when the officer there reported gunshots and asked for a backup. Somehow, I knew you two would be in the thick of it again." He kicked the gun away from where Harper lay.

"We're both fine," Diana answered, "but I'm not climbing down that broken ladder."

"We'll find a safe one for you, don't worry." He gestured to one of the officers, who nodded and trotted off. "You know, if I was prone to ulcers you'd have given me the granddaddy of them all by now," Don added, shaking his head.

Diana nodded gently. "Well, cheer up. There's a silver lining in all this. Although we were wrong about the *church* custodian, we were close. Harper's the killer. I think you'll find the things he stole from the church inside that sack," she pointed to the bag on the ground a few feet from Harper.

Hearing the injured man moaning as he started to regain consciousness, Don turned his gun on Harper. "I don't think he'll be going anywhere. From the looks of his legs, I'd say he's broken both of them. I have to call in for an ambulance," Don said as the other patrolman concentrated on Harper. He glanced back at Diana and Greg. "Don't either of you try to climb down until we get a good ladder here. And don't go anywhere until I get back. I want to find out *everything* that happened here tonight."

AN HOUR LATER, Diana and Greg sat in Don's office. "That's the whole story," Diana said, finishing the tale of that night's adventures.

"What exactly was inside the bag?" Greg asked. "Was the hide painting there?"

"Yes, the frame's been damaged, but the *Madonna* seems to be in good shape. There's also a set of silver candlesticks, a jeweled cross, several other gold crosses, a chalice, and some *santos* cast in gold." He rested his elbows on the desk and regarded them for a moment. "The bag showed signs of having been dragged by one of the heavy loaders that hauled in the gravel. It ended up reburied directly over a coffin, of all the crazy places. We had to get permission from the city and the Archbishop to move the remains."

"How did Joe Martinez find the murder weapon? Did Harper plant it near Coin's Realm hoping to throw suspicion on the gang?" Greg asked.

"That's right. Harper's telling us everything. He's hoping it'll go easier on him if he cooperates. He admits to trying to frame you after his brother was caught in the area. It was a halfhearted attempt to take the heat off Eric. He said he felt it was his 'duty' to do something, since Eric really wasn't guilty this time." Don paused as if trying to find the right words. "I've been wrong about you, Marten. You did okay tonight."

Diana laughed. "Don, you're the prince of understatements!"

Don scowled. "I still can't figure out who the cowboy was or where he fits in," he added quickly, eager to change the subject. "Harper doesn't have a clue, although he's still cursing the man for making him lose his balance on the ladder. He says when you first told him about the guy, he thought you were both nuts."

"That cowboy saved our lives more than once. I wish I could thank him. Whoever he is, he's a very special man." Diana leaned back in her chair and rubbed her eyes. "Will you need us much longer?"

"You can go now if you want." Don walked with them to the front door of the station. "I'd like both of you to come back at ten tomorrow morning so you can sign your statements. Will that be a problem?"

Diana glanced at Greg, then, after seeing him shake his head, agreed. "We'll see you then."

Diana and Greg walked out to the parking lot slowly, each lost in their own thoughts. Finally Greg broke the silence between them. "Would you mind if we stopped by the school before we call it a night?"

"You're hoping we'll see the cowboy again, right?"

He nodded. "I don't like walking away from this without even thanking him."

"I know exactly what you mean," Diana agreed. She led the way back to the school. "Maybe there's something we can do for him."

They arrived a few minutes later and Greg walked around the school grounds with her, staying alert for signs of the cowboy. But he was nowhere to be found. Only the hum of night insects broke the silence.

"I'm not surprised he's gone," Diana admitted at last.

"You had the feeling he was saying goodbye too, when he tipped his hat?" Greg asked, hugging her lightly.

Diana nodded. "I hate goodbyes, but even more than that, I hate not being able to say them." She looked at Greg speculatively and started to ask him the question foremost in her mind, but her courage failed her. Greg still hadn't said if he'd be staying on, now that the murderer had been found.

"Well, there's no use in hanging around here," Greg said at last. "I've got a great deal of work to finish tonight."

"Can I help?"

"Not this time," he replied gently.

He was shutting her out, and the realization made Diana feel as if her heart was being squeezed by a cold hand. As in her past, had she found someone to love only to have him leave her behind? "Greg, what happens to us now? Will I lose you?"

"You can't lose me, Diana," his voice was husky with emotion. "I'll always be a part of you, as you are a part of me."

She slammed her hand against the wheel impulsively. "But does that mean you'll be staying?" she blurted. Then, horrified, she said "Don't answer that." She took a deep breath. "You said once that we need to adapt to each other's needs. Let me at least try to do that. I know you like time to think things through, and I'm always the one who's impatient. Right now I've backed you into a corner trying to get answers, and that's not what I want to do at all. Please don't say anything tonight. You bring this up when you're ready to talk about it."

Greg smiled gently. "You see? It's like I said, it's all a matter of making room for the other person in your heart. Then, everything else follows naturally."

Diana pulled up near the side entrance to Greg's apartment complex. "I'll say good-night here."

"That's probably best. I'd never finish what I have to do tonight with you there to distract me." He smiled.

He reached out and wove his hand beneath the curtain of her hair, to pull her close. His mouth closed over hers in an achingly tender kiss that told her more about his feelings than brutal passion could have. "I'll see you at the police station in the morning."

Diana watched him walk inside the building and for a moment considered going after him. Surely no man could give a woman a kiss like that without having surrendered a part of his soul!

But perhaps he didn't see it that way. Maybe to him it had simply been a way to say goodbye. In her eagerness to believe differently, had she made it into something much more? Diana took a deep breath, put the car in gear and drove slowly home.

That night sleep eluded her. She must have picked up the receiver by her nightstand and set it down again at least a dozen times before dawn finally came.

By eight-thirty she was showered and dressed and ready to go to the police station. Only she wasn't supposed to be there until ten. Remembering Greg's van was still at her print shop, and unable to resist the chance to see him, she grabbed her purse and drove to his studio.

She hesitated only a second before knocking on his door. Greg answered almost immediately. Beard stubble covered his jaw, and he looked as if he'd been up all night. His eyes were red, but they burned with a curious intensity. "I was hoping it was you, Diana. Please, come in. I have something for you."

She walked inside and saw countless wood shavings littering the floor.

"I've been up all night," he explained, "working to finish a very special carving. I told you once before that all my carvings are a part of me. This one is a very private piece of my soul. No one's ever seen it." He placed a hand over the oil-soaked cloth that covered a statue about fourteen inches high.

He lifted the cloth away, revealing an intricate wood sculpture of a rugged cowboy, seated on a crude wooden bench, holding a newborn baby in his outstretched hands. Hesitation and uncertainty showed in his features as he struggled to find a way to support the delicate infant. A woman sat by his side, love resplendent on her face as her gaze rested on the two people she loved most in her life.

"This is my dream, Diana, and since I never knew what it was until I found you, it seems right that you should have it."

A lump as large a fist formed at the back of her throat. "It's exquisite," she managed. She hadn't meant to cry, but somehow the tears began to stain her face.

"You hate it," he muttered.

She laughed, tears still rolling down her cheeks. "No, I love it, and what it represents. I'd all but given up on having dreams that come true," she answered, a tender smile on her lips.

He reached out for her, and her tears moistened his chest as she pressed herself against him.

He tilted her head and covered her mouth in a long, passionately tender kiss that left them both trembling. "We belong to each other."

He kissed her again, needing the taste of her and wanting to surround her with the love that filled his heart. "Life has been hard for you, but I need you to believe in 'happily ever after' and 'forever' again."

"I do," she murmured, as his kisses left a moist trail down the column of her throat. "You've given me that."

"It's only one of many gifts we're going to give each other." He rained kisses over her face.

Suddenly, the alarm on his watch began to go off. He muttered a curse. "We're due at the police station in ten minutes," he said. Then he bent down to nuzzle her neck again. "What the heck," he growled. "We'll be late."

Diana pushed him away, laughing. "No, we'll continue this later. We don't want Don dropping by, wanting to know what's holding us up."

Greg exhaled softly as she slipped out of his grasp. "Then let's get this police business over with as soon as possible," he said, picking up a cordless razor. "Come on. By the time we get there, I'll be presentable."

Ten minutes later they walked through the station's doors. Greg was clean shaven and no one would have guessed from all his energy that he'd been up all night.

As they reached the main desk, Don came out. "I just got the copies of your statements from clerical." He led the way to his office. "They're ready for your signatures."

"By the way," he continued, "we made an interesting discovery this morning. Remember the coffin Harper accidentally unearthed?"

The two of them nodded.

"The desert sand preserved the wood somewhat, but when the men started to lift it out, the old pine box fell apart. Among the remains, they found an old badge. It turns out the person buried there was a former sheriff of Santa Fe. We've had him reinterred at Las Almas Cemetery." He gestured toward the door. "We've got pictures of all the sheriffs dating back to the mid 1800s along the walls in the hall, so he's probably out there somewhere."

Greg and Diana signed the statements, then returned them to Don. "Will you need us for anything else?" Diana asked.

"You're both free to go. There will be a hearing and probably a trial but the courts will notify you in plenty of time if your testimony is needed." He walked with them down the hall.

Diana casually glanced at the pictures that lined the wall. Suddenly her gaze fastened on a faded photo of a cowboy. He was wearing a Stetson hat and holding a pipe in his left hand. "Greg, look!"

He stood beside her and read the caption beneath it. "Sheriff Samuel Givens. This was taken in 1883."

"There's a bright button on his vest, which I bet was his badge. Notice the way his coat bulges out slightly over the revolver on his hip?" Diana looked over at Don. "What do you know about him?"

Don gave her a puzzled look. "Not much, but I can check. His name does sound familiar, maybe he was the one they reburied today." He walked to a bookshelf directly beneath the photos and pulled out a small volume. "He didn't hold the position of sheriff for too long. I guess he— Wait, here's why. You know those candlesticks that were taken in the theft? I think they're the same ones mentioned here. Robbers broke into the home of a prominent local silversmith, murdered him and his family and took everything they could carry including the candlesticks. Apparently those had been crafted especially for the church."

Don filled them in as he read through the material. The story was the same one Greg and Diana had found in the church records. "Givens went after the outlaws and killed them all. But the gunfight eventually cost him his life, too. One bullet pierced his throat, another his side. Mortally wounded, he rode back to town and collapsed on the steps of the church. He died in the arms of a priest there at 6:00 p.m., only a few hours after the gun battle."

Diana looked at Greg, then stared at the photo.

"Wait a minute," Don said incredulously. "The cowboy you've been seeing might resemble this guy, but Givens has been dead a hundred years. It's just a coincidence. Let's not go off the deep end here."

"Whatever you say, Don," Diana replied with a shrug.

Don gave Greg a pat on the back. "Take her home, Marten. I think she's been out in the desert sun too long."

As they walked out of the station, Greg cleared his throat. "He's right, you know. It's got to be coincidence."

"But you know it isn't, don't you?" Diana observed softly. She got into the car, then waited for Greg to fasten his seat belt. Placing the car in gear, she pulled out into the street.

"Where are we going?" he asked, noting that she wasn't heading to either his studio or her home.

"To Las Almas Cemetery. It isn't far."

"What do you expect to find there?" he asked cautiously.

"I don't know, but I have to do this. It's for my own peace of mind, I guess." She paused, her voice so soft it was almost inaudible. "I want to say goodbye."

He nodded, but said nothing. He didn't think there was anything to say at this point. The whole idea sounded preposterous, but a feeling deep down told him their questions about the cowboy were about to be answered.

When they arrived at the small cemetery, Diana parked and got out. "That must be it," she said after a moment, pointing out a recently cleared place with a temporary metal marker and identification plaque.

As they reached the marker, Diana read Sheriff Givens's name out loud. "If it was you, cowboy, then thanks from both of us," she whispered.

They stood there silently for a few moments, then the air around them came alive with the scent of a familiar, strong blend of tobacco. Diana's eyes widened as she glanced at Greg, but before either of them could say a word, the scent faded and was gone.

# A CENTURY OF
# 1890s AMERICAN 1990s
### ROMANCE

**A CENTURY OF AMERICAN ROMANCE** has taken you on a nostalgic journey through time—from the turn of the century to the dawn of the year 2000.

Relive all the memories . . . the passions . . . of
**A CENTURY OF AMERICAN ROMANCE.**

1890s #345 AMERICAN PIE by Margaret St. George
1900s #349 SATURDAY'S CHILD by Dallas Schulze
1910s #353 THE GOLDEN RAINTREE by Suzanne Simmons Guntrum
1920s #357 THE SENSATION by Rebecca Flanders
1930s #361 ANGELS WINGS by Anne Stuart
1940s #365 SENTIMENTAL JOURNEY by Barbara Bretton
1950s #369 STRANGER IN PARADISE by Barbara Bretton
1960s #373 HEARTS AT RISK by Libby Hall
1960s #377 TILL THE END OF TIME by Elise Title
1970s #381 HONORBOUND by Tracy Hughes
1980s #385 MY ONLY ONE by Eileen Nauman
1990s #389 A > LOVERBOY by Judith Arnold

# HARLEQUIN'S WISHBOOK
## SWEEPSTAKES RULES & REGULATIONS
### NO PURCHASE NECESSARY TO ENTER OR RECEIVE A PRIZE

1. To enter the Sweepstakes and join the Reader Service, affix the Four Free Books and Free Gifts sticker along with both of your Sweepstakes stickers to the Sweepstakes Entry Form. If you do not wish to take advantage of our Reader Service, but wish to enter the Sweepstakes only, do not affix the Four Free Books and Free Gifts sticker; affix only the Sweepstakes stickers to the Sweepstakes Entry Form. Incomplete and/or inaccurate entries are ineligible for that section or sections of prizes. Torstar Corp. and its affiliates are not responsible for mutilated or unreadable entries or inadvertent printing errors. Mechanically reproduced entries are null and void.

2. Whether you take advantage of this offer or not, on or about April 30, 1992 at the offices of Marden-Kane Inc., Lake Success, NY, your Sweepstakes number will be compared against a list of winning numbers generated at random by the computer. However, prizes will only be awarded to individuals who have entered the Sweepstakes. In the event that all prizes are not claimed, a random drawing will be held from all qualified entries received from March 30, 1990 to March 31, 1992, to award all unclaimed prizes. All cash prizes (Grand to Sixth), will be mailed to the winners and are payable by check in U.S. funds. Seventh prize to be shipped to winners via third-class mail. These prizes are in addition to any free, surprise or mystery gifts that might be offered. Versions of this sweepstakes with different prizes of approximate equal value may appear in other mailings or at retail outlets by Torstar Corp. and its affiliates.

3. The following prizes are awarded in this sweepstakes: ★ Grand Prize (1) $1,000,000; First Prize (1) $25,000; Second Prize (1) $10,000; Third Prize (5) $5,000; Fourth Prize (10) $1,000; Fifth Prize (100) $250; Sixth Prize (2,500) $10; ★ ★ Seventh Prize (6,000) $12.95 ARV.

   ★ This sweepstakes contains a Grand Prize offering of a $1,000,000 annuity. Winner will receive $33,333.33 a year for 30 years without interest totalling $1,000,000.

   ★ ★ Seventh Prize: A fully illustrated hardcover book published by Torstar Corp. Approximate Retail Value of the book is $12.95.

   Entrants may cancel the Reader Service at anytime without cost or obligation to buy (see details in center insert card).

4. Extra Bonus! This presentation offers two extra bonus prizes valued at a total of $33,000 to be awarded in a random drawing from all qualified entries received by March 31, 1992. No purchase necessary to enter or receive a prize. To qualify, see instructions on the insert card. Winner will have the choice of merchandise offered or a $33,000 check payable in U.S. funds. All other published rules and regulations apply.

5. This Sweepstakes is being conducted under the supervision of Marden-Kane, Inc., an independent judging organization. By entering this Sweepstakes, each entrant accepts and agrees to be bound by these rules and the decisions of the judges, which shall be final and binding. Odds of winning in the random drawing are dependent upon the total number of entries received. Taxes, if any, are the sole responsibility of the winners. Prizes are nontransferable. All entries must be received at the address printed on the reply card and must be postmarked no later than 12:00 MIDNIGHT on March 31, 1992. The drawing for all unclaimed Sweepstakes prizes and for the Bonus Sweepstakes Prize will take place May 30, 1992, at 12:00 NOON at the offices of Marden-Kane, Inc., Lake Success, NY.

6. This offer is open to residents of the U.S., the United Kingdom, France and Canada, 18 years or older, except employees and their immediate family members of Torstar Corp., its affiliates, subsidiaries, and all other agencies and persons connected with the use, marketing or conduct of this Sweepstakes. All Federal, State, Provincial and local laws apply. Void wherever prohibited or restricted by law. Any litigation within the Province of Quebec respecting the conduct and awarding of a prize in this publicity contest must be submitted to the Régie des Loteries et Courses du Québec.

7. Winners will be notified by mail and may be required to execute an affidavit of eligibility and release, which must be returned within 14 days after notification or an alternative winner will be selected. Canadian winners will be required to correctly answer an arithmetical skill-testing question administered by mail, which must be returned within a limited time. Winners consent to the use of their names, photographs and/or likenesses for advertising and publicity in conjunction with this and similar promotions without additional compensation.

8. For a list of our major winners, send a stamped, self-addressed envelope to: WINNERS LIST, c/o MARDEN-KANE, INC., P.O. BOX 701, SAYREVILLE, NJ 08871. Winners Lists will be fulfilled after the May 30, 1992 draw date.

---

**ALTERNATE MEANS OF ENTRY:** Print your name and address on a 3″×5″ piece of plain paper and send to:

| In the U.S. | In Canada |
|---|---|
| Harlequin's WISHBOOK Sweepstakes | Harlequin's WISHBOOK Sweepstakes |
| 3010 Walden Ave. | P.O. Box 609 |
| P.O. Box 1867, Buffalo, NY 14269-1867 | Fort Erie, Ontario L2A 5X3 |

LTY-H491RRD

**Back by Popular Demand**

# Janet Dailey
## Americana

A romantic tour of America through fifty favorite Harlequin Presents® novels, each set in a different state researched by Janet and her husband, Bill. A journey of a lifetime in one cherished collection.

In June, don't miss the sultry states featured in:

Title # 9 - FLORIDA
         **Southern Nights**
  #10 - GEORGIA
         **Night of the Cotillion**

### *Available wherever*
### *Harlequin books are sold.*

JD-JR